DM

MURDER OF INNOCENCE

MURDER OF INNOCENCE

Veronica Heley

Severn House Large Print
London & New York

This first large print edition published in Great Britain 2004 by
SEVERN HOUSE LARGE PRINT BOOKS LTD of
9-15 High Street, Sutton, Surrey, SM1 1DF.
First world regular print edition published 2003 by
Severn House Publishers, London and New York.
This first large print edition published in the USA 2004 by
SEVERN HOUSE PUBLISHERS INC., of
595 Madison Avenue, New York, NY 10022.

British Library Cataloguing in Publication Data

Heley, Veronica
Murder of innocence - Large print ed.
1. Quicke, Ellie (Fictitious character) - Fiction
2. Widows - Great Britain - Fiction
3. Detective and mystery stories
4. Large type books
I. Title
823.9'14 [F]

ISBN 0-7278-7384-9

Printed and bound in Great Britain by
MPG Books Ltd, Bodmin, Cornwall.

One

Smoke seeped under the door.

She'd always been afraid of fire. She got the boy to help her, and in the dark they felt around for something, anything, to prevent the smoke suffocating them. Any old towel would do. The sides of the door fitted pretty well. Not so much smoke came in now. Would it be better to die of suffocation than to burn alive?

Ellie tried the door again, and again. Immovable.

The house was empty except for the two of them, shut into that tiny room with no means of escape. There was no window, and the fire was gaining ground around them.

It would be easy to give way to hysteria.

Calm down.

How long since that fiend in human form had shut them in? How long would it take for the fire to reach her ... or the smoke to suffocate her ... and the boy?

Breathing wasn't getting any easier...

For the recently widowed, some days are better than others.

This had been a bad day from the start. Ellie had woken up and asked her husband

Frank the time. Only to remember that he wasn't going to answer.

Ouch.

Some days she looked forward to a future in which she wasn't just the 'little woman' at home. Today was not one of those days.

She laddered her tights. She dressed in yesterday's cream jumper and blue skirt because it was too much trouble to sort anything else out. Anyway, with her short silvery hair and clear complexion, she'd always looked good in blue and white.

She used the last of the loo paper.

There wasn't enough milk left to have cereal and tea. One or the other. Midge the cat needed feeding, so he took most of the remaining milk.

Ellie tried to cheer herself up. She would spend the morning making a list of plants for her new conservatory. It wasn't finished yet, but the builders were making good progress and it would give her something to do. Frank's early death had left her a comparatively wealthy woman, but she wasn't used to spending money on herself and still felt guilty about doing so.

She was making herself a pot of tea when the phone rang. At the same time the foreman of the builders barged in through the back door.

'Seen this, missus?' He was brandishing a soiled piece of paper with figures on it. It was obviously bad news.

'One moment ... the phone.' She lunged for

the phone in the hall.

'This can't wait, missus.'

'Is that you, Ellie?' Her husband's elderly aunt Drusilla was on the phone sounding less imperious than usual. 'I've had a fall ... I need you...'

Ellie tried to hush the builder, who was saying, 'Time's money, you know, and these aren't what you ordered.'

'Aunt Drusilla, I...'

The doorbell rang and as it did so, Ellie's daughter Diana turned her key in the lock and entered, manoeuvring the pushchair in front of her. Ellie could see that her daughter was in a foul mood, while baby Frank was yelling, red-faced. Ellie covered her free ear in an effort to hear her aunt, who was explaining how she'd come to fall.

'Mother, what's going on? You promised we'd discuss my moving back here this morning...' Diana could be very intimidating.

'Please!' said Ellie. 'Everyone...'

No one was prepared to give way to anyone else. Builder, daughter, aunt: all spoke at once, demanding attention.

Ellie reflected that a water cannon might have quelled the disturbance. Might. What chance did a fiftyish widow have? Especially one who liked a quiet life.

'Ellie, are you still there?' quacked Aunt Drusilla on the phone. 'Did you hear what I said?'

The builder wasn't going to be put off by a crowd of silly women. 'You see, missus, we opened up...'

'Mother!'

The front door burst open again. Diana couldn't have shut it properly. Mrs Coppola, a near neighbour of Ellie's, fell into the hall. 'Tod, have you got him? You have, haven't you?'

Brittle blonde, single-parent mother of Ellie's young friend Tod who lived just up the road. Mrs Coppola was usually immaculately turned out. Today she'd forgotten her careful make-up and was actually wringing her hands.

Ellie blinked. She hadn't seen the boy Tod for a couple of days. He spent a lot of time in her garden shed, at her kitchen table or on her computer, because his mother was out all day at work, but ... missing? No, impossible!

One thing at a time. She spoke into the phone. 'Aunt Drusilla, listen. Ring the doctor – get an ambulance if you think it's bad enough. There's a spot of trouble here. I'll ring you back as soon as I can.'

'Mother...'

'Missus, it's like this...'

Mrs Coppola screamed, a thin sound. Even baby Frank stopped yelling and looked at her.

Tod's mother had bedroom slippers on but no eyebrows. She made a blind sweeping gesture. 'You've got to help me! I was out last night ... office do ... thought he was asleep ... lights were all out when I got back. Not in his room. Hasn't been to bed. He's never ... I can't think where. I thought he might be here

... with you for some reason? Camping out in your garden shed? It's my last hope!'

Ellie felt the blood recede from her own head. Tod missing? It didn't bear thinking about. Ignoring Diana's furious face, Ellie took Mrs Coppola's hands in both of hers. Fear of what might have happened to a ten-year-old boy flowed from one woman to the other. They'd never touched one another before, never even liked one another much.

Ellie struggled to keep calm. 'Sit down.' She pressed the distraught woman on to the hall chair. 'We'll find him. Have you rung the police? No? Well, you must, if ... Diana, just run down the garden and look in the shed, see if he's there. Take Frank with you, let him run around outside for a bit.'

'Are you mad? I'm not taking Frank out there, not with all the builders' materials around. Besides, I have to get to work. I'm going to have to leave him with you anyway, since the babysitter's taken the day off to go to the doctor's.'

Ellie couldn't take this in, had no room in her head for anything but the news that Tod was missing. She turned on Diana. 'Shed, now!'

Diana didn't usually take any notice of her mother but this time she sped out through the kitchen and half-built conservatory to the garden, leaving Frank behind in the hall. As Diana went out through the kitchen Ellie heard a thump, followed by the clatter of the cat flap. Midge – Ellie's ginger tom cat –

didn't like Diana.

The builder leaned his massive weight against the kitchen wall. 'That the boy I seen here a lot? Dark-haired, cheeky? Climbs trees?'

Mrs Coppola opened her mouth, but no words came out. She was in shock.

Ellie flicked a glance at the builder. 'Could you put the kettle on? *Tod is missing?*'

He shrugged but obeyed. Outside the kitchen window work had stopped. The gaunt framework of Ellie's new conservatory stretched across the back of the house, enclosing both the kitchen and living room. The roof of the conservatory and most of the windows had been glazed, but the doors to the garden beyond were propped up against the interior wall. Concrete had been laid on the floor and concrete steps led from the conservatory down into the garden.

A pedestrian alley ran along the bottom of Ellie's garden, dividing it and the neighbouring gardens from the grounds of the church beyond. The lawns around the church were criss-crossed with paths and shaded by mature trees. It was an outlook people paid good money for, but it didn't contain a missing small boy.

Tucked into the bottom corner of Ellie's garden beside the alley was the substantial shed which Tod used as a playhouse.

Back in the kitchen the kettle boiled and Ellie refreshed her pot of tea. She poured out a mug for Mrs Coppola, took it into the hall and thrust it into her hands. That took the very last of the milk. Mrs Coppola sipped, shuddered and made a face. 'Ugh! Sugar.'

'Drink it.'

Ellie darted back into the kitchen to peer out of the window. Diana was shading her eyes to peer through the window into the shed. She rattled the door. The door was padlocked, just as it should be. Tod had a key, but obviously hadn't used it or the padlock wouldn't be on.

Frank wailed in his pushchair in the hall. Diana plodded back up the path, calling, 'Not there.'

The builder said, 'You tried his friends, missus?'

'They haven't seen him. He went swimming as usual yesterday, was still in the baths when they left. No one's seen him since. Oh...!'

Ellie dialled 999. 'Police, please.'

Mrs Coppola ignored her mug of tea, staring wide-eyed at the parquet floor. She was shivering.

'He's not there.' Diana, repeating the obvious. 'Look, I've got to go.' She hesitated, looking at Mrs Coppola. 'So sorry. Dreadful thing. Sure he'll turn up.' And to Ellie, 'I've got an appointment in half an hour. Ring you later. Kiss, kiss.'

As she left the house Frank opened his mouth and yelled. Ellie passed the phone to the builder and grabbed the biscuit tin, thrusting something, anything, into the toddler's hand to shut him up. The builder passed the phone to Mrs Coppola, who tried to speak into it but failed. Her shivering became convulsive.

Ellie took the phone off her. She pressed one hand to her forehead. One of them must keep calm. It would do no good to give way to tears.

'Police? We need to report a boy missing. Oh yes, my name is Ellie Quicke, Mrs.' She gave the address while joggling the pushchair with one hand. 'The boy is called Tod. His mother is Mrs Coppola, she's here with me, but not in any fit state to talk to you ... yes, she lives nearby, three doors away. Our gardens back on to St Thomas' Church grounds, Ealing. His mother's tried his school friends, but no go. He hasn't been seen since he went swimming after school yesterday.

'Description? He's aged ten and three months, smallish for his age, dark hair, brown eyes, goes to the primary school just across the road from the church ... we can almost see it from here. Last night – it was Tuesday, wasn't it? He would have gone on to Swimming Club straight from school. His mother works. She leaves supper for him though he often comes here to spend the time after school with me. She came home rather late, lights weren't on, everything looked normal, so she went to bed...'

The woman had probably had too much to drink and wouldn't have noticed if the place had been turned over by a burglar.

'What's that? What would he have been

wearing? School things, I suppose. The uniform is grey sweatshirt with the school logo on it, white shirt, grey trousers. The school tie is yellow and blue and he wears black shoes, not trainers. His jacket is olive brown, padded. He'll have a school bag with him, brown plastic, I think, quite ordinary. And swimming things, probably in a separate plastic bag.'

She put the phone down. 'They'll come straight round.'

The builder said, 'Like us to look round about, missus?'

Mrs Coppola gasped and put her head down between her knees.

Ellie realized the builder meant that Tod's body might be out there. She leaned against the wall. At the second attempt she managed to say, 'Yes. Would you? Back gardens, the grounds around the church.'

He nodded and left, calling for his two workmen to drop everything and go with him.

Ellie thought, Doctor? Brandy? Dear Lord, help. What do I do? TOD!

Little Frank began to scream, growing purple in the face, trying to get out of his pushchair. He'd covered the lower part of his face with chocolate and was now smearing it on the hall table.

Ellie thought, I can't cope. I'll go to pieces. Tod ... Mechanically, she tore open a banana and gave it to the boy.

Mrs Coppola's eyes were wide open and her

lips were moving. She was still shivering. Ellie plucked an overcoat from the hallstand and put it round Mrs Coppola's shoulders.

The woman looked up. 'What do you think's happened to him? You hear such things. His dad'll kill me!'

'No, no, of course not.' The woman didn't mean it literally, of course, but from the little Ellie knew of the long-ago divorce, Mr Coppola had possessed a lively temper.

Mrs Coppola shrieked, 'Tod!' and began rocking backwards and forwards. Frank mashed his banana against the hall table and joined in. Ellie joggled Frank's pushchair but he failed to respond. She tried to undo the straps that held him into the pushchair, but he fought her off. Till Christmas he'd been a cuddly little toddler, but with the advent of teething problems, he'd turned into a little monster, rejecting her every advance. And strong with it, too. She gave him another biscuit to keep him quiet.

Bedlam, thought Ellie. Oh, Tod. Where are you? She had a flashing picture in her mind of a broken body lying in the shadow of her shed. She shook her head to drive it away. She made herself take one deep breath, and then another. She told herself to breathe deeply, think clearly, pray for help.

Please God, not that. Oh, please ... I beg you...

Moving stiffly she manoeuvred the pushchair away from the hall table and dialled the number of the charity shop in the Lane. She had worked there for many years and made some good friends, one of whom she still saw on a regular basis. She needed help and with any luck, dear Rose might be there and have time to spare.

She wasn't. Madam, who managed the shop, was extremely surprised – she meant displeased – that Ellie should ring there to speak to one of her friends on a busy day like this. Ellie apologized, put the phone down, couldn't think which day of the week it was. Dialled Rose's home number and thank God, she was there.

'Rose, dear. Something terrible's happened. Tod ... you know, the little boy from down the road who comes round here a lot ... yes, the one you're so fond of ... well, he's been missing since last night, the police will be at his house in a minute and Mrs Coppola's in no fit state to be left alone. And I'm looking after little Frank. Could you come and help me look after him, take him for a walk or something till his babysitter gets back?'

Rose was shocked, but willing to help. 'Oh, my dear, how awful. I'll be there in two ticks, just wait till I get my coat on, and as it happens, I was meaning to call you today because we've run into a spot of bother over the wedding arrangements...' Rose's daughter was getting married in six weeks' time. '...but this is more important, of course...'

Action helped. Ellie phoned little Frank's babysitter, left a cry for help on the answerphone. Phoned Aunt Drusilla – how awful to have forgotten her – and got no reply. The old bat hadn't even got an answerphone even though she was as wealthy as Croesus ... Ah, at last someone had answered. The cleaning woman. Limited English. Polish. Probably.

'Hello-oh? Miss Quicke? No, she cannot come to phone. Is resting. Who is? Ah, niece, Ella. I tell her, yes. You come soon, no?'

'I'll try.'

Mrs Coppola was rocking to and fro, her face blank.

Oh, Tod. Where are you?

Try not to think about him. Try to think about practical matters. Stop Frank yelling. Give him a drink ... there, there, now ... splash some water on your own face ... cold water ... bracing, very. Pull the coat back over Mrs Coppola's shoulders. Coax Frank to hold his cup.

Mrs Coppola started up. 'I must look ... perhaps our attic...?'

'Wait a minute and I'll come with you.' Clean Frank up. Chocolate and banana mash everywhere.

The front door opened and banged shut as Mrs Coppola flew out. Frank threw his cup at the wall. The lid came off and water splattered everywhere. The builder came to the door.

'He's not in any of the gardens that go down to the alley along here. Nor in the church grounds. My lads found a drunk in the porch there, sleeping it off, that's all.'

Ellie covered her eyes with her hands. I

must not give way. Frank howled. The builder put his big hand on her shoulder and patted it. That was nice of him. If only my dear husband Frank were still alive, he'd know what to do.

She straightened up, ran her fingers back through her hair. 'Thank you. I'm waiting for my friend Rose to come and take care of Frank and then I must get round to Mrs Coppola's. The police will be there in a minute.'

'Your friend Mrs Rose that was with you the other day? I'll let her in. Look, I've got grandchildren of my own. Let me take the laddie out into the garden till she comes. We can't work with this on, anyway.'

'I've just had a thought. The park's not far away. The river ... perhaps he's there?'

'We'll have to wait for the police. They'll tell us what to do, right, missus?'

She nodded, tried to put her overcoat on, got the sleeves the wrong way round, and was helped by the builder to get it right side out. 'You wanted to see me about something?'

'They've sent the wrong hinges for the door and windows. Don't you worry yourself. I'll sort it. Off you go.'

What a nice man. It's a good job Diana's not here to hear him, or she'd accuse me of flirting with him – oh dear, oh dear, as if I would...

She made sure baby Frank had his favourite toy within reach but attached to the push-chair, and left.

* * *

Mrs Coppola had left her front door open. Her house had the same layout as Ellie's, but in reverse. It looked different because the garden was under concrete back and front whereas Ellie's was full of plants. Instead of a parquet floor in the hall, Mrs Coppola had a cheap dark-red carpet. The woman seemed to like red. There were red-and-black curtains in the sitting room disagreeing with a flower-patterned green carpet. The three-piece suite was rather the worse for wear.

Oh, Tod. Are you dead?

There was no sign of Mrs Coppola, but looking around, Ellie thought she could interpret what had happened. Two wine glasses were on the floor by the settee, one overturned. An empty wine bottle and corkscrew. A pair of very high-heeled shoes kicked off here, a crumpled blouse there, a man's handkerchief wadded under the settee.

Humph! thought Ellie, with a sour taste in her mouth. A lift home in someone else's car, a nightcap of wine, followed by a roll on the settee. I suppose that handkerchief might contain traces of what had happened, if one needed to find its owner.

She sighed. No trace of Tod.

She made her way up the stairs to the landing. Mrs Coppola was using a pole with a hook on the end, vainly trying to reach the catch of a trapdoor which gave access to the attic. It was a similar arrangement to the one in Ellie's house. Mrs Coppola's face was streaked with dirt, the pole coated with cobwebs, as was the catch on the trapdoor. It was clear no one had attempted to open it for ages.

Suddenly there was a shout. 'Police! Missus, are you there?'

Mrs Coppola allowed Ellie to take the pole off her and be led downstairs to face officialdom.

It was mind-numbingly awful. Questions ... a policewoman summoned. More questions. Tramping up and downstairs. They assumed Ellie was Mrs Coppola's mother and when she explained they told her not to go, they'd need to talk to her, too.

Ellie made herself useful. She washed all the dirty plates in the sink and made cups of coffee for the police and Mrs Coppola.

The phone rang and rang till Ellie answered it.

'Loose, are you there?' A man's voice, peremptory, annoyed.

Ellie was wryly amused. Loose, indeed. Short for Lucy? 'This is a neighbour speaking. Who is it?'

A policewoman appeared at her elbow, took the phone off her, held a short exchange and put the phone down before reporting to the man in charge. 'Someone from Mrs Coppola's office, asking why she hadn't come in.' And to Ellie, 'I'll answer the phone in future.'

They think it might have been a demand for ransom? Dear Lord, no. Please.

* * *

Later the builder and his workmen came to the door offering to help search the park. The police said they'd search this house first. Then they'd see where else they might need to go. The builder was annoyed. Hadn't he offered to help?

Ellie managed to get him to one side. 'Baby Frank?'

'Mrs Rose took him off for half an hour. Made us a cuppa first and fed the toddler. Said she'd call round here later if you hadn't got back home by the time she returns. She could talk for England, that one, couldn't she?'

Ellie tried to smile, because it was true. Rose did talk a lot.

The builder dropped his voice. 'Look, we'll just have a look round the park on the quiet like. Can't wait for the police to get organized. Right?'

She thought, This is a judgement on me. I love Tod more than I love my own grandson. I have left my own flesh and blood with a builder whom I hardly know, consigning him to the care of a friend. I wouldn't have done that to Tod. He's dearer to me than my own grandson. Oh, I can't bear it.

Mrs Coppola was reviving a little, not unconscious of the fact that the police sergeant was a youngish man with astonishingly blue eyes. Talking non-stop. 'No, no, you've got that wrong. Tod's father and I were married, of course we were, but he went off years ago, thought he wanted a child but when I got pregnant decided he didn't. By the time he finished agonizing about whether he did or didn't, I was too far along to do anything about it and anyway, his real passion in life was football, wouldn't talk about anything else. So he took a job in Glasgow when Tod was barely a year old, and I went back to work, of course.

'What's that? No, his father hasn't taken any interest for years. Doesn't even send him a present at birthdays or Christmas. He wouldn't kidnap the boy, really he wouldn't.'

Ellie said to the policewoman, 'Look, I've got my grandchild to see to. A neighbour's taking him for a walk but I really have to get back.'

'In a minute.'

Mrs Coppola's voice went on and on, all on one note, monotonous. 'Tod's a good boy, not mixed up in any gangs, no bullying, nothing like that...'

Ellie needed to go to the loo. She went upstairs; the loo wasn't particularly clean, but it wasn't really dirty. Then she peeped inside Tod's bedroom. She knew his bedroom was at the front of the house overlooking the road. He'd told her he kept a notebook there with his dad's old binoculars, watching the neighbourhood for signs of burglars or foreign spies or men from Mars.

The decoration here was not as strident as in the living room, but it was furnished and decorated with the same colours. A plain dark-green carpet, stained here and there, inexpertly put together from offcuts. Thomas the Tank Engine wallpaper, young for a ten-year-old who was into computers.

Tod's own computer – an ancient and unreliable model – sat on a wide desk under the window, surrounded by the detritus of a busy schoolboy's life. A stool nearby held binoculars and a notebook. The floor and bedside table displayed comics, stamp catalogues, stamp album, science-fiction paperbacks, a dilapidated old dictionary which had lost its outer covers ... a dented portable radio/cassette player/alarm, with batteries scattered around it...

The duvet cover pictured Star Trek characters. The bed was neat. A large toy panda looked out of place, peeping out from under the bedclothes. Ellie smiled; she'd given him that panda for Christmas a couple of years ago.

There was a grey jumper slung over the back of a chair and muddy football boots in a torn plastic bag under it. The built-in wardrobe door was ajar. Most of the clothes inside were on the floor instead of on hangers.

Ellie told herself that she had to be strong, she must not give in to the temptation to throw herself on the bed and have hysterics. Dry eyed, she went downstairs to make yet another round of cups of tea. At least Mrs Coppola had plenty of milk in her fridge. Not much else, but plenty of milk. Some of it had gone off.

Ellie had another mental flash of her padlocked shed.

She told herself that Tod couldn't be inside if the padlock were securely fastened on the outside. It was his favourite place to play, that was the reason she kept thinking of it. But thinking of it wouldn't get him back.

Two

The room had once been a nursery at the top of the house. It had barred windows overlooking a large garden below. The boy hadn't been able to see anything from the windows because they'd been blacked out when the room had been converted to a photographic studio and dark-room. Once upon a time, children had played here and been happy.

Now there were splashes of blood on the flowered wallpaper.

Ellie said, 'I must go home. My grandson needs me.'

It was past lunch time but no one was interested in food.

The policewoman volunteered to return home with Ellie. Taller than Ellie, big-boned, mid-thirties, long hair tinted to that peculiar mahogany colour which never quite convinced. She seemed efficient.

They reached Ellie's gate just as Rose hove into sight, taking one step at a time, pushing the baby buggy. Frank was fast asleep.

'I walked him all along the shops and back, but was he a handful! Why don't young mothers of today have those reins like the ones we had when we had our children? He wouldn't go in his pushchair and I had to keep running after him and bringing him back and then he'd yell. It tired him out nicely, thank goodness. I bought some of those nice sausage rolls from the bakery, thought you wouldn't have had anything to eat. Phew, is he heavy!'

'Dear Rose.' Ellie hugged her friend, who hugged her back. 'Go and sit down. I'll warm the sausage rolls and make some tea while you put your feet up. We'll leave Frank in his buggy in the hall while I tell the police everything I know in the kitchen, and then you can tell me about whatever it is that's been worrying you.'

'Oh, my dear, I couldn't bother you with all this that's going on. Mine is such a little problem when all is said and done.'

The policewoman was about to do a 'goo-goo' act over Frank, till she took a good look at his frowning, pudgy face. Instead, she produced a notebook and seated herself at the kitchen table.

It was Ellie's turn to explain herself. No, there was no Mr Quicke – he'd died last November. No, she wasn't Tod's grandmother, merely a neighbour with whom he often spent an hour after school before his mother returned from work. Yes, she lived alone. Her daughter Diana lived not far away and occasionally Ellie looked after her grandson when Diana was working. As had happened today.

Then they got down to the nitty gritty. What was the boy Tod like? Ellie thought, His hair sticks up at the back, no matter what he does with it.

She said, 'Normal, nice-looking. Impulsive, imaginative, inquisitive, confident but not brash. Into computer games.'

She thought, My cat Midge adores him and Midge is supposed to be a good judge of character. But she won't want to know that. Nor that Tod's interested in spiders and knows the difference between a plant and a weed.

When had Ellie last seen him? Saturday morning. He'd arrived early, about nine, told her his mother was working. But in truth he made any excuse to go round to Ellie's, play with the computer, the cat, get a cooked meal. That day he'd come round to see if he could 'help' the builders, who tolerated his presence surprisingly well.

Ellie and Rose – they were old friends – had already arranged to go shopping in Oxford Street. They were shopping for Rose's wedding outfit because her daughter was getting married in six weeks' time. Ellie had agreed that Tod might stay and play games on her computer if he wished. She'd given him a couple of biscuits and warned him not to make a nuisance of himself with the builders. Then the taxi had arrived to take her and Rose to the tube station. That was the last she'd seen of him.

'Builders?' said the policewoman.

'A reputable local firm, building a conservatory on the back of my house. Their premises are just off the Avenue, down a side road. Everyone uses them.'

'Workmen?'

'Two. Been with the foreman man and boy. When they heard Tod was missing they searched our gardens here and the church grounds. They're out looking in the park now, I think.'

Ellie said she hadn't seen Tod on Sunday as she'd been to church – where she sang in the choir – and then out to lunch with an old friend. No, she didn't mind giving his name. Bill Weatherspoon, her solicitor, and they'd gone to the Carvery.

She hadn't seen Tod on Monday, either. It had rained. She supposed he'd gone straight home after school. Tuesday afternoon – was it only yesterday? – she'd been working in the front garden. She'd been half expecting him, as he was always hungry after swimming and would often drop in on her afterwards for a cuppa and some biscuits. But she hadn't seen him.

'Tod has keys to his own house, of course. The quickest way home from school for him would be across the main road by the zebra crossing, over the Church Green, into the alley and up his back garden to the kitchen door. The same if he'd gone swimming. He'd take the bus from the swimming pool to the stop by the school, or even walk. It's not that far. Working in the front garden, I wouldn't expect to see him but the builders know him and they knew where I was. If he'd wanted me, he'd have asked them if I was in and then come through the house to find me.'

I don't know how I can keep so calm ... Dear Lord, be with him...

Frank woke from his nap, stretching, making grunting noises. Oh dear, that meant a full nappy. Diana didn't believe in early toilet training, which was all very well when dear little babies could be lifted with ease, but another matter altogether when they were struggling, kicking toddlers.

The detective sergeant recoiled as the stench filled the kitchen and Ellie explained, 'I'll have to change him.'

Dear Rose was fast asleep in the sitting room, her coat unbuttoned but still on, her knitted tea cosy of a hat squashed over her permed grey hair.

Ellie heaved Frank out of his buggy, changed him on the kitchen table – she was not going to struggle upstairs with him, despite the distaste on the policewoman's face. She put Frank in his chair seat at the kitchen table, rescued the sausage rolls from burning and made a pot of tea. There wasn't any fresh milk of course, but she had some long-life which would do if you were desperate. And she was desperate. Frank ate more than her but she managed two cups of tea, and the policewoman had one, too.

'Did anyone see you working in the garden yesterday?'

Ellie flushed. The sergeant was actually considering the idea that she, Ellie Quicke, had been responsible for the boy's disappearance?

She thought back. 'Well, yes. Several people. Everyone stops to talk when you garden by the roadside. I'd promised Mrs Dawes – she's the head of the flower-arranging team at church – some variegated ivy from my front garden, and she came by to collect it.

'She brought along her lodger. Gus, that was his name. She thought I might be able to find some odd jobs for him to do. My garden gate had come off its hinges. The builders would have done it eventually but Gus was on the spot, so I asked him to repair it. He was at it, on and off, for most of the afternoon. The hinge was broken. He had to go and buy another and then fit it. He finished about five, I suppose.

'I promised to ask my builders if they could find some work for him, but it was getting dark and they'd gone by then. I don't know who else might have seen me. Oh, I remember. My next door neighbour, Armand, teaches at the High School, he came back about five and we talked a bit about my conservatory, and his. He's going to have one done soon, too. That's when I remembered that I had to get to B&Q that night. They were out of stock of the floor tiles I'd ordered, so I needed to get an alternative before the tiler comes. Armand was kind enough to run me down there – I don't drive. I said he'd no need, I could get a cab, but he insisted on taking me and bringing me back. I suppose we got back about six fifteen. Something like that.

'Then there was a slide show and talk at the church hall. My friend Rose – she's the one who took baby Frank out for me this morning – she dropped by and we had a quick snack together beforehand. The talk finished about half eight, quarter to nine, I suppose. Then we had coffee, and Rose and I washed up. I think that's all.'

'We'll have to check, names and times.'

'Of course,' said Ellie, trying not to mind. She gave names and addresses, hoping that Armand next door wouldn't be too sharp with the sergeant. He could be abrasive, but there, a teacher's job was not an easy one.

The sergeant stared at Ellie. 'Where would you look for the boy?'

The answer was, In my shed. But Diana had looked there. Ellie lifted her hands and let them drop. 'I'm trying not to think about it.' She went to wake Rose, to have some lunch.

Rose was excited by all the hoo-ha but very concerned for Tod, whom she liked. She was in a high old state when the sergeant wanted her to confirm what she and Ellie had done together recently, and when she'd last seen Tod.

'Oh dear, oh dear! When did I last see him? On Saturday. You really want to know what we did after that? Shopping is so tiring, but we did manage to buy a nice royal-blue suit for me, practical for all occasions. To think of dear little Tod going missing. I can't hardly believe it!'

'What do you think has happened to the boy?' asked the sergeant.

Rose gaped, her tongue still for once. She shook her head and replaced the sausage roll she had been eating on her plate.

Ellie looked out of the window. She didn't dare put her fears into words, either.

Frank wouldn't settle after his lunch, so the two women struggled to insert him back into his buggy and took him for a walk. Ellie called at Mrs Coppola's on the way.

The policeman who came to the door said that Mrs Coppola's sister had arrived to look after her. The woman came to the door. Another brittle blonde, but older, cigarette-stained, putting on weight and straining at the seams. Tears all round.

As Ellie and Rose made their way slowly to the park they met Mrs Dawes, the flower arranger, on her way to the shops. She'd heard about Tod's disappearance and was distressed, as was everyone who knew him. She was also in a bit of a state because her lodger Gus had been out all night and not returned. Someone at the shops said they'd seen him reeling down the Avenue last night, very much the worse for drink. His smoking was bad enough – those hand-rolled nasties, ugh! But drink she could not be doing with.

Uh-oh! What was that about a drunk sleeping it off in the church porch this morning? Was it only this morning? Gus had told her he'd had a problem in the past with the drink, but said that he'd been on the wagon for months and months. He looked so respectable. Ellie had paid him in cash for mending the gate, so he might just have taken that money and got drunk with it. Oh dear.

'I would never have taken him in if I'd known that he was likely to get drunk and disgrace me,' said Mrs Dawes. 'He came to me through the church, you know. The curate asked us in the Women's Guild to be a friend in the community to someone from a hostel. Since my nephew left last month, I could do with the rent and of course it's all paid by the DSS, so I didn't think there'd be any problem. But out all night and drunk in the Avenue! Ugh! I suppose he's sleeping it off somewhere now, but when he comes back, I'll tell him to mend his ways or get out.'

'So you didn't see Tod yesterday?'

'Can't remember the last time I set eyes on him, to tell the truth.'

Ellie and Rose plodded on to the swings in the park. There was a group of men leaving the park as they entered. Some police, the builders. They looked as tired and depressed as Ellie and Rose felt. And it was only three in the afternoon.

'What was it you wanted to talk to me about, Rose?'

'Such a little thing it was, not to mind, it'll

get sorted. Not today of all days, right?'

Frank made them push him and push him on the swings. Then he ran around while they collapsed on to a nearby seat. Finally they coaxed him back into the buggy and made their way back. Mrs Coppola's house was all lit up, a police car outside.

Ellie's house was dark and quiet. The builders weren't there, knocked off for the day – or else gone to help the police search further afield. There was a message on the answerphone to say that Frank's babysitter was back from the doctor's with some antibiotics and would ring again if she felt well enough to work the next day. Also a message from Diana to remind Ellie that they still needed to discuss a projected house and flat swop, and to do this Diana proposed to have a meal with her that evening.

'Can't,' said Ellie to herself. 'Won't.' The prospect of a fight with Diana did tend to sink the heart rather. It was beyond her to understand where Diana had got the idea from that Ellie would calmly vacate her own home to let Diana move in.

Diana had moved down to London to take a job managing a block of flats owned by her great-aunt Drusilla, leaving her husband Stewart to sell their house up north and follow her down. Diana was in a perfectly good rented two-bedroomed flat locally at the moment and when their house was sold, they would no doubt find something to buy. But Diana seemed to have been born greedy. Ellie sighed. If only her dear Frank were still alive ... but there. If wishes were fishes...

At present Stewart was still working up north and living in the marital home, while commuting south at weekends. He was a nice man and devoted to Diana but his failure to gain promotion at work was putting a strain on their marriage. Ellie banished the suspicion that Diana was tiring of a husband who couldn't provide her with the lifestyle to which she aspired.

As for the idea of Ellie meekly handing her house over to Diana, Ellie told herself for the umpteenth time that she only had to stand firm, that Diana couldn't make her do anything she didn't want to do and she did not, repeat *not* wish to leave her own little house. Why should she, for heavens' sake?

Rose made some tea for them both while Ellie hauled Frank out of his buggy and let him run around the sitting room. Neither of them had enough energy to talk.

Ellie told herself she needed to shop, to get some food in for herself. Milk. Loo paper. Instant coffee and tea bags. Fresh fruit and veg. She made a list and sat down to rest her aching head for a while. She had promised to get round to see Aunt Drusilla. But how? She tried to pray but found it difficult. Went into the kitchen and wept a little with her back carefully turned so that Rose shouldn't see.

Rose called from the sitting room. 'He's just done another pooh!'

Ellie cleaned Frank up. Again. He was fractious, wanted to pull all the books out of the bookcase, switch the telly on and off, sweep the flower vase off the mantelpiece. When prevented from doing what he wanted, he kicked and screamed. 'No!' was the only word in his vocabulary at the moment. Ellie tried to hold on to the fact that before he started teething, he'd been a different child. It was hard to remember that when he was throwing a tantrum.

Ellie decided that this was one time she could reasonably expect Diana to get home early and resume her motherly duties. Diana had a mobile, of course. Ellie hated mobiles. All that technology was frightening. And how anyone remembered those long sequences of numbers, she couldn't think. Diana had programmed her mobile number into Ellie's ordinary phone memory, so it should in theory be easy to contact her. Not so easy to explain to Diana that she must leave her very important work and return home. Now!

Diana said she couldn't possibly leave, as she had a site meeting with the decorators in half an hour at Aunt Drusilla's block of flats down by the river. And no, nobody else but her could deal with them. Diana loved playing at being an executive and had taken to power-dressing in a big way.

'I don't care what meetings you have,' said Ellie. 'I have to go out to get food and I must see to Aunt Drusilla.'

'She's making a fuss about nothing, as

usual. The sooner she goes into a home, the better.'

'I'm afraid she wouldn't agree,' said Ellie, tired to the point of feeling faint. 'I'll give you half an hour to finish up and get home. Then I'll order a minicab, take Rose back home, get some food and pay a quick call on Aunt Drusilla.'

'Well, if you're going to the shops, you might as well get me some—'

Ellie put the phone down with a clatter and to stop Diana ringing back, booked herself a minicab. Rose had painfully managed to get down on her knees to stop little Frank from jamming a biscuit into the video recorder. Frank was going to start screaming at any minute. He was also very smelly. Again.

'I'm getting too old for this,' said Ellie, changing the little boy. He stared up at her with hard dark eyes, clutching a wooden spoon and banging it on the table.

Rose was uncharacteristically terse. 'Do you think he does it on purpose? Oh, my back!'

Ellie tried to cuddle Frank but he would have none of it. He struggled out of her arms so she set him down on the floor where he made a beeline for the cat Midge, who was curled into a circle on top of the boiler. Without opening an eye, one inch of Midge's tail began to twitch. Rose and Ellie watched as Frank tried to grab it. Both women were too exhausted to stop him.

'My money's on Midge,' said Rose, who was a fan of Ellie's formidable cat.

Ellie hesitated. 'We mustn't let Frank get scratched.'

Rose sighed. 'I suppose we'd never hear the end of it.'

Frank went purple with rage at not being able to reach the cat. He stamped his feet and banged the boiler. Midge rose to his feet, stretched himself into an upside-down U shape, turned round with his back to them and returned to sleep.

'What is my darling getting so upset for?' Diana had swept in, unheard. She picked Frank up and he turned off the tears and gooed at his mother, hitting her with the wooden spoon he still held in one hand.

Ellie and Rose made their escape. As the minicab passed the Coppola house, they turned their heads to see the police car still outside.

They were quiet for the rest of the journey.

Ellie's husband had left her very comfortably off so while she did not drive a car, she had recently opened an account with a local minicab firm. The driver waited while she dropped Rose off at the council flats, did a quick shop in the Avenue, and then took herself and her packages on to Aunt Drusilla's.

As they drew up on the gravelled driveway of the large Victorian house, Ellie straightened her back and tucked her chin in. For years during Frank's lifetime she had been at his Aunt Drusilla's beck and call so that now even the sight of the building made her feel cowed. The house had actually been left to Ellie in her husband's will, but both women knew that Ellie would never turn Frank's aunt out.

'Wait for me. I shouldn't be more than half an hour.'

There was a nice-looking Jaguar in the drive, which meant that Aunt Drusilla's son Roy was visiting. Roy was Aunt Drusilla's illegitimate son who had been adopted at birth and risen to become a successful architect. He had reappeared in his mother's life a while back, hoping that some family money might come his way. He had stayed for all sorts of reasons: because he'd found a property in the neighbourhood suitable for development, and because he'd grown to admire his mother.

He'd also stayed to court Ellie, at first because she was a wealthy widow and after that because he'd become fond of her. Some of Ellie's friends likened him to a second-hand-car salesman; others thought him quite charming.

As Ellie mounted the steps to the great front door, Roy opened it to leave. Tall, well-built, silver-haired, Irish blue eyes, well dressed.

'Ellie, my dear. I was just thinking about you.' Voice and eyes were warm. Ellie liked him, found him entertaining and was wary of his effect on her. She wasn't sure she should trust a man who cast sexual lures over a woman of her age.

'I came as soon as I could. How is she?'

'Shaken. Slipped on the third step up and fell. Gave herself a black eye and a sprained knee. She's resting in bed, now. The daily's just gone. Left her a foul-looking stew for supper. I said I'd fetch in some fish and chips, unless you've got something better with you...?'

Ellie couldn't help grinning. Aunt Drusilla eating fish and chips out of newspaper would indeed be something. 'Will you get her a take-away?'

'She's refused my offers of Chinese, Indian and pizzas. With disdain. Any other suggestions?'

'She should have some frozen meals in her freezer. If not, try Tesco's frozen meals. She hasn't got a microwave, but you could use the oven.'

'If you'll help me light it...?'

She laughed. 'Not tonight. I've got to get back.' With a pang she remembered. 'Young Tod's missing, not been seen since last night.'

'Oh, he'll turn up. Boys are like that. Shall I bring a bottle round and share it with you later on?'

'Sorry, Roy. I'm flaked out, just dying to get to bed. Also Diana's supposed to be coming for supper.'

'Ah.' He liked Diana as little as Diana liked him.

Sometimes I like you, Roy, sometimes I don't. You might have pretended to be worried about Tod.

She went into the great dark house, turning on lights as she went. From floor to high ceiling, double-lined velvet curtains kept out the dusk.

She climbed the wide, shallow stairs to the first floor and entered the long, parquet-floored main bedroom with its hand-blocked blue-and-white Chinese patterned wallpaper, and intricately carved mahogany bedroom suite. No built-in fitments for Miss Quicke. She'd been born in that boat shaped bed, her father had died in it and she intended to do the same.

The old lady was propped up with pillows, looking as small as a child, a wet flannel draped across one eye.

'You took your time.'

Ellie drew a chair up to the bed and took the old lady's hand in hers. The skin was only slightly too warm. Not much of a temperature, if any.

'There was a problem. Young Tod's missing since last night. His mother's hysterical. We had to call the police. Also, Diana dumped baby Frank on me. His babysitter had to go to the doctor's and is now on antibiotics.'

'And I chose today to fall down the stairs. Bad timing.' At least Aunt Drusilla could laugh at herself.

'How are you?'

'Bruised. I don't hold with painkillers but Roy got me some and they seem to be working. He even made me some tea, not that I could drink it.'

Ellie smiled, looking at the mismatched teacup and saucer on a rough wooden tray nearby. Aunt Drusilla liked the best china, silver, expensive trays, thinly cut bread and butter, shortcake biscuits from Fortnums.

'Shall I get you some more?'

'In a minute.' Aunt Drusilla had left her hand in Ellie's. For years Miss Quicke had treated Ellie as her own personal slavey, but after Ellie's much-loved husband – and Miss Quicke's nephew – died, Ellie had gradually emerged from his shadow. Of course she still missed Frank, but she'd discovered that she could manage all sorts of things quite well by herself, thank you. In consequence, Miss Quicke had begun to treat Ellie more as an equal.

'The boy Tod. You're fond of him, aren't you?'

'Yes.'

'Do they know why...?'

'No.' Ellie sniffed. 'I must be getting a cold.' She had yet another flash of the tool shed. Tod couldn't be there though, because the padlock was on. Diana would have noticed if it hadn't been properly fastened.

Roy had tried to draw the bedroom curtains but left gaps between. Ellie remedied this, shutting out the night.

'You might get me a hot-water bottle, too. My feet are like ice.'

Ellie took the tea tray downstairs and returned with a fat hot-water bottle and a china mug of hot tea, no milk, weak, with two slices of lemon in it.

'I must go. I have the minicab waiting. I keep thinking about Tod and my garden shed. It's no good. I'll have to go and check for myself.'

'Don't worry about me. Roy's bringing me in something decent to eat. Take care of yourself.'

Ellie bent to kiss the old woman's cheek. 'Thank you, Aunt Drusilla.'

'For what, girl?'

'For understanding. I'll be in tomorrow.'

In the cab going home, Ellie relaxed, closing her eyes. A padlock which was secure. A key in Tod's possession. How could he be inside, if the padlock were on and properly fastened?

He couldn't. Could he?

Think, girl, think.

Suppose he'd wanted to hide himself away? He could open the padlock with his key and go in. Dump his school bag and swimming things. He'd made a sort of den in there, where he kept a lantern with a stub of candle – he preferred it to a torch. He even had some stick insects in a closed jar. His mother wouldn't allow them in her house.

He would sit there for hours, reading in an old reclining chair with a rug on it. Under the window there was a table which Ellie used for potting up seeds. There was a very special smell in there, of fertilizer, potting compost, earth. Garden tools hung on nails from the wall.

How could you close the door and put the padlock on from the inside? Well, you could not, obviously. You'd have to find another way out of the shed ... by the window? A window kept firmly latched shut on the inside.

But the window was not that high off the ground. Suppose Tod had wanted to hide himself away for a bit. To scare his mother. As a prank, maybe. A prank that might have gone wrong.

Suppose that he'd taken the padlock off, opened the door and gone inside. He could then climb on the table and open the window as wide as it would go. Perhaps he might have wedged it open with something, a flower pot, a bamboo stick.

He could go outside again. Close the door. Feed the padlock through the hasp and snap it shut.

Then climb in through the open window. It wouldn't be that easy, but it could be done. Once inside again, he could have shut the window tight and latched it securely.

Hey presto. He was inside a locked room.

Oh, it was clearly a prank that had gone wrong. Once inside, he must have been taken ill, gone down with flu perhaps. Something must have happened to prevent him from leaving once he considered he'd frightened everyone enough.

Yes, that was it.

Thank you, Lord, for helping me to work it out.

When I get hold of the little brat, frightening everyone silly like that...!

But Diana looked in through the window. She would have seen him if he were there, wouldn't she? Perhaps. Perhaps not. If he'd hidden in a corner, under the rug...

Ellie signed for the minicab and carried her purchases indoors.

Diana met her in the hall with a fractious Frank in her arms. 'Mother, what have you been giving Frank to eat? He's done nothing but fill his pants since I got here and—'

'I won't be a minute.' Ellie unearthed her big torch in the cupboard under the stairs, ignoring Diana's complaints. Midge wandered in from outside, letting the cat flap clang to behind him. He wanted to be fed but she couldn't wait any longer.

The framework of the conservatory was stark against the night sky. Perhaps there would be a frost that night? There was a lamp post in the alley at the bottom of the garden and that, with the torch, helped her to see where she was going as she made her way down the path. Midge followed her.

The shed was in darkness, no candle alight inside.

'Tod?' She shook the padlock.

No reply.

Perhaps she had been wrong. Perhaps he wasn't there, after all.

She shone her torch through the window and played it around. Everything looked normal, except ... except that the rug wasn't on the chair any more.

Midge pressed his nose to the door of the shed and Ellie felt the hairs rise on the back of her neck.

Tod was there, all right. Midge sensed it. Perhaps could hear him breathe.

She unlocked the padlock and took it off.

Pulled the door wide open.

A dense shadowy interior, barred with light from the lamp in the alley.

Midge disappeared inside.

Ellie pointed the torch after him.

Three

At first she couldn't see anything unusual, but Midge darted forward and disappeared behind the stack of plant pots under the table by the window.

Ellie listened for breathing, but heard none. She sat on the garden chair and shone her torch on to the ranks of pots. She couldn't see anything to cause her alarm. Then she caught the flash of Midge's eyes reflected in the torchlight. She looked for the lantern but it wasn't there. Nor was the box of matches.

'Mother, where are you? Don't you realize it's bedtime for poor little Frank...?'

'Not now, Diana,' muttered Ellie.

Dead or alive, Tod could be hidden behind those plant pots. He was small for his age and wouldn't take up much space. If he'd wanted to hide himself away, he could have pulled the stacks of pots out from the wall of the shed by the light of the candle in the lantern, crawled in there with the rug to make himself a comfortable nest and pulled the pots back in front of him.

Diana was coming down the path with little Frank in her arms, calling for Ellie. The toddler was wailing. Diana was getting angry.

Ellie put the torch down on the floor, aiming its beams at the plant pots, and began to pull them away from the wall. One stack. Two stacks. Lift them clear and dump them on the table. Three ... and there was the faded tartan of her old rug. Also there was Midge, curled up on top of the boy, staring down into his sleeping face.

'Mother, what on earth are you doing?'

'What I ought to have done this morning. Finding Tod.'

'Well, he can't be there. I looked.'

Ellie didn't reply. Four stacks. Five. She lifted the pots and put them on the table. A terracotta pot crashed to the floor and broke. Midge decided he'd had enough and strolled out of the shed, darting between Diana's legs to shoot back up the garden. Still there was no sign of movement from the bundle of rug.

'He's here.' She knelt down. 'Tod. Tod, it's me.' Pray God he's alive.

'Mother, come away, for God's sake. Frank, please! Just be quiet for a moment and I'll get you your drink. Mother, if the boy's been hidden there, he's probably...'

'Dead?'

The lantern was there, the stub of candle burned out. And his school bag. Ellie tugged at the rug and it flopped down over her hands, revealing a grubby small boy in a foetal position.

Diana drew in her breath. 'Oh, my God...'

Ellie told herself she was not going to faint. There was a nasty dark stain on the rug around the boy's body. Dried blood? He was wearing his school clothes, but there was no sign of his jacket. His clothing looked dishevelled, the buttons on his school blouse not done up correctly, as if someone else had dressed him in a hurry.

I must keep calm. Dear Lord, help me to do the right thing.

She felt for a pulse in his neck. 'He's alive. Phone for an ambulance.'

Diana hissed something between her teeth and ran back up the garden path.

'Oh, Tod.' She must not cry.

There was no movement from the bundle under the table. Gently she tried to pull him out by means of the rug. He didn't resist. He wasn't stiff. He was floppy, so he couldn't be dead. But he didn't open his eyes.

Ellie began to pray aloud. 'Dear Lord, don't let him die. Tod, dearest, it's all right now. I'm here. The ambulance is coming, any minute now. Just hold on, there's a good boy...'

Dear Lord, how could you let this happen to him? No, I know I ought not to question whether you know best, but ... I can't bear this. Dear little Tod. Such a bright light in my life. Yes, Lord, I know I'm being selfish, thinking only of myself, but he is a nice boy and ... just save him, will you? And I promise I'll...

No, that's stupid. No bargains. That's not the way. I'm not thinking straight.

She managed to pull Tod clear of the table and lift him into her arms. It wasn't easy to do but she managed it, somehow. She held her cheek to his, feeling his cold skin gradually warming to hers. There was blood on his face from a head wound. As she moved him, fresh blood began to seep from deep cuts on his wrists, so he must be alive. Yes, he was still breathing, if shallowly. The rug was stiff with dried blood, as were his trousers. She didn't want to think what had caused his injuries.

Dear Lord, she prayed. If it is your will, let him live. Give him strength and courage to meet whatever is to come. Give us all strength and courage. We're going to need it.

There were more footsteps coming down the garden path. Not Diana, but her next-door neighbour, the teacher Armand. Sharp-voiced, foxy-faced, practical.

'Ellie, are you there? I was just parking the car when your daughter shot out of the house screaming something about ... oh, my God. Is he...?'

'No. But in a bad way.'

'Shall I take him off you?'

'I'm keeping him warm. Besides, it doesn't matter about my clothes, but you might get blood on your suit.'

He hesitated, and then to his credit stooped down and took the boy from her.

'He's too heavy for you. I'll carry him up to the top. We mustn't waste any time getting him to hospital.'

She let the boy go and as she did so, the tears came. Armand carried the boy gently up the slope.

Ellie couldn't move. Didn't want to.

The knowledge of what was to come was too much for her to bear.

The room wasn't used very often but when it was, you could understand why the windows had been closely sealed and the fireplace, too. The houses in that road were detached, set well apart in a pleasant neighbourhood to provide privacy for the fortunate owners. The back gardens were long and well fenced. Across the bottom of the gardens ran a tube line. No one walked their dogs that way, or kicked a football over into the garden by accident or on purpose.

When dusk came, lights were switched on in the kitchen and sitting room of number thirty-four, as usual. Curtains were drawn. There was the scent of curry from the kitchen. Then the television was turned on until it was time for bed.

There was absolutely nothing abnormal about all that.

Only the stains on the wallpaper in the nursery told a different story.

So it was a police matter again, but with a different slant.

Tod lived. At least, his body did. His mind was another matter. On Thursday he opened and closed his eyes but didn't respond in any other way. The doctors were wary. There'd been a blow to the head, they said, apart from the – er – other injuries, which had been stitched up. Tod was young and strong, yes. But they couldn't say how soon he might become fully conscious.

Mrs Coppola was hysterical. The police said that she and her son – if he lived – would be given counselling.

Ellie wasn't offered any counselling but definitely needed it. She reflected that it was all very well for people to come to her with their troubles – which they did – but when you were a strong person and needed help for yourself, you didn't get it. She was distracted with worry about Tod and to add to her misery, Diana had brought baby Frank and decided to sleep over at Ellie's. Diana said that there was a nasty smell of gas in the kitchen at the flat, and she couldn't expose her little baby to such a dangerous situation. Anyway, said Diana, she was sure that Ellie would be glad of the company, with a homicidal maniac in the neighbourhood.

The police cordoned off the shed as a crime scene, though Ellie pointed out that the keys were found in Tod's pocket, so he must have locked up and then crawled through the window to hide. The police found blood on a corner of Ellie's potting-shed table, where Tod must have struck his head while scrambling through the window. They took the table and the rug away for tests.

The only bright spot on the horizon was that baby Frank's babysitter was back on the job.

Ellie was frantic to be quiet on her own in her own house. By the time she'd done the rounds of visits to Tod at the hospital, to a gradually recovering Aunt Drusilla and liaised with builders she was too tired to fight with Diana. So at night she threw some food together and washed up, agreed with whatever Diana said – more or less – and went to bed early. Though not to sleep well.

By Friday morning Ellie had had enough. Diana's husband Stewart would be coming south to join them that afternoon. Diana had said that naturally he would also expect to sleep at Ellie's. Ellie liked her son-in-law well enough but if he were to move in, too, Diana's temporary move might harden into a permanency. Just to get some peace and quiet, Ellie might find herself forced to leave. Fudge and fidget, it was *her* house and not Diana's, wasn't it?

This was one problem too many so she rang the Gas Board and asked them to check out a possible leak at Diana's – they could get a key from the managing agents in the Avenue – and to leave a message about it on her answerphone. That done, she arranged to meet an old friend up in town for the day.

Liz Adams was the wife of the ex-vicar at St Thomas' Church on the Green. An experienced counsellor who worked with the victims of abuse and trauma, she'd been a tremendous comfort to Ellie when Frank died. Ellie had kept in touch with Liz and her husband after he'd been promoted to a larger parish on the other side of London, and every now and then Liz and Ellie enjoyed a day out together.

Liz had also got a promotion to a better-paid job recently, so her grey hair was well cut and she wore a stylish trouser suit. Otherwise, she was the same dear old 'horse-face'.

They met at the Wallace Collection in Manchester Square, which had free entrance, superb pictures – Ellie usually skipped the armoury section – delightful restaurant facilities and excellent toilets.

As they looked at the Flemish interior pictures, Ellie unburdened herself of her grief about Tod. 'Do you know, I think I was a suspect for a time? It was my shed, my padlock, my garden. They worked it out that I'd no motive and wouldn't have had time, anyway. By great good fortune I had an alibi all Monday afternoon and evening. That weird odd-job man was with me till dusk – I'll have to tell you about him sometime, talk about "odd", the word might have been invented for him – then Armand from next door took me to B&Q to choose some more tiles for the floor of the conservatory – my first choice was out of stock and of course he wanted to see what was available because he's going to have a conservatory, too. Actually he was very helpful, and I did get some more tiles though they are not quite what I wanted. Then dear Rose came with me to the slide show and talk in the hall.'

'Do you feel guilty about that?'

Ellie paused in front of a small picture of a

woman sitting with her back to the viewer, looking into space. What was she thinking about, that still, quiet woman?

She sighed. 'Yes, I suppose I do. If I'd been at home he might have felt able to come and tell me what had happened. We'd have saved a day.'

Liz pressed her arm. 'What do the doctors say?'

'They can repair the damage to his poor little body, though there may be scars. The bang on the head is another matter. He did come round but...' She scrabbled for her handkerchief. 'Oh, Liz! He's not really "there" any more. His eyes are open some of the time, but he doesn't seem to recognize us.'

Liz moved away to examine a seascape. 'It's early days. Children are resilient.'

'You of all people know better than that.' Ellie blew her nose.

Silence.

Ellie mopped her eyes and turned to ask Liz why she hadn't responded. Liz was staring at a painting of a lad with a cheeky grin on his face. There was a bright sheen of tears in her eyes.

Liz said angrily, 'His hair always stuck up at the back.' She was not referring to the child in the picture.

Ellie remembered with a jolt that Liz had had young Tod in her Sunday-school class. Liz had been fond of Tod, too.

Ellie closed her eyes. She wanted to scream.

She'd been depending on Liz to prop her up but it seemed that Liz wasn't able to cope, either. Which meant that Ellie would have to 'pick herself up, dust herself down, and start all over again'. By herself.

She couldn't do it. She wanted to burst into tears, lie down on the floor and weep herself insensible. She. Could. Not. Do. It.

Yes, she could. If she made an enormous effort, she could control her own feelings and not batten on Liz.

Ellie took a deep, calming breath, deliberately pushing her own tearing grief down and out of sight. Without speaking they moved on to another room, and stopped in front of a big canvas showing a celebration following the birth of a child. Here was a Flemish interior with people crowding around a table and a fireplace. They were toasting the father, proudly holding up the newborn baby.

Only if you read it aright, there were clues to what the picture was really about. Broken eggshells, etcetera. Meaning broken virtue. The comely wife was smirking, her lover leaning over her shoulder to whisper in her ear, the husband holding up a baby who was probably not his.

'Lucky they didn't have DNA testing in those days, or there'd have been all hell to pay.'

'Every picture tells a story.'

She hadn't realized she'd spoken aloud till Liz replied.

'What? Oh, yes. I wonder if the husband

ever found out. Was there any ... on Tod, I mean...?'

'Yes, if they find the man responsible they'll be able to get a conviction.'

'No suspects?'

'No. Except ... well, Mrs Dawes – remember our flower lady? I swear she had white roots to her hair showing on Sunday, but yesterday it was all black as jet again – anyway, she said there was a rumour that a paedophile's been seen in the area, though no one seems to know who it is. Someone from the bail hostel the other side of the shops. I expect Mrs Dawes got that item of gossip from her lodger.'

'Didn't she take in a nephew of hers? No, wait a minute, he left some time ago, didn't he?'

'He went off to share a flat with some friends, so Mrs Dawes took in a poor sort of creature from the hostel instead.'

'He's not the paedophile?'

Ellie had to smile at that. 'Oh no. Not the sort.'

'Hm? Sure about that? The unlikeliest people...'

Ellie laughed. 'Poor Gus. He told me "Gus" is short for "Gustave". Anybody less like a "Gustave" ... No, definitely not the sort.'

'What's your idea of a paedophile, then?'

'Well, for a start, Gus is too old...'

'That means nothing.'

'Too frail, honestly. And he stank of those horrid hand rolled cigarettes. Tod didn't smell of cigarettes when we found him.'

'Ah. Reasonable.'

They passed on to eat in the restaurant. Pretty plates of unusual salads. Waiter service. A little too noisy to be entirely comfortable, but the glassed-over courtyard was a delightful place in which to eat.

Ellie struggled to finish her plateful. Struggled to maintain a bright manner. Talked about going to the National Gallery to see a newly opened exhibition. Talked about where she would like to go on holiday that year.

Liz followed her lead. But when they were leaving, they passed back through the Flemish pictures again and Liz stopped short, looking up at that busy picture of celebration, with the husband holding up a child who was possibly not his own.

Liz touched Ellie's arm. 'You said every picture tells a story. You're good at that, Ellie. Reading the picture, I mean. Can't you find out who did that awful thing to Tod?'

Instinctively Ellie rejected any further responsibility. She laughed as if Liz had made a joke.

Liz sighed, shaking her head. 'Sorry, sorry. I'm no help to you today, am I?'

'You've had to counsel all sorts in your time. What sort of man does that to a young boy?'

'Paedophiles think sodomy is absolutely natural. The blow to the head, the damage inflicted on the boy – that's not usual. Sometimes...' she hesitated and then braced herself. 'Sometimes they take photographs or even video their victims. Pass the evidence around, put it on the Internet even.'

'Ugh! That's creepy. Can you generalize what sort of man it might be, off the record?'

'Off the record and in general terms ... an older man, you'd be surprised how old sometimes. Usually a solitary sort of person. Quite often they're unemployed because the pursuit of what they call their "hobby" takes up all their time. If Tod didn't smell of cigarettes, did he smell of drink or aftershave?'

Ellie closed her eyes and thought back. 'He smelt faintly of chlorine from the baths. He'd been swimming just before. Someone – the man responsible I suppose – must have given him a lift afterwards. The police have interviewed the staff on duty at the swimming pool and talked to Tod's friends, who'd all left earlier than him, apparently. The police are going to try again next Monday, see the regulars, you know.

'Did Tod smell of anything unusual? Not that I can remember. It was twenty-four hours before we found him. He smelt of Midge, who often sleeps on the rug Tod had wrapped around himself. And potting compost, dust and spiders.'

'Do spiders smell?'

They both smiled. Leaving the gallery, Ellie looked back at the picture of the quiet girl, sitting with her back to them, gazing at ... what? 'I wonder if she was praying, or just accepting whatever life had in store for her?'

'Ah, acceptance. The secret of a contented life?'

The two women embraced at the tube station.

'Love to your dear husband,' said Ellie, remembering their former vicar with fondness and respect.

'I've not been much help to you today, have I?' said Liz. 'Gilbert will want to know the latest. He was fond of Tod, too. Ring us when you hear anything?'

'Promise.'

One went east, and the other went west. Ellie shuddered, trying to face the immediate future ... Tod, Aunt Drusilla, Diana...

She would put off going home for a bit, by doing her sick visiting on the way.

Ellie sat by Tod's bedside, holding his hand in hers. They'd shaved part of his head to treat the gash on it and he looked a proper little wounded soldier. It also looked to her as if he'd lost weight. He was hooked up to a Walkman – his mother's idea – but though it was playing loudly enough for Ellie to hear the scratchy beat, his eyes were still unfocused. Ellie wondered why his mother hadn't brought his toy panda. It might have been more comfort to him.

She turned down the volume on the Walkman and stroked the back of his hand. 'What say I get you a brand-new Playstation? You'd like that, wouldn't you? Or would you prefer a new PC with access to the Internet? You can play a raft of games on it, but also use it for finding out things, for school, homework ... generally play around with it?'

Not a flicker of interest.

'The builders have nearly finished my conservatory. I'm having a water feature inside, a trickling sort of fountain for soothing background. I couldn't get the tiles I originally wanted for the flooring – you remember helping me to pick some out of the catalogue? Well, they were out of stock so Armand helped me to get some others. I thought they weren't quite as nice at first, but I'm growing to like them...'

She talked on and on, about this and that and nothing in particular. His hand grew warm in hers but his eyes never focused.

For the first time Ellie allowed herself to speculate what would happen to Tod if he didn't come back to full consciousness. Would he be left so brain-damaged that he'd never walk or talk again?

Would he ever play with the cat Midge again? Eat all her chocolate biscuits at the kitchen table? Laugh...

She closed her eyes and prayed a little.

When she finished, she kissed his forehead, turned up the Walkman a little – but not to screaming pitch – and left.

Next was Aunt Drusilla.

Aunt Drusilla was up and about, but using her stick to lean on more than usual.

'Well, girl? Have you brought me my Bath

Oliver biscuits? I told my daily – fool of a woman, but what can you expect – that you'd make me some tea. So what's the news from the hospital?'

Ellie sighed and shook her head, unpacking the goodies she'd bought on the way home in the Avenue.

Aunt Drusilla poked at a box of chocolate biscuits. 'They're not the sort I usually have.'

'They were out of stock. I thought you might like to try these instead.'

'They'll be too hard on the teeth.'

'Dunk them in your tea, then.'

'The idea!' But the old lady's lips twitched. 'Well, what about the boy?'

'They say he's showing signs of returning consciousness but his eyes are still unfocused.'

Aunt Drusilla tutted. 'Taking his time. Have they arrested the man responsible? It was on the local radio, my cleaner said. Or did she hear it from a neighbour? What's his name? Something stupid. Can't remember it for the moment but it'll come back to me. I hear he's roaming the streets bold as brass. I'm not leaving this house till he's caught, and that's flat.'

'They suspect someone from the hostel. I suppose he'll be easy enough to pick up.'

'I objected when they first wanted to turn that big house into a hostel. Asking for trouble. I said, "We'll all be murdered in our beds," and look what's happened.'

'Surely the people who live there are not let

out into the community till they're safe?'

'They're cunning enough to play sane till it's too late and you land up in hospital. The government wants to get the prison population down, so what happens? Paedophiles and murderers roaming our streets. We're lucky he's only attacked one boy so far.'

'I suppose paedophiles look just like everyone else. I've only met one man from the hostel and he seemed just, well, inadequate. A rather pathetic little man. His mother called him Gustave, of all things. Can you imagine lumbering a child with such an odd name?'

'But that's the man. Gustave. That's the one who did it!'

'Nonsense, he couldn't hurt a fly.'

Aunt Drusilla banged the floor with her stick. 'Stupid girl, what do you know about such things? The sooner they get him under lock and key the better.'

Perhaps I am stupid, thought Ellie, as she walked back home. Perhaps I am naïve and trusting and a little simple, but I really don't think that poor creature Gustave was responsible for harming Tod.

He's too, well, gormless. And frail.

Of course, Liz said they could be all ages, but...

Liz believed in my judgement, anyway. She said I was good at 'reading the picture', and I really think I do have a small talent in that direction. I may not have been to university or be a Brain of Britain, but I'm usually right about people. As far as I'm concerned, Gustave is not in the picture.

I hope.

It would be terrible to be defending someone who had torn a small boy apart and left him to die.

Oh, I can't bear it ... Tod, Tod ... Lord, if it is your will, let him recover.

She was not someone who went in for anger, much. Anger roiled the contents of your stomach, giving you acid heartburn. But she realized that, for the first time since Tod's disappearance, she was extremely angry with the man who had abused the boy. If she could lay her hands on him ... but of course she couldn't. She hadn't a clue who he might be. Well, not Gus, obviously. But when they did catch the person, she wouldn't mind having five minutes alone with him. That core of anger stayed with her, though she kept pushing it down and telling herself it did no good to be angry with someone you'd never even met.

She took the pedestrian crossing across the main road and crossed the Green in the shadow of the church. It was getting lighter in the evenings. Forsythia bushes were springing into yellow magnificence, daffodils shone under the trees and bird-song was everywhere, competing with the noise of the traffic.

Bother the traffic. How lovely it would be to live in the country, gently greening over at this time of year ... with primroses to be hunted in the hedgerows and catkins.

And mud. At this time of year, the countryside was awash with mud.

Ellie shook her head at herself. In times of trouble she allowed herself to daydream of living in the country, although she knew perfectly well that she'd be a fish out of water there. One bus a day if you were lucky, not a bank in sight and no shops within walking distance.

When she reached the alley at the bottom of her garden, she stopped and looked about her.

Tod would have come this way home on Tuesday afternoon. His swimming club finished about five but for some reason he'd been the last of his group to leave. No one had admitted seeing him go. It was a ten minute walk home from the swimming baths, which were on the far side of the park. It would have been getting dark and he wouldn't have risked walking through the unlit park. Not in the dusk. There'd been a couple of cases of indecent exposure there recently...

Oh. Did those who exposed themselves indecently go on to rape and mutilate children? Ouch. She must ask Liz. Well, the police would no doubt be following up that line of enquiry.

On the whole it wasn't likely Tod would willingly have gone into the park. To walk round by the streets took much longer, so usually he took the bus home. It was only two stops and he'd be getting hungry after swimming. His lunch would have seemed a long time ago. His mother usually left something out for him to eat, or he'd delve into the freezer. Or come round to see what Ellie had to offer.

Suppose he'd left the baths about quarter past five and been standing at the bus stop when along came ... who? Someone in a car, offering a lift? He'd never get into a stranger's car. He'd been too well taught for that.

Or was he walking along home with someone he knew, and then...?

Well, you couldn't exactly rape and mutilate a boy in full view of everyone on a busy bus route.

So, he must have been taken off the roads, somehow.

And how long would the attack on him have taken? An hour? Possibly two hours? Possibly even more? Really, no one knew how long. Tod might have been kept there all evening, or even all night for all they knew.

She was standing in the alley by now. The back garden of her own house rose gently in front of her, the skyline blocked by the tree. And the builders. They were working by floodlight, fitting doors, singing along to a transistor radio which was blaring out pop music. Armand would be around to complain about the noise in a minute.

To the right the alley meandered along past Armand and Kate's house – there was a light in their back room, where Armand was no doubt getting down to his nightly task of correcting pupils' homework – he was a master at the High School. His wife wouldn't be home yet, because she worked in the City. Their garden was a muddy slope, cleared of its previous cover of weeds and overgrown shrubs. When the builders finished at Ellie's they were due to start next door, building Armand and Kate an almost identical conservatory. When that was finished, Ellie was to mastermind the creation of a new garden for them. She was looking forward to that.

It crossed Ellie's mind that if Tod had been abducted straight from the swimming pool and taken somewhere to be abused, it would all have taken time. If he'd come this way home afterwards, the earliest he could have arrived would be, say, about half past six. Armand had taken Ellie to B&Q about a quarter past five, say, and they'd got back home about half past six. Armand would then have got down to marking homework and preparing lessons.

If Tod had reached the alley at any time after half past six, he'd have seen Armand's lights on. Armand was not a particularly sympathetic character, though Ellie was getting to like him, the more she knew of him. Tod had never taken to him. Tod wouldn't have gone to Armand for help.

Tod had been in a bad way. He'd known his mother would be out till late. Normally he'd have gone straight up the garden path to

Ellie. Ellie had been out with Armand from just after five till about half past six. Then she'd been at home from half past six to a quarter to eight, making and eating a light supper for herself and Rose before they went off to the slide show at the church hall. If Tod had seen the lights on in Ellie's house, he'd have come to her for help. But he hadn't.

Which meant either that he hadn't reached the alley till after Ellie had gone to the slide show ... or he'd been too distressed to ask anyone for help. He ought to have gone home and phoned his mother at work. Their house was three along to the left.

Dark, as usual. As it would have been on Tuesday night.

Mrs Coppola had gone back to work today, of course. Or, she might be at the hospital. One must be charitable. She might be at the hospital.

But Tod hadn't gone home. He'd hidden himself in a dark, safe corner. Curled up in a rug, hidden himself away. To die?

Ellie shivered. It was getting cold. The builders were knocking off for the day. Ellie saw Diana appear in the conservatory. The builder was showing her something and to judge by her body language, Diana was saying it wasn't acceptable.

Ellie felt tired at the very sight of Diana and the problems she represented. The builder closed the outer door to the conservatory, fading out the noise of the transistor.

Ellie pushed open the gate to her garden

and felt Midge the cat brush around her legs. She stooped to stroke him but he bounded away into the dusk, chasing who knew what ... a field-mouse? A spider? He was an indiscriminate hunter.

Ellie plodded up the path to the conservatory and went in. The place smelt of new wood and undercoat and one of those strong man-made glues that you weren't supposed to use in enclosed spaces. It made her sneeze.

'Mother, there you are! Where have you been? Stewart's got a couple of days off, remember, so he'll be here any minute and I thought we'd go out after supper...'

'Missus, do you want to have a look at this?'

'...while you babysit.'

Baby Frank was wailing. The builder was looking grim – what else could go wrong? The phone was ringing, but nobody was bothering to answer it.

Stewart appeared in the kitchen doorway. He was a tall, well-built man with an endearing mop of blond hair. He looked harassed. 'Hello, everyone! Hi, darling!' He kissed his wife, catching her on the side of her jaw.

Frank began to scream. Stewart dropped an evening paper on the table and as it flopped down, Ellie saw the headline, 'SEX MANIAC HELD!'

'What's that? Is that about Tod?'

The builder nodded. 'Hadn't you heard? It's all round the shops. I hope they chop off the bastard's whatsit!'

'It's that nasty dirty old man who was

hanging around here the night Tod was attacked,' said Diana. 'Really, mother. You can't be trusted on your own. Fancy employing such a piece of garbage.'

Ellie thought, This is terrible. They've got the wrong man!

Then her usual lack of confidence kicked in. I'm being stupid. Of course they wouldn't have arrested the man if he weren't guilty. I must just be thankful that they've got him.

Four

One of the messages on the answerphone was from the Gas Board, saying they'd checked out Diana's flat and there was no trace of a gas leak. The other message was from Liz's husband, Gilbert. He said Liz had come home in a state, feeling she hadn't been able to help Ellie at all. Would Ellie please remember that he was always there and wanted to hear from her, any time of the day or night?

Ellie didn't return the call, because she had to entertain Diana and Stewart and then babysit for little Frank. Worry mixed with anger was so tiring...

Gustave was taken in for questioning at the police station. Mrs Dawes gave interviews to the press saying she would never have guessed, she'd never been so taken in, and if he wanted his stuff – not that there was much of it, sniff – he could get someone to collect it from her front lawn.

The following morning Tod opened his eyes and focused on his surroundings. His first intelligent action was to paw the Walkman off his head.

* * *

In the interregnum since their own vicar, Gilbert Adams, had been promoted to a larger parish on the other side of London, their curate had been enjoying himself. His nickname – not an affectionate one – was Timid Timothy, and the parish was looking forward to the day when he would be superseded in the pulpit by someone more, well, up to the mark. The congregation was not, on the whole, intolerant. But when Timothy preached that Sunday a rather weak sermon about forgiving your enemy, no one was impressed.

'What we wanted today,' said Aunt Drusilla's son, Roy, delivering a cup of coffee into Ellie's hands after the service, 'was some good, old-fashioned Hellfire and Slaughter condemning the paedophile to outer darkness. Preferably something with boiling oil in it.'

Ellie sighed. 'I know I shouldn't feel so angry and that we ought to forgive our enemies, but I agree with you. When I think of poor Tod...'

'Recovering, I hear,' said Roy, angling to look down her cleavage.

She pulled the lapel of her blouse across. She'd wondered if she'd been showing too much when she'd put it on but she'd been in a hurry, what with Diana and Stewart having somehow arranged to stay for the weekend and baby Frank teething. And she really hadn't thought anyone would want to peep down her cleavage at her age. The very idea!

She gave Roy an old-fashioned look.

Roy waggled his dark eyebrows in appreciation. Silver haired, silver-tongued, six foot of charm and a cousin of her dead husband. You couldn't get rid of Roy Bartrick with a frown. Anyway, did she really want to?

She tried to put some frost into her voice. 'Visiting Aunt Drusilla again today? How does it feel to have a long-lost mother?'

He grinned. 'You forgot to add "unmarried mother". I rather like the old bat, you know. She's nothing if not gutsy. I wish I'd come looking for her years ago. Yes, I'll be going round there this afternoon, after she's had a little nap. She wants me to look at her computer. The email is playing up again.'

Nothing that Aunt Drusilla undertook ought to have surprised Ellie by now, but this did. Ellie herself was only just beginning to come to terms with the very basic word processing side of her dear husband's computer, and here was his aunt tackling email? Aunt Drusilla was *ancient*. Was she really playing around with email at her age? Ellie herself hadn't dared try it.

Roy removed a cat hair from Ellie's blue jacket. 'Hadn't you heard that silver surfers are the fastest growing group of people to use the Internet?'

With an attempt at insouciance Ellie asked, 'What on earth does she use it for?'

'Checking out her bank accounts? Buying and selling shares? Surfing the net for new tax fiddles? Checking up on your Diana in her work at the flats?'

Ellie put down her cup with a clatter. Diana had said her new job was a doddle, but Diana was always looking out for the main chance. Once or twice Ellie had suspected Diana's business methods of being unethical. Did Aunt Drusilla share the same suspicion? 'Are you trying to tell me something about Diana?'

'Possibly.' He was serious, staring at the floor. 'I know she's your daughter, but...'

There was a sour taste in Ellie's mouth. 'She cuts corners, tries to make a bit extra on the side? Yes. I'll warn her. Thank you.'

He shrugged. 'By the way, I expect you'll hear soon enough, but my mother has agreed to back me in redeveloping the site opposite the church. The plans come up for approval at the town hall next week and I think they will be accepted. It's a safe investment for her, I assure you.' Grimly, but amused, 'My mother's tied the money up well enough. Even if I come a cropper, she'll come out of it smelling of roses.'

Ellie laughed. 'You're one as bad as the other, you and her.'

He flashed a blue glance at her. 'Yes, but Diana may say ... well, you know.'

'That you've been fortune-hunting again?'

He lowered his eyes. 'She was wrong, about me wanting to marry you just for your money.'

'I know. But I also know that my money helps.' She buttoned her blue jacket firmly over the too-revealing blouse. 'Oh dear, it's started to rain, and I haven't brought my umbrella. Mrs Dawes is giving me the eye, ready to go. No doubt she wants to tell me all over again how badly she was taken in by Gus, and how she'll never trust a man again, etcetera.'

'Supper tonight? I'm out and about this afternoon – thinking of applying to join the golf club, but you can get me on my mobile.'

She shook her head. 'If you ever gave me the number, I've lost it. You'll have to stand over me while I write it in my telephone book. Anyway, I've got the family staying, though I'm not quite sure how that happened. Maybe one night next week?'

Mrs Dawes usually went back to Ellie's house for a sherry on her way home from church, and she wasn't going to make an exception just because Diana and her family were there. Mrs Dawes glared at Stewart because he was occupying the biggest armchair – the one that had been Ellie's husband's and which Mrs Dawes considered fitted her bulk best. Stewart had buried himself under a coverlet of Sunday papers and didn't notice.

Diana fidgeted, turning her laptop on and off, frowning as Mrs Dawes accepted a refill of sherry. Little Frank was asleep in his buggy in the now waterproof conservatory and the rain was tipping down. Ellie was trying to think what she could feed everyone for lunch, while appearing to be engrossed in Mrs

Dawes' story.

'...and my friend who was at school with me, you know, the one who lives at the top of the next road, overlooking the park? Well, she said to me that our dear curate had tried it on her – about having someone to lodge with her from the hostel, you know – and there's no denying that she's got a bedroom to spare, same as I have, but then I needed the money more, so I said I'd have him, of course. But Never Again!'

'No, indeed,' said Ellie, shuddering at the thought of poor little Tod. Also thinking, Shall I take them all out to the Carvery for lunch? Surely they'll all go back to their own flat this afternoon...?

Mrs Dawes drained her second glass of sherry, chasing the last drop around her scarlet-painted lips. A widow of a certain age with jet-black hair, she'd recently taken to wearing earrings which grazed the shoulders of her heavyweight Burberry mack. She was a brilliant flower arranger, frequently asked to act as judge in local flower shows. And an avid gossip.

Diana snatched the empty glass from Mrs Dawes. 'Shall I get your umbrella?'

'Oh, is that the time? Well, I suppose I'd better be...'

The front door bell rang. Stewart rose from beneath his papers. 'I'll get it, shall I?'

Mrs Dawes and Diana were squaring up to one another. Ellie wondered, reprehensibly, who she'd back in a fight.

Mrs Dawes said, 'Back from the north so soon, Diana? I thought you had a good job there.'

Diana didn't even attempt to smile. 'There's better opportunities down here for a businesswoman.' There was more than a touch of the feline in the emphasis on 'business', since it was well known that Mrs Dawes had never soiled her fingers with a wage packet in her life. She'd been brought up to believe that husbands did the providing while they were alive, and the state did the rest.

'I suppose,' said Mrs Dawes, showing large teeth, 'that it must ease the situation, being able to rely on your mother for so much.'

Ellie thought, Ouch. One All.

Ellie smiled, shepherding Mrs Dawes out into the hall. Stewart was holding the front door ajar, creating a horrible draught and letting in the rain. He beckoned to Ellie. 'Someone wants the lady of the house. I said you never bought anything at the door.'

Mrs Dawes reeled back, clutching her bosom. 'It's Gustave!'

'What?'

Ellie thought, Dial 999 ... But no, it can't be. They arrested him.

The front door flew open with a bang. Little Frank woke up and wailed. On the doorstep stood an unshaven, red-eyed waif of a man wearing a cap and what appeared to be a torn bin bag over his clothes. He was shivering with the cold, dripping rain all over the porch. Ellie gasped, finding it hard to recognize the trim, neatly dressed man who had mended her gate, in this vision from Wino City.

Gus recognized Mrs Dawes and launched into a tirade which would have been powerful if his voice hadn't been so weak and querulous. Ellie automatically filtered out his use of four-letter words.

'What you done with my things, eh? I couldn't get in, and that nosy neighbour of yours said you'd had the locks changed and my stuff's been dumped somewhere; but I know my rights and you got no right to throw me out and, about my stuff, I'm going to sue.'

Mrs Dawes made a strangled sound in her throat and looked wildly around for protection. Stewart gaped. He really had been born a few pence short of a pound.

'Is that the paedophile?' said Diana. 'How dare he come here! Shut the door, Stewart, and phone the police.'

'Wait,' said Ellie, as Stewart dithered. 'Gus, you came here to see me?'

Gus took his eyes off Mrs Dawes and transferred them to Ellie. 'I din't know that old cow would be here...'

That old cow sank on to the hall chair and fanned herself with her scarf.

'...but when I found I was locked out, I thought you was straight with me the other day, cash down, no problem, cuppa as well. She said you was friends with her, so I thought you'd know how to get my stuff back that she stole...'

Mrs Dawes gave a little shriek and threw her scarf over her head.

Ellie said, 'Let's get this straight. You were arrested for interfering with a neighbour's small boy...'

'Sure, they took me in. But I never, no, not me. That sort's dirt beneath my feet, should not be allowed to live, give them the chop down there is what I say. The police know me, a course they do. Polite they are. Always a clean cell and breakfast thrown in. I don't mind them. But locking me out and stealing my stuff's not on, and I'll have the law on her, I will.'

Mrs Dawes wailed. 'You didn't come home all week and then I heard you'd been arrested for molesting Tod, so what was I to think? I put your things in a dustbin bag and they're under the laurel bush at the front of the garden. I'm not letting you back in my house, I couldn't, no I really couldn't.'

Diana said, 'Yuk. The man stinks of drink and nicotine.'

'And Tod didn't,' said Ellie thoughtfully. 'I believe Gus when he says he didn't hurt Tod.'

'Then where's he been all this time? Getting drunk? Sleeping it off somewhere?'

Gus shifted his attack to Diana. 'What if I have? And what do you know about anything, you uppity bitch? I know your sort. Never a moment's thought for anyone but yourself. You need a damn good seeing to, you do. If I were five year younger, I'd give it you an' all.'

Now it was Diana's turn to shriek, though

Ellie noticed that while Stewart looked nervous, his lips twitched. In the background Frank's wails had turned to cries of fury.

The rain was now beating into the hall. Lightning shot across the sky.

Ellie made up her mind. 'Please come in, Mr .... er, Gus. Take off that bin bag and give it to me. There. And your overcoat. Now we can close the door and discuss this in a civilized fashion.'

Mrs Dawes showed the whites of her eyes. 'If he's coming in, then I'm going.'

'No, you're not, dear. Come back into the sitting room, all of you. Stewart, could you attend to little Frank? Diana, would you put the kettle on for a cuppa?'

'I'd prefer something stronger, if you've got it,' said Gus, eyeing the remains of the bottle of sherry. 'To keep the cold out. Wet through, I am, and likely to get it on me chest, if it ain't attended to immediate.'

'I think not,' said Ellie, putting the bottle away. 'The other day when you mended my gate, you told me you'd been on the wagon for twenty months. You said that in the past you'd had a "little problem with the drink" that kept you from holding down a proper job. I paid you in cash for the work you did for me on Tuesday. I suspect you went straight down to the supermarket, got a bottle of something alcoholic and drank it then and there. You were so drunk that you couldn't find your way back to Mrs Dawes' but slept it off in the church porch. Am I right?'

'Could be.' He lowered himself gently on to the settee. His boots, once stout and polished, were now broken and stained. The laces of one had broken and been awkwardly knotted together. He was still wearing the neat windcheater, blue pullover and grey trousers that she'd seen on Tuesday, though they were now rather the worse for wear. The overcoat that she'd hung up was far too large for him and torn in a couple of places. He'd probably picked it off a skip somewhere. His hair was lank and he reeked of stale booze and cigarettes.

'So that accounts for Tuesday. You didn't return to Mrs Dawes' on Wednesday. So what happened then?'

'I din't want to go back to Mrs Dawes with a hangover, did I? I were going to sleep it off, clean meself up in the public toilet in the park first. But I met a coupla mates. They'd had a bit of luck, come by some bottles of the good stuff. It was blowing a gale so we made ourselves cosy with another mate of mine in a lock-up garage we know of, t'other side of the park. A course we had to sleep it off. 'S only natural, innit? Then the police picked us up. Talk, talk, talk. All day. But we'd all bin together, all the time. So we couldn't have done it, none of us. They had to check us out, I see that. I'm a reasonable man, I am, and the food ain't bad at that nick.

'This morning they shoved us out in the rain, wouldn't even keep us in the dry till tomorrow. So I went back to the old cow's place and found she'd changed the locks. But I know my rights and I'm due some compensation, right?'

'For wrongful arrest?' said Diana, slamming a mug of coffee in front of him. 'You must be joking.'

He tasted, and spat. 'No sugar. Haven't you any biscuits? Chocolate, if you've got any.'

Ellie tried to take charge of the situation. 'Mr ... er, Gus. The most important thing now is to rescue your belongings and find you somewhere to stay.'

'Don't look at me,' exclaimed Mrs Dawes. 'Oh, my heart! It's banging away in my chest so's I can hardly breathe. I'm not having him back, and that's flat. They told me he was a nice, quiet man who wouldn't give me any trouble, and look at him...'

It was true that Mrs Dawes' colour was bad. Gus spooned sugar into his mug and pointed the spoon at her. 'You oughta be ashamed of yourself, dishing up so little food you can hardly see it on the plate, and no hot water for washing...'

'Huh! You wouldn't know what to do with soap if it was—'

His voice rose to a scream. 'I couldn't work the bloody shower, could I?'

There was silence. Mrs Dawes had gone a most peculiar plum colour. Ellie remembered her friend's boast about taking out her old bath to install a new moneysaving shower unit, and how when her nephew had been staying with her, he'd often complained about the small portions Mrs Dawes doled out at mealtimes. It was a mystery how Mrs Dawes maintained her bulk as she did. The contrast between weedy little Gus and the majestic Mrs Dawes was very marked. If she fell on him, he'd be squashed flat. But size wasn't everything and neither was respectability. Mrs Dawes really was afraid of the little man.

Ellie sighed. 'It seems you need some alternative accommodation. If you'll give me the name of the hostel, I'll ring them and see...'

'They're full. I been round there already.'

Impasse. Stewart was now playing with Frank, dandling him on his knee. Mrs Dawes' colour was gradually fading to normal.

Diana was tapping her teeth. 'Mother, this has gone on long enough. What are you doing about lunch?'

Mrs Dawes heaved herself to her feet. 'I almost forgot. I've got a pot roast in the oven but I'm that shaky I can hardly keep my feet.'

Ellie took the hint. 'Stewart, would you be so kind as to run Mrs Dawes back home in your car? It's only just round the corner and it's still raining hard. And retrieve Gus's belongings? There's a dear.'

Diana frowned. 'What about lunch? Stewart will have to start back up north in an hour's time, so's he can do most of the journey by daylight.'

Little Frank was hitting Ellie on the knee, so she picked him up. He screamed and jerked backwards. 'Diana, please will you take your son and I'll see what I can find in the cupboard ... make some pasta or something...'

'What about me, missus?' Gus had lost all his fire. He looked shrunken, pathetic and miserable.

'I'll see what I can do.' Ellie thrust Frank into his mother's arms and would have escaped to the peace and quiet of the study, but that the doorbell rang again. This time it was a welcome visitor, her next-door neighbour Armand's wife, Kate. A thirtyish Amazon in designer casual clothing and Ellie's very good friend.

'A bad time to call?' asked Kate, frowning. 'I just wanted to know if there were any news about Tod. Also, Armand's out on school business, so I thought we might share a take-away?'

A dilemma. Ellie knew she could rely on Kate in nasty situations and this was undoubtedly a nasty situation. On the other hand, Kate and Diana – both businesswomen – disliked one another. Both were tall, dark and handsome. Kate was also honest and compassionate. Diana was ... well, best not to think exactly what Diana was. Decision time.

Ellie beckoned Kate in, shouted to Diana that it was just a neighbour enquiring about Tod and drew her friend into the study. Shutting the door behind her, she explained in a few sentences what had happened. Kate stripped off her jacket and dumped her handbag. 'What would you like me to do?'

'Phone the police, check if Gus's story is

true. I don't really doubt it, but we ought to check. Find out what they do about homeless people on a Sunday.'

Kate pulled the phone towards her while Ellie darted into the kitchen to work out what she could make for lunch. Macaroni cheese and tinned tomatoes seemed best and quickest. She set the water to boil for the pasta, put some marge on to melt for the sauce and scrabbled for breadcrumbs in the freezer. The study had once been a dining room and there was a hatch between it and the kitchen. Ellie opened the hatch to see how Kate was getting on.

Kate swivelled round to report. 'His story checks out OK with the police. They just laughed when I said he'd been refused re-entry to his digs. They said drunks can't be trusted.'

'He says he was on the wagon for twenty months...'

'But fell off in spectacular fashion.'

'Does that mean he doesn't deserve another chance?'

'Dunno. Depends how charitable you're feeling, I think.'

Ellie glanced out of the window. It was still raining hard.

Kate shrugged. 'Shall I try the local hostel?'

'Mm.' Ellie rescued the marge, which had melted by now, added flour, pounded it up together, added milk little by little and kept beating as it thickened to a sauce. Salt and pepper. Threw the macaroni into the boiling water. Grated cheese, threw that into the sauce, stirred frantically.

Kate appeared in the hatchway. 'Hostel's full. They said the only hope was the Salvation Army, which might take him in and might not. I've tried ringing them. They're engaged.'

'I've had an idea. You stir this and I'll try the vicarage.'

'You're mad,' said Kate, but took the spoon and began to stir.

Their curate Timothy had been most persuasive in urging his congregation to befriend the men and women leaving the local hostel. He had played on the fund of goodwill that often exists in a church where fundraising for charity is the norm. Their previous vicar, Gilbert, had frequently taken in homeless teenagers and stray visitors from other countries. Also the odd man or woman sleeping rough. The main body of the large Victorian vicarage was now empty, awaiting the appointment of a new incumbent, while Timothy and his young family occupied the curate's flat at the back.

Surely Timothy couldn't refuse to take Gus in – just for the time being, till something better could be sorted out?

Timothy was delighted to hear from her, as he had been intending to call to see her soon. He was not so delighted to hear what she wanted him to do. In fact he refused. He was mellifluous in his self-justification. His wife was due to have her second baby within the next fourteen days, he wasn't sure he had the right keys to the vicarage proper, he was very sure the police would find Gus somewhere suitable to stay, and he must rush because he was due to take his mother-in-law back home for her afternoon nap.

Ellie crashed the phone down just as Kate drained the macaroni and dumped it into a large dish. 'No luck? Do I shove the sauce over it, like this? And what about the bread-crumbs?'

'Sprinkle on top, dot with butter and put it under the grill. I'll warm up some tinned tomatoes, see if we have anything for pudding. Are you staying?'

'You've got enough on your plate. I'll try the Sally Army again.'

'Come off it. You wouldn't miss this for anything. I'll set a place for you, too.'

Diana came to the kitchen door and exploded. 'Well, isn't this a cosy little meeting! What's that woman doing here and where's our lunch? Mother, I didn't expect you to...'

Ellie pulled Diana into the kitchen. 'Kate is trying to find somewhere for Gus to go. Lunch is nearly ready. I was intending to take you all out to the Carvery...'

'Stewart's back. We can go straight away.'

'...but I can't leave poor Gus here on his own. And the macaroni cheese is nearly ready.' Opening the tins of tomatoes, tipping them into a bowl, shoving them in the micro-wave and hoping she'd got the right setting on. The microwave still intimidated her but

Kate said it was handy and indeed it was, in its own peculiar way.

'Of course you can't leave that man here,' said Diana. 'He knows the drill. Let him find himself somewhere to doss down.'

'Would you take him in, looking like that, with no money?'

'I suppose he must have some money.'

'Want a bet on it?'

Silence. 'Well.' A shrug. 'None of my business.' And she walked away.

Ellie sighed.

Kate crashed the phone down again. 'The Sally Army will take him in if he's sober, on a night-by-night basis. In other words, if he turns up sober tonight, they'll give him a bed. If he turns up drunk tomorrow, they won't. The only thing is, the nearest hostel's miles away. It's still raining. Shall we foot the bill for a mini cab to take him there?'

'A night-by-night basis,' said Ellie. 'If he's sober. That sounds reasonable.' She clattered spoons and forks on to a tray, took it through into the living room and swiftly laid the table in the bay window overlooking the road.

Stewart was in the conservatory, looking out at the rain. Gus appeared to have fallen asleep. Baby Frank was investigating the contents of a large bin bag which had unfortunately been left on the floor where he could get at it. The relics of a poor creature struggling to maintain respectability lay on the carpet: a roll of bedding, a tote bag, a toilet bag and threadbare towel, a couple of paperbacks – one of them a Bible – an opened roll of biscuits, Polos, shirts, underpants, socks, another pair of shoes with a brush and tin of polish stuck in them, a newish cap, a plastic raincoat, even a small radio/clock, a used hankie, a tin of tobacco and a packet of cigarette papers, a disposable lighter and so on. Frank was chewing on a hairbrush, yuk!

Diana swooped on her son with a cry of horror and retrieved the brush, which made Frank yell and Gus start to wakefulness. He gazed around, bleary-eyed. All the fire had gone out of him. He looked sixty and was probably forty.

Ellie returned to the kitchen, where Kate was assembling plates and glasses.

Ellie said, 'I've just had what my mother would call a very naughty idea.'

Kate stiffened. Ellie had a silent conversation with the back of Kate's head. It was surprising how expressive the set of a head and shoulders could be, even when the face was turned away.

Ellie: *I'm going to offer him a room for the night.*

Kate: *You know the risks. He's a drunk.*

Ellie: *But reformed for twenty months. Isn't that worth something? Besides...*

Kate: *It's one in the eye for Diana. You'll make it an excuse to get her out of here.*

Ellie: *YES! YES! It's perfect.*

Kate turned her head and winked at Ellie. 'You're a wicked girl, do you know that? And a bad influence on me. But before I egg you on, one last throw for sanity. Shall we find out why he fell off the wagon?'

Ellie nodded. She carried the macaroni cheese through into the living room and set it on the table. Kate brought in a tray containing plates, glasses, a jug of water and the tomatoes.

'Grub up,' said Ellie. 'Stewart, fetch Frank's high chair from the kitchen, will you? And Gus can sit at my right hand.'

'Mother, really! You aren't expecting us to sit down at table with him, are you?'

'Certainly, dear. Feed the hungry, you know. All that Christian stuff. And I wouldn't turn a dog out on a day like this.' Gus was surveying his possessions, strewn over the carpet. Ellie patted the chair next to her. He levered himself out of the armchair, then passed his hand over his chin. Looked at himself in the mirror over the fireplace, and winced.

'I don't think I...'

'You shall have a bath and a shave after we've eaten,' said Ellie.

'Hrrrm!' said Kate. 'First things first...'

'Yes, indeed,' said Ellie, dishing out steaming macaroni cheese. 'First things first. How did you come to fall off the wagon on Tuesday, Gus? Something happened after you'd finished mending my gate?'

'There was some big boys, off the bus. Teasing a little un. Hitting him. Made the little un cry. I knew I oughta keep out of it. But I shouted at 'em and they turned on me instead. The little un ran away. I'd been shopping, got some food. Always hungry at that woman's place. The boys took my food, smashed it up. Too many of 'em. All over me. When they'd done, I sat there in the gutter and thought, What's the use...?'

Diana wrenched her chair back, sitting as far from him as she could. 'You should have called the police.'

He laughed, lifted his spoon and fork and hesitated. Looking at Ellie he said, 'Gonna say a grace, missus?'

Ellie felt a shiver run down her back. When had grace last been said at that table? She didn't know how to say grace, herself. Had never been asked to do it before. She held Kate's eyes. Kate folded her hands in front of her and bowed her head. When had Kate last been to church, or heard grace said at table? Beyond Kate, Stewart finished strapping Frank in and sat down with bowed head.

Ellie had a moment of inspiration. Stewart had been brought up in a church-going family, hadn't he? 'Stewart, would you say grace for us?'

Without a flicker of surprise Stewart folded his hands and said, 'For friends, fellowship and good food, we give thanks to you, O Lord.'

Ellie dumped a helping of macaroni cheese on her own plate and sat down.

'Well, isn't this nice. I'll put the immersion heater on after lunch so that Gus can clean up while Stewart takes Diana and Frank back to their flat. Kate can help me change the sheets so Gus can stay the night. Tomorrow – well, we'll see what happens then, shall we? Tomatoes, anyone? Just peaches and tinned custard for afters, I'm afraid.'

Five

Ellie was enjoying herself.

Diana threw down her spoon in a fury but couldn't speak properly because her mouth was full. Frank imitated her. Stewart tucked his head in, and got down to demolishing his plateful. Kate mopped up little Frank, grinning to herself. Gus looked from one to the other, bemused.

'Mother, you can't possibly!'

'Of course I can. Eat up while it's still hot.'

'I won't let you!'

'Try me.' Ellie put some ice in her voice. Gus followed Stewart's example, tucking his head in, picking up his fork and starting to eat as if there were no tomorrow.

'You know I can't move back into the flat. There's a gas leak...'

'No, there isn't. I had the Gas Board check it out. There was a message on the answerphone about it being all clear. You could have rung them yourself, if you'd thought about it.'

'You can't invite a ... a criminal ... to stay in your own home.'

'Gus isn't wanted for any crime that I know of so why shouldn't I invite him to stay the night, if he behaves himself? Anyone for seconds?' said Ellie, brightly.

'I'd love some,' said Stewart, handing his plate up. 'It'll set me up nicely for the drive back.'

Diana bit her lip and toyed with her food. Ellie scraped the dish out for Stewart. 'Any news on the sale of your house up north yet?'

Stewart glanced at Diana for permission to give out information. She sulked, hunching her shoulder at him, so he said, 'Yes, we have a buyer, should be exchanging contracts tomorrow. The furniture removers are booked for Friday, if everything goes according to plan.'

This was news indeed. Ellie wondered if Diana had intended her furniture to come down to this house ... while Ellie and her bits and pieces would be shoved out to their furnished flat? Forewarned is forearmed.

'That's good news,' she said, bracing herself to be cheerful. 'I suppose it will all go into store till you've found yourself a place to buy down here.'

Stewart reddened. He glanced at Diana, who was refusing to eat, glaring out of the window at the rain. 'We haven't decided yet.'

'You'd better hurry up, then,' said Ellie, determined not to read the subtext. 'Storage costs money, though I suppose it's cheaper to store the furniture up north than it is to bring it down here. We don't seem to have had any time to talk lately. How's your job going? How are you getting on by yourself up there? Have you got yourself some digs to move into?'

Stewart concentrated on pouring himself a glass of water. 'Didn't Diana tell you? I've been made redundant. I finish on Friday. Diana says jobs down here are few and far between. She wants me to look for a new job up north.'

Ellie said, 'I see.' In fact, she saw rather more than Diana perhaps wished her to. The sale of Stewart and Diana's big house up north would release capital which Diana could use for a better lifestyle, while Stewart – being no longer the breadwinner – might be quietly sidelined. Ellie collected dirty plates and took them out to the kitchen, with Kate helping her.

Kate hissed, 'Is Diana planning to dump him?'

'Over my dead body.' Together they collected the peaches, custard, bowls, spoons and took them back to the dining table.

Ellie felt a quiet fury building up inside her. First Tod, and now this! She hadn't realized before how fond she was of her inoffensive son-in-law. Aunt Drusilla had foretold that Diana would get rid of Stewart if he couldn't keep pace with her. Aunt Drusilla had also wondered aloud about giving him a job managing some of her other properties, if the worst came to the worst. Something about setting up a dummy company to run them, so that neither Diana nor Stewart would know who employed him.

'Stewart, I heard only the other day of a job

going down here that might suit you. Something similar to what Diana is doing, but managing bedsits and flats in large converted houses. Being old, the houses need a lot more maintenance than the block of flats which Diana looks after, but I don't suppose you'd mind that. In fact, I think your flat is in one of the houses concerned. Would you be interested?'

'Indeed I would.' Stewart was hearty. 'Thanks, mother-in law. You're a brick.'

Diana turned a nasty shade of grey. Little Frank watched her face in fascination and hit her on the arm with his spoonful of food to attract her attention. Diana gave an angry squawk and tried to rub the custard off with her hankie.

Someone banged on the front door and rang the bell, hard.

Everyone at table jumped. Ellie got to the door first. Mrs Coppola, wearing outdoor clothes with court shoes this time, but still in a state.

'Sorry to bother you again, but – yes, I'll come in for a minute, if I may – I did ask my sister but she's got her own family, had to go back home again, her varicose veins are playing up, of course. Anyway, they said I had to take him home, they needed the bed, and he is eating and drinking and toileting and that, and it's all outpatient appointments now and I may be able to get some time off tomorrow, I think, but I can't leave him alone in the house, I just daren't, so then I thought of you, and you will do it, won't you?'

'Tod is home? With you? He's all right?'

'All right is not what he is but there, what can you do when they say they need the bed, and I had to get a cab there and back and the day after tomorrow I have to go back to work, or I'll lose my job and what with the mortgage to pay and having had so much time off to look after him last week, I'm at my wits' end, I really am.'

'You've got him home, but he has to go for outpatients' appointments, is that right?'

'It's only during the day, when I'm at work. I think I can get time off to do it tomorrow, because there's three different people he has to see, doctors and shrinks and police and that and yes, of course I can get time off for that. I'd resign if they didn't give me it – though I daren't resign really, you never know but they're looking for an excuse to get you out nowadays. But Tuesday on? You could just sit with him, couldn't you? I really don't like to leave him on his own, poor little tyke. He could come round here. He likes it here and at least your house is warm, which mine isn't with the central heating on the blink and they say it all needs tearing out and I'm not made of money, am I?'

'You want me to look after him for you while you're at work? And take him to these hospital appointments? You know I don't drive.'

'He won't talk yet, you see. Shakes his head when he's asked what he can remember. So it's going to be all playing about with his head and I've heard these people always want to know if you've been abused as a child, which as you know he never has been, well, not up to now he hasn't, and I've never held with them, but what can you do?'

'Counselling?'

'Therapists, they call them. They say it will do him a power of good because he won't speak or even watch the telly. Nor listen to his Walkman, and I spent a fortune on those CDs for him...'

'His father...?'

A bitter laugh. 'Couldn't care less. Not even living in this country, now. Got a job in Spain.'

Ellie thought of all the problems current in her life: Diana and Stewart, baby Frank, the builders, Aunt Drusilla ... With a start she remembered that she'd missed her weekly computer lesson last Wednesday when they'd found Tod had gone missing. She'd been getting on so well with it, too. What a pity. But she couldn't take Tod to that, or to visit Aunt Drusilla, or shopping or ... anything. Or could she?

'Say you'll do it?' The woman had tears in her eyes. Useful weapons, tears.

'I'll come over to have a chat with you this afternoon, and then I'll decide whether I can cope or not.'

'Of course you can! Oh, bless you, I knew I could rely on you. I'll tell him you're coming round straight away.'

‘In about an hour...’ But the woman had gone, clop clopping on her high heels up the drive. The rain appeared to be slackening off.

It was only then that Ellie remembered she’d just taken in a new lodger.

The rain stopped and the sun came out. But inside the nursery, it was still dark. The digital camera lay on the workbench. The video camera and tripod had been pushed into a corner and covered with a sheet. The locked drawers of an old fashioned green metal filing cabinet contained innocuous material: tourist brochures, family papers and photographs. These photographs were unremarkable. They could be shown to anyone. But nearby there was a crack in the skirting board and if you knew how to press and pull, a large section of the woodwork came away. Behind it was a cache of videos and discs. The images on those were not at all innocent.

Stewart got back into his car to drive north again – for the last time, he hoped. Diana complained she’d never get the custard stain out of her new blouse and took Frank back to their flat. Kate rummaged next door for some of Armand’s old clothes, then helped Ellie clear away, wash up, put all Gus’s clothes through the washing machine, make plans.

Gus had a bath and shave. He put on some of Armand’s old clothes and came down, he said, to make himself useful. Of course, the washing-up had been done by then. Now that he’d cleaned himself up, he looked less like a tramp and more like an OAP down on his luck. He blinked a lot, bewildered by the turn of events.

Kate said, 'What do you do with yourself all day, Gus?'

'Old soldiers' club up the Avenue. Lunches at the Catholic church down the other end of the park. Sit in the public library where it's warm. Do you want me to leave, missus? I don't want to cause no more trouble.'

'You're staying tonight, and tomorrow we'll talk about it again. Maybe you can stay for a bit if you behave yourself,' said Ellie, though she was far from certain that she'd done the right thing. 'Take a kitchen chair into the conservatory with the papers, if you like. It's nice there now the sun's out. Don't use the sitting room; that's mine. I shan't give you a key for the moment but I'll provide breakfast and supper on a day-to-day basis. We'll have a chat tomorrow morning, work out how much you pay me. I have to go round now to visit someone, be back in about an hour, all right?'

'That woman's not coming back, is she?'

'My daughter? No, I shouldn't think so. Look, I'm only going three doors up the road to visit the little boy that got hurt the other day. You can come round for me there, if you need me.'

Kate left the house with Ellie. Rain was scudding along the road, driven by an east wind. Phew! They turned up the collars on their coats.

Ellie said, 'Have I done something really stupid? Shall I get back to find all the silver and Gus missing?'

'Nah. He can't believe his luck. He'll be all right for a day or two, then I suspect he'll either make a pass at you...'

Ellie snorted. 'You're joking.'

'...or go on another bender and disappear.'

'He was sober for twenty months. Why shouldn't he be so again?'

They paused at the gate.

Kate said, 'The trouble with you, Ellie, is that you still think a good woman can reform her man. And don't remind me that I reformed Armand when he was beating me up. True, I did. But only by scaring the daylights out of him. You couldn't throw a scare into that little runt; he might die of a heart attack.'

Ellie went along to the Coppolas'. Mrs Coppola, still wearing her outdoor coat, let her in. 'What took you so long? He's upstairs in his room. You know the way, don't you? I'm just on the phone...'

Ellie shivered. It really was cold in this house. She kept her coat on to go upstairs into Tod's room. He was half lying and half sitting on the bed, as limp as a rag doll. He no longer wore a helmet of bandages on his head and they'd done a neat job with stitches, but he still looked rough. The bruises were fading around his eyes and mouth, and only one wrist was still taped up. They said he must have been tied up with wire at some point.

His eyes were empty and he didn't stir when

she came in. His panda was on the floor under the chair. She picked it up and tried to put it in his arms, but he made no move to accept it. She touched his hand. His skin was chill. She wanted to howl with grief, to snatch him up in her arms and take him home with her. She took off her coat, wrapped him in it and pulled him on to her knee. He didn't resist in any way but she thought his breathing quickened a little. She rocked him to and fro, humming – how absurd we are at times like this – humming a lullaby.

Down below she could hear his mother on the phone, talking – no, chatting. Laughing. Flirting. Oh well. What else could one expect of her? Divorced, having to work for a living. Single parent. Difficult.

Ellie's back began to ache but she ignored it. Tod was getting warmer by the minute. His legs were outside the coat. She rubbed them, careful to avoid the bruises, the marks of a whip. How could he treat a little boy so badly, that man, that pile of filth, that murderer of innocence? Anger stirred again, deep inside her.

His mother was coming up the stairs, calling out, 'Whoo hoo!' His mother would hate to see her son being cuddled like a baby in Ellie's arms. She managed to get Tod back into his original position. Then found that somehow or other he had got one of his hands into hers. A warm hand. A hand that clung. A hand that was hidden under the coat. Ellie shivered. Without her coat she was chilled to the bone. The house was icy cold. She could even see her breath.

'How are we doing?' asked Mrs Coppola. 'I've just got to pop out for half an hour. We're out of all his favourite foods and a friend's just offered to give me a lift to the supermarket, won't take long, you can leave him if you like.'

The hand inside Ellie's strengthened its grip on her. 'No, I won't leave him.'

'Suit yourself.' The phone call had rejuvenated the woman. A little while back, she'd been unwilling to leave the lad alone and now listen to her!

Ellie shivered. 'If you've got to be out for a while – it's rather cold in here – do you have any form of heating we could use?'

'I told you. Boiler's knackered. Can't afford a new one. I'm not made of money. Not like some people.' An acid smile for Ellie, who had been left very well off by her husband. 'I thought, well, spring's on the way. I've got a little blower heater down below. Shall I bring that up here?'

Ellie thought, She's conning me. She wants me to buy her a new central-heating boiler, and she thinks I will because I'm so fond of Tod. Ouch. But I can't let Tod suffer, and I'm not staying a minute longer than I can help in this icebox. It's true that I have a warm house and enough money to pay the gas bills. It's also true that when my dear Frank was alive, I used to pile warm clothes on because he always turned the heating off from the first of

May till the first of October, no matter how cold it was. And now I can switch it on whenever I wish.

'Yes, do bring up the extra heating,' said Ellie. 'Let me have a front-door key and tomorrow, if you agree, I'll have my own central-heating engineer look at your boiler, see what can be done with it. Otherwise we'll have Tod back in hospital, won't we? No, don't thank me...' Though the woman had shown no signs of doing so. 'We'll come to some arrangement about repayment. Zero interest, twenty pounds a month, or whatever you can afford.'

The woman's mouth drooped. She'd thought she could get it for nothing.

Ellie said, 'So in the meantime, do you think I could take him back to my place, give him tea?'

'Oh, I wouldn't have dared ask you to take so much trouble.'

Ellie ignored the sarcasm in the woman's voice. 'No trouble, provided Tod can make it? How do you feel about it, Tod?'

By way of answer he got off the bed, still holding her hand. Under her coat he was wearing an old jumper over even older jeans, dirty trainers. Ellie reflected that it was her day for rescuing waifs and strays. To go outside, he'd need a coat or jacket and some kind of cap. Ellie opened his cupboard. The majority of his clothes were still on the floor, but an ancient anorak hung on a peg, and a baseball cap peeped out from the stir-fry on the floor. They'd do. She had to dress him as if he were a toddler, thrusting his arms into sleeves, zipping up the anorak, pulling the cap over his half-shaved head.

Gratefully she huddled back into her own coat, accepted a front-door key from Mrs Coppola and with Tod walking in her shadow, went back home. Then realized that once again she'd forgotten Gus.

In the porch she paused. Tod was stuck to her side like glue. 'Tod, I've got someone else staying. A poor man who has nowhere else to go tonight. If he makes you feel uneasy even for a minute, I'll get rid of him, send him on to a hostel. You've only got to let me know. Right?'

He shrank against her. She hoped it was only because he didn't want to face a stranger. But suppose ... just suppose Gus was the man who had harmed Tod? No, she must be sensible. The police had cleared him. Gus was not the man. Everything she knew about him, everything he'd said himself, reassured her that he was not the man. But if Tod showed any sign of fear then he'd have to go.

She opened the door and let them into the warm, quiet house. At least, it ought to have been quiet but someone had turned her kitchen radio on. Not loudly, not offensively. But it was definitely on. And someone was whistling along to the music.

Tod allowed her to take off his anorak but jerked his head away when she would have removed his cap. Ah well, lots of boys wore baseball caps indoors, and he'd be sensitive about that shaved area of his head.

Ellie went into the kitchen and Tod followed her, clutching a fold of her skirt.

The back door was open into the conservatory and Gus was sitting there with the easy crossword. Ellie tensed. Tod stared at Gus from under the peak of his cap, but didn't react.

Ellie said, 'Well, I'm back. Gus, would you like a cuppa?'

Gus started. 'Why, missus, you gave me a jump.'

Ellie tested the atmosphere and found it relaxed. Tod's breathing hadn't changed. Gus had been uneasy when she brought Tod in, but was now only as concerned as he ought to be. There were no undercurrents.

'Cuppas all round,' she said. 'This boy needs something warm inside him. Hot chocolate, Tod? Soup? Tea, coffee?'

He nodded, which wasn't particularly helpful, but when she put the kettle on he got out mugs, hot chocolate, the chocolate biscuits and a teapot. He sat at the kitchen table as he had so often over the years, drank his cup of hot chocolate and ate two biscuits. So far, so normal. At least he wasn't clutching her skirt any more. She took a mug of tea out to Gus, who seemed embarrassed about her running round after him.

She pottered around in the kitchen, wondering what she could make them for supper, talking to herself, making it seem normal that Tod didn't reply. Turning the radio down. The next thing she knew, Gus had come into the kitchen for a refill and seated himself opposite Tod. Ellie waited for Tod to show signs of alarm, but he didn't. When Gus eyed the biscuit tin, Tod even pushed it an inch in the old man's direction. Ellie considered that a good sign.

Gus had brought the crossword with him. 'What's the capital of Peru, then? Four letters. Might begin with an M.'

Tod's eyes sparkled. He knew all right. He'd always been interested in far-off lands and collecting stamps had helped. Ellie trudged through her mind, but couldn't remember. Her brain was like a sieve nowadays. 'There's an atlas in the bookcase in the sitting room, Gus. Bottom shelf, right-hand side. Take a look in that, if you like, but put it back where you found it.'

Gus scraped back his chair and left. Tod was looking through the hatch into the study where the computer was. Ellie guessed he wanted to play a game. Could she make him ask for it?

'We've got bacon and eggs and some potatoes and onions. Shall I make a sort of Spanish omelette for supper?'

Tod sidled off his chair and to the door, then turned to look at her for permission. So he couldn't talk yet. He would in time.

She nodded permission and he disappeared into the study. In a while she heard the whine and ping of a game being played. Good for him. Losing himself in something else. Of course when he played Minesweeper usually he accompanied himself with howls of despair and whoops of glee. This time he played in silence. But it was a step forward.

The phone rang. It was Aunt Drusilla.

'I'm so sorry, aunt. I did mean to get round to see you this afternoon, but...'

Aunt Drusilla sounded amused. 'Diana's been on the phone. I hear you've taken in an escaped criminal. Thought I'd better check that you were still alive.'

'Wait a minute...' Ellie shut the door to the study with her foot, and reached a long arm to shut the door into the sitting room. Now both her visitors were behind closed doors. 'That's better. It was like this...' She explained what had happened.

Aunt Drusilla gave her dry laugh and then coughed. 'Drat it. This east wind never agrees with me. I told Diana that you usually knew what you were doing, but she seemed distraught, babbling now about you offering Stewart a job and then about this paedophile...'

'Ah. I'd better explain. It was just as you thought. Stewart's job has folded up north and Diana wanted him to stay up there...'

'So you thought I'd bail him out and save his marriage?' She sounded amused, rather than angry.

Ellie relaxed. It was going to be all right. You never knew which way Aunt Drusilla would jump. 'How do you feel about it?'

'Stewart's honest and hard-working. He always looks for the best in people. Perhaps a trifle naïve? He wouldn't know all the latest scams that builders use...'

'Well, *you* do, and you only use firms you can trust. Will you give Stewart a chance? It's working out cheaper for you to have Diana managing the block of flats than relying on those estate agents, isn't it? I know you've been thinking of finding someone else to manage the rest of your properties, the ones in the older houses. And of course Stewart isn't to know that you own them.'

'Get that tame solicitor of yours to draw up a contract. Tell Stewart he can start at the end of the month and meanwhile I'll get the present people to bring their files up to date and hand them over to your solicitor. Stewart can collect them from him. If anything goes wrong, you'll have to act as go-between. I don't want him knowing all my business.'

Tod shot out of the study, making a desperate lunge for Ellie. She held on to him, telling Aunt Drusilla that she'd ring her back. Tod buried his head in her arm, knocking his cap on to the floor. His breathing was far too rapid. He'd lost so much weight that he felt bony.

He tried to scramble on to her lap, but the chair in the hall was too small to hold them both comfortably. Half carrying and half leading him into the sitting room, she got him on to the settee with her to give him a cuddle.

Gus looked up from the atlas he was studying and made as if to withdraw. Ellie smiled at him, indicating he should stay. Tod burrowed into her armpit. Maybe he was crying. She clucked and soothed him.

A quiet time. A time apart from all that had happened and all the terror that was to follow. A golden time. The phone rang several times. She didn't move. The answerphone would take messages.

A time for prayer. Gus's eyes were closed. Perhaps he was praying, too. Perhaps not. It didn't matter. The rain had stopped and a shaft of sun thrust through the window behind her, glanced off the bevel of the mirror over the mantelpiece, and set a prism of colour dancing on the wall. She smiled at herself for thinking it an omen, but recognized that it had lifted her heart.

Eventually Tod's shakes subsided and he slept.

Eventually her arm went to sleep. Eventually Gus appeared at her side with a mug of tea, which he'd made for her, unasked. She smiled her thanks.

Gus lowered his voice to say, 'I thought at first he might be one of the lads that set on me the other night. I wouldn't mind giving them a taste of the old strap. But he wasn't one of them. Reminds me of when I was little.' He shook his head, remembering. 'Our dad used to beat us, all four of us. It takes the heart out of you.'

'That's terrible.'

He shrugged. 'Mum went off. Can't blame her, except for not taking us with her. There wasn't no one to cuddle us, after. Likely you'll see to it the lad gets proper help.'

'His mother's taking him to all these appointments tomorrow. Doctor, hospital and police. He'll need counselling, too.'

'Hospitals! National Waste of Time. Wait three hours, busy doctor says, "What are you here for, we've lost your notes, come back in six weeks." '

'I can't go over the heads of ... no, you're right. If I square it with his mother, perhaps I can. When Tod wakes up, I'll ring a therapist friend of mine, see who she can get him in to see privately. Then I must get some supper.'

'Don't you bother with that home cooking, missus. Fast food is what the lad'll want. Pizza. McDonalds.'

Tod stirred and yawned. 'Pepperoni,' he murmured.

'Pepperoni it is,' said Ellie, delighted to think she didn't have to cook, and even more delighted to hear Tod speak.

Six

By seven o'clock Ellie was at screaming pitch. Despite all her good intentions, everything Gus did irritated her. She made herself be pleasant, though. It was her own fault entirely that she was landed with him. She had taken him in off the street and offered him a bed, provided he behaved. He had behaved, more or less, but he'd left his belongings where they'd fallen, strewn across the carpet. The very sight of him sitting in what had been her dear husband Frank's chair was enough to drive her to the sherry bottle – except that she daren't drink in front of a man who admitted to a problem with alcohol.

She could see him assessing her assets. Widow, nicely placed. Bound to be lonely. Might be worth buttering up. 'Nice place you've got here, missus.' His eyes went from the television and video to the stereo, from the silver vase and christening cup on the mantelpiece to her handbag lying open on the floor beside the settee.

He picked up the framed photo of her dear dead Frank, and she nearly yelled at him to Put It Down! He smirked at her. 'Your better half?'

'My husband. He died late last year. But I have lots of friends, keep myself busy, people drop by, church business, you know how it is.'

He got the message but continued to register the more valuable items in the room. The crystal glass in the corner cupboard. The rather good art-nouveau clock which had been her mother's.

Tod had gone to sleep again, having eaten two thirds of his pizza. Ellie began to feel, not afraid of Gus, exactly. But wary. He sat there, cracking his finger joints, looking at her in a speculative way. She didn't like it.

'Mind if I smoke?' he asked.

'I'm afraid I do mind.' She couldn't put up with him smoking, that would be the last straw. She wasn't a big woman and if he were to jump her ... but no, the thought was ridiculous. On the other hand, perhaps it had been foolish of her to invite him into her house just to spite Diana. Which is why she'd done it. Ouch.

The phone rang again, and again the answerphone clicked in. That made three calls she hadn't answered – or perhaps it was four. Gus must think that she usually let the phone go unanswered. In which case, he might well be thinking that if he were to knock her on the head, steal whatever was in her handbag and scarper, then no one would find her for hours. She must stir herself, show him he was wrong.

She eased herself out from under Tod and stood up. 'Suppose you collect your belongings and I'll show you your room. You could smoke up there, if you kept the window open. I'm afraid there isn't a television up there, but there is an old radio. You may use the bathroom tonight before I go up, and after I've been in there tomorrow morning. I have to get Tod back home or his mother'll be worrying, and I must see to the messages on the answerphone, or they'll all be coming round to see what's wrong with me.'

Prompt on cue, the doorbell rang. Impatiently. Three times. It would be Roy, he never had the patience just to ring once. Tod stirred and rubbed his eyes. Gus got down on the floor to gather his things together.

Ellie opened the front door, her finger to her lips. Roy shook rain off his umbrella and burst in without ceremony.

'Ellie, thank God. I was afraid ... but I see you are quite all right. I was round at my mother's and she told me you'd taken leave of your senses.' In a lower voice, 'Yes, yes, I understand that he's still here. I rang you a couple of times and when you didn't answer I thought I'd best come round. So, tell me what's going on. I promised I'd get you to ring my mother back. She's really anxious about you.'

Ellie raised her voice so that Gus could hear. 'How nice of you to come round, Roy. Do come in. Is it raining again? Oh, dear. Roy, this is Gus. He's staying the night in the spare room. Of course, you know Tod. Little sleepy-head. Roy, could you get him back into his anorak? And I don't know where his cap's got to. Can I borrow your umbrella for a minute? It's bigger than mine. I'm just going to take Tod back to his mother's while Gus takes his things upstairs ... the room straight across at the back of the house, Gus ... and then, Roy, you and I can sit down and have a coffee, right?'

Ellie delivered a still sleepy Tod back to his mother's care – his bedroom was still as cold as ice, but there was a hot-water bottle in the bed. Ellie tucked Tod up with his panda beside him. His mother had company in the sitting room and that was the room where she'd got the small heater running, but she came out to say goodnight to Ellie and moan that she'd forgotten to give Ellie the antibiotics which Tod was supposed to be taking, but she didn't suppose it would matter, and yes, she had managed to get tomorrow off, so it was doctor's first thing, then the police and counselling and goodness knows what else.

Oh well. Ellie trudged back through the rain to her own cosy house. Only it didn't seem so cosy now, with Gus upstairs.

Roy had turned up the central heating and found a bottle of brandy from somewhere. She sank into her favourite chair and eased off her wet shoes. 'Don't tell me I'm a fool to take Gus in. I know it.'

Roy poured her a brandy. 'My mother said you did it to get Diana out of your house, but surely you could have thought of something less drastic.'

'I suppose I could have used a kitchen knife on her? Or a slab of paving stone? No, you're right. I could have got rid of her another way, I suppose, but ... well, I just didn't like the thought of the man being turned out into the rain like that.'

'He could rob you blind.'

'Yes.'

He took a gulp of his own drink. 'He could, well, try it on with you.'

'Yes, I expect he will.' She sighed. 'But refusing to take him in would be like turning a stray cat out into a thunderstorm. The local hostel's full. The nearest Salvation Army hostel that's got room for him is miles away. Roy – you've got a nice flat, only one bedroom but you do have a good settee in the living room. Will you take him in?'

'Good God, no!'

'The curate wouldn't, either. So I have. And no, I'm not sure he's perfectly harmless and yes, I will have to lock up my treasures and be careful about my handbag and my keys. If he gets drunk tomorrow, I'll throw him out. Come to think of it, I'm going to have to push him out of the house tomorrow because I'm right out of food and need to visit your mother and see to Mrs Coppola's central heating and oh, a hundred different things.'

Roy stood with his back to the rarely used gas fire, in the age-old position of The Man of the House Laying Down the Law. 'Ellie, you're not thinking straight. You can't possibly allow him to stay.'

'You sound just like my dear dead husband.'

'If he were still alive, he'd knock some sense into you.'

'So he would.' Ellie put her glass down with a hand that trembled. 'So he would,' she repeated, quietly. She thought, Yes, Frank would have forbidden me to take Gus in, and I'd have gone along with it because Men Know Best. Only, he's gone and left me and I don't like being bullied, even by Roy. Roy means well, I know, and part of me would love to fall at his feet and cling to his knees and have a little weep and have my shoulder patted and be told, There, there, now; you poor little thing, let me take care of you. The other half wants to use a very rude word to him.

She said, 'Sit down, Roy. You're giving me a crick in my neck, looking up at you.'

Roy sat on the arm of her chair, putting his arm along her shoulders and taking one of her hands in his. She could see he had decided to turn on the charm.

'Well, I won't allow it, letting all and sundry take advantage of you.' He treated her to one of his long-lashed blue-eyed stares. It was supposed to reduce her to a simpering heap of pliant womanhood.

Unfortunately it reduced her to the giggles. 'Oh Roy, you are funny.'

His thick black eyebrows – which all her friends thought a delicious contrast to his silvery hair – did their famous up-and-down trick. Now he could either laugh or be angry. He chose anger.

'You simply have no idea of the real world, Ellie. You're so naïve. Taking this man in against all our advice puts you at risk. You haven't considered anyone but yourself. Think of the anxiety it's going to cause your friends. We're all going to be worrying ourselves sick about you till he's gone. I'll have to put off half my workload to keep dropping in on you to make sure you're all right...'

'I'm hardly ever alone,' she said. 'There's the builders and Diana, and Aunt Drusilla and Kate and everyone. And Tod, too.'

'Now that's another thing...'

Ellie stifled a yawn. 'Sorry, Roy. Too tired to think straight. Thanks for coming and thanks for making me drink the brandy. I shall sleep now.'

'Ellie...!'

'That's enough, Roy. I must ring Aunt Drusilla and reassure her. Take care how you go.'

'If that's your attitude...'

'So sorry, Roy. It is.' She handed him his coat and umbrella and saw him out into the cold wet night. She returned the calls on the answerphone – two calls from Roy, one from Aunt Drusilla, one from Rose and one from Kate – with soothing words and a promise to ring on the morrow. Then she rang Gilbert. He might already be tucked up safely in bed with his dear wife Liz beside him. Or out at a parish meeting. But he wasn't. He was there and anxious to hear what had been going on.

She told him everything, about Tod and taking Gus in, and all her misgivings.

He was silent for a while. She waited, secure in the knowledge that he would give her good advice.

'I'm proud to know you, Ellie Quicke. You've done a fine thing but you've poked the Devil in the eye and he might well poke back. There's often a price to be paid for living your life as a Christian. Sometimes other people don't like it. It shows up their own shortcomings, you see. In this case I worry because you're not a professional who's been trained to deal with the homeless. There are precautions you can take, removing valuables from open view, keeping your handbag and keys with you at all times. But you'll have thought of all that.'

'Yes, I have. Pray for me?'

'Of course. And Liz does, too. She sends her love.'

'See you both soon.'

She rang off and went to bed.

It took only a day and a half for the news to get around the parish. 'Did you hear that Ellie Quicke has taken that paedophile into her own house...?'

Ellie was the last to hear the gossip, of course. She was busy with the builders, who had the usual tale of woe to tell.

Sorry, the plumber couldn't come to fit the water feature in the conservatory till Wednesday, which meant the tiler couldn't start yet. The central-heating engineer who was supposed to be extending the radiator system had sprained his thumb and couldn't work for a while but of course he would try to drop in at Mrs Coppola's to inspect her little problem with the boiler, but couldn't guarantee to do anything about it, and could she be there from ten to twelve as he wasn't sure when he'd get there.

She left Mrs Coppola's key with the builders and dashed out on her rounds.

Aunt Drusilla needed assistance. 'I'm totally bereft of help, that stupid daily hasn't turned up and I'm completely unable to move, so would you...'

Diana: 'We simply must talk, mother...'

Kate: 'Are you still OK?'

Dear Rose: 'How is Tod, and how are you coping, my dear?'

And Gus grumbling about going out in the rain and borrowing dear Frank's umbrella and coming back in a terrible temper without it, saying it had been stolen – oh, how that hurt, Gus losing Frank's precious umbrella. Something so taken-for-granted, something that still reminded her so vividly of him – gone for ever. She would never see it again.

And Midge the cat deciding that the only place for him in this appalling wet weather was on her bed, which meant she had to find a big towel to cover her duvet with, because when he came in all wet, he left paw prints on everything...

And she got out the hoover to do the ground floor and the bag burst. And she couldn't find a spare. And when she managed to get to her solicitor's, he was busy and could only spare a moment to say he'd ring her later...

And the builder wasn't happy about having Gus around. 'I know you said he'd been cleared of attacking the little boy, but that don't mean he's got the conscience of a new-born babe.'

Ellie suppressed a smile. No, Gus and that sort of innocence didn't seem to go together.

And then when Jimbo, the central-heating man, did come – late – he said it was only Mrs Coppola's pump that was knackered and he could install a new one if she wanted, but he couldn't personally do anything for at least a week because of his sprained thumb and what did she want to do about it, he might be able to recommend someone to do it for her, though he didn't like letting old customers down ... and the man he recommended couldn't do anything for three days at least...

And Gus enthroned himself in Frank's chair and moaned that Mrs Dawes had stolen a pair of his socks and he'd have the law on her, he would.

Ellie thought, What a misery this man is. Then she wondered if she would have been any more gracious in his situation. An out-cast, really. No home, no property, no real friends. Despised and rejected. She sighed and made a resolution to try harder with him.

A tiresome day, but at least it was a day in which she wasn't being asked to track down a murderer on top of her everyday duties. Although, come to think of it, being a free-lance investigator would mean a lot quieter life than the one she was having to live at the moment. She would have an office all to herself, and tell her awful family that she was working and far too busy to attend to their trivial problems, and perhaps there would be a girl to dictate reports to and...

She giggled. What a fantasy!

Frank would have said she was getting above herself, girl. And of course she was.

It was a considerable relief to go to choir practice at church on Monday evening and think about something else for a change. She didn't notice that two of the choir were whispering about her at the back of the pews or that one of them ostentatiously moved away from her side afterwards.

Tuesday started badly and descended into farce.

First of all, Mrs Coppola rang to say she had to leave for work but couldn't get Tod out of bed, he just refused point-blank and she had to go, she really did. She'd told Tod if he wanted any breakfast he'd just have to get himself along to Ellie's, but he showed no sign of having heard her and she was at her wits' end she really was, because she'd taken a day off work yesterday to get him to the hospital and the police and he wouldn't help them, not a word could they get out of him, no matter how hard they tried, and she couldn't think what to do about it, she really couldn't.

Ellie thought, No builders here today. Dare I leave Gus in the house alone? I have to, I suppose. I can't leave Tod at his house all by himself.

Ellie let herself into the chilly Coppola house. Dust on every surface. Muddy foot-marks on the carpet. Well, she was *not* going to do any housework in here. She had enough to do at home.

Tod was hunched up in bed under his duvet. The little electric blow heater was working manfully away, producing a nice old fug. The curtains were still drawn at the window.

Ellie sat on Tod's bed and tried to stroke his head. He pulled himself further down the bedding till only the top of his head was visible. She looked for his panda, but couldn't see it. Perhaps he had it under the bedclothes with him? Was that a good sign?

'Tod, dear one. It's only me, Ellie. What would you like for breakfast? Eggs, bacon, porridge? I think I've got some porridge oats somewhere, if they're not out of date.'

No reply. She didn't think he was even listening. No, he wasn't. He'd put his Walk-man on under the duvet. She could hear the beat through the bedding. Contrary child. First he didn't want it, then he used it as a weapon against her.

Impasse. If he didn't want to get up, she couldn't physically make him. She got off the bed, pulled back the curtains and started picking clothes up off the floor. 'This lot need washing, and what you wore yesterday ... this is only fit for the rubbish bin ... I suppose this needs dry-cleaning...'

She opened his cupboard door and sighed anew. What a stir-fry on the floor. Everything seemed to have been thrown in regardless. Shoes, trainers, socks. Pants. Sweatshirts, shirts. School books. Yuk. A heavy waterproof jacket with a fleece lining had a torn sleeve and a nasty stain down the front. She pulled it out, wondering if it might be possible to get it invisibly mended, but decided it was only fit for the dustbin. Where was his good jacket? Missing. He hadn't been wearing it when he was found, so probably he'd lost it. Or left it at school. Or left it at the place where ... the bad thing had happened. Shudder.

It was automatic to empty the pockets before she threw the ruined waterproof away. Chocolate egg wrappers, a toy from a breakfast-cereal packet, stamp hinges, something which looked remarkably like chewed-up chewing gum, ugh! A screwed-up paper tissue containing something so disgusting that she exclaimed in horror.

She put the stamp hinges on his table and tipped the rest of the stuff into a plastic bag to take downstairs because the waste-paper bin was full. Then set about folding jumpers and hanging up shirts.

At last she could see the floor of the cupboard. She needed a cup of coffee.

There was silence in the room now. He'd turned the Walkman off but hadn't come out of his cocoon.

Now was the moment to get through to him, but what words could she use? She found herself getting angry with him, which she hadn't intended to do. 'Tod, I know you've been badly hurt, but it really isn't necessary to commit suicide because of it.'

He threw his Walkman at her. It hit her on her wrist and rebounded on to the floor. It hurt. How dare he! She wanted to give him the walloping of a lifetime.

'I'm not,' he said. Or at least, that was what it sounded like, muffled by the duvet. There was more, but so indistinct she couldn't make it out. Then something about a promise.

'What promise?'

'You lied to me.' His head emerged from the duvet. 'You said you'd buy me a new computer. You said you'd mend the central heating.'

'Yes, I did, and I meant it, both times. I'm so pleased you've remembered about the computer. I hoped you'd hear what I said, but I wasn't sure if you were awake then or not. We'll go and have a look at them after we've had some breakfast, shall we?'

He scowled. 'Don't want any breakfast. What about the central heating?'

'The man came to look at it. It needs a new pump, but he couldn't fix it himself, so he's given me the name of another man who'll come as soon as he can to put it right.'

She held out a T-shirt and he reached for it, taking it under the bedclothes to put on.

'You promise not to go on at me to remember? Because I can't. It was the knock on the head that did it. Concussion. It's made me forget.'

She thought, It might have. Or on the other hand, it might be that he simply can't bear to remember and so has blocked it out. I don't blame him for that.

'Jeans? Sweatshirt? Trainers? I suspect you've grown an inch or two while you've been in bed. Do you think your mother would mind if we did a bit of a shop for clothes as well?'

He got out of bed, shivering, to put on his trainers. Wrists and ankles stuck out of his clothes and he had to jam his feet in hard to get his trainers on. 'Bathroom.'

He stuck his baseball cap on over his ruined haircut, sighed but obeyed. She used a disreputable T-shirt of his to wipe the dust off the furniture, stacking his books neatly on the wide window ledge, chucking more sweet papers into the bin. The broken computer was so old it would have to be thrown. She went to add some screwed-up paper hankies to the bin before she remembered it was full. It was filled with sheets torn from his cherished stamp albums, with the stamps still on them. A dark-blue looseleaf album lay open on the worktop, devoid of its sheets of stamps.

She pulled the torn sheets out of the bin. Surely they must have been put in there by mistake? But who would...?

'Tod, why are these in the bin?'

He didn't even glance at them. 'I don't want them any more. Can we go now?'

Anything to get out of that chilly house. She switched off the blower heater and they left. But she couldn't forget those torn-up sheets of stamps. Only last week he'd been bragging about completing a valuable set from some obscure part of the world. South America? South Africa? Ellie hadn't really paid attention, except to be pleased that he was enjoying himself. Mauritius? Can't remember.

There'd been stamp hinges in his heavy-duty anorak. All the paraphernalia of an enthusiastic collector littered his worktop. Magnifying glass, catalogues, albums.

She tried to picture the worktop as it had been on Sunday evening when she'd collected him and brought him back. There'd been much the same clutter, but the dark-blue album had then been ... where? She rather thought it had been lying flat under one of the catalogues, complete with its full complement of sheets. Sometime between Sunday evening and Tuesday morning Tod had discarded his previously much loved stamp collection.

So what did all that mean?

Liz had told her that she was good at 'reading the picture'.

Well, if Ellie were a fanciful sort of person, she supposed that she could read something into what she'd seen. Or not. The sort of experience Tod had been through might well have brought about a new maturity in him. A shedding of childish values, and with them a shedding of childish hobbies. Off with the old. On with the new. Out with collecting stamps. On with a new computer.

'Cereal, porridge, eggs?'

He nodded so she got busy.

Or, she thought, if you had a suspicious turn of mind, it could mean that the events of his rape were linked in some way with collecting stamps.

Midge clattered in through the cat flap and made a leap for Tod's lap.

'Grrm, prrm,' said Tod, hugging the cat close. Midge responded by nibbling his ear. Tod laughed. 'Gerroff, you! Ouch, you're heavy! And wet, ugh!'

Ellie proffered a clean tea towel. 'Dry him off, will you? Or he'll leave paw marks over everything. Oh, that reminds me. I think I had a letter the other day with a foreign stamp with a cat on it. Sri Lanka or something? No, not Sri Lanka. Where was it? Australia? Now where did I put that envelope?'

He hunched his shoulders, finished rubbing down the cat and got down to his cereal without replying. She had half expected an airy, *Oh, I've got bored with stamps*. He ate two mouthfuls, pushed the bowl away.

Ellie thought he might eat some more if she

left him alone. Besides, she wanted to make a phone call. She told herself she was being nosy and over-suspicious, but it wouldn't do any harm to phone a friend and ask a question or two about stamps, would it? Hadn't Kate once mentioned that Armand had an interest in collecting stamps before he met her? Something about going to a stamp fair – whatever that might be. Neither Kate nor Armand would be at home on a weekday morning, but they had an answerphone. Ellie left a message for whoever got home first, asking for information as to who might collect stamps locally.

When she went back into the kitchen, Tod had almost finished his bowl of cereal, so that little ploy had worked. Gus loomed in the doorway from the half-finished conservatory and at that same moment the doorbell rang.

It was Mrs Dawes on the doorstep, panting with the effort of shaking drops off her umbrella.

'Ellie, thank God you're in. I've just heard the most terrible – oh, not that I believe it for a minute, but...' She stamped her boots clear of the wet on the doormat and then caught sight of Gus lurking in the kitchen. Putting her hand to where her heart might be under layers of clothing, Mrs Dawes whispered, 'I didn't believe it. He's not still here? Ellie, don't you realize...?'

'Come in, dear. Let me take your coat. I'm just making breakfast for Tod...'

'You've got the boy here? But...!'

'Yes,' said Ellie in a false, cheerful voice. 'I've got company, as you can see. Tod, can you put the kettle on for me? And put some toast under the grill for yourself. Gus, you're on your way out, aren't you?'

Gus cringed. 'Got no umbrella. And what's that woman done with my socks, eh? Tell me that.'

'I'll ask her,' said Ellie, soothing Mrs Dawes into the living room and shutting the door on the others. 'Is it too early for a sherry, dear?'

Mrs Dawes gobbled, her shaking finger pointing at the door. 'You don't know? No, you can't know or you wouldn't have let that man...'

'He's staying here on a day-to-day basis till he can move into the hostel. If he's sober, I give him a bed. If not, I throw him out. All right?'

The threads of red on Mrs Dawes' cheeks began to glow. 'How can you take such a man into your house and expose that poor lad to...?'

'Come off it, dear. Gus is not the one who—'

'He may have pulled the wool over your eyes, but—'

'He didn't do it!' Ellie rarely raised her voice, but she considered the circumstances exceptional. 'The police cleared him. He had an alibi. His being here doesn't worry Tod and I wouldn't turn a cat out unprotected into this weather.'

'You didn't see him when he was blind

drunk and vomiting all over the place.'

'Did you?'

The doorbell rang again, a key turned in the lock and in came Diana, dressed in her black and white professional gear, looking even angrier than usual. 'Mother, we have to talk. I've just heard that...' She was facing the kitchen and so caught sight of Gus. Diana was not normally the screaming type, but this time she did give a little yelp of horror. 'Mother, he's not still here?'

'Come in, dear. Shouldn't you be at work at this time of day? That's right, Tod, make a pot of tea. I'm sure Gus will have one as well, if he's not going out straight away.'

'Mother, I can't think what came over us on Sunday to let you take that man in for the night, but...'

Mrs Dawes nodded. 'Just what I was saying to your mother.'

'...when I thought he was just a drunk, well, as I told Stewart on the phone, you've always been a sucker for lame ducks and would pass him on to the appropriate agency the next day, and he agreed with me that it was a good idea for you to learn from experience that these people never repay your generosity with anything but insult and you were a grown woman and had to make your own mistakes...'

'Thank you, dear.'

'...but when your builder – he's doing a little job for me today at the flats – told me that this pervert was still with you and making himself quite at home, well, it's time to put my foot down...'

Mrs Dawes was nodding. 'Absolutely, I agree. A pervert. They used to flog them.'

'Oh, really.' Ellie tried to keep her voice down. 'Gus is not a pervert. He's no saint, probably. I don't say I particularly like him...'

'I should think not!' said Mrs Dawes

Tod came in, carrying a mug of tea with enormous care not to spill it. Through the open doorway, Ellie could see Gus standing in the hallway, sagging at the knees, listening. Despairing.

'Thank you, Tod,' said Ellie. 'That was very kind of you. Finish your breakfast and we'll go shopping in a minute.'

Tod didn't look at the other two women. He kept his eyes on the floor and went out, closing the door behind him.

Diana and Mrs Dawes broke out together, 'You can't let—'

'This is just not—'

'Sensible?' said Ellie sweetly, sipping her tea and not bothering to offer either of them any. 'I must remind you that this is my house and I invite whom I wish to stay. Gus is harmless enough, poor creature.'

'A stinking pervert!'

'Mother, it's all around the neighbourhood, everyone's talking about it. You just don't realize how upset people are about this. Get rid of the man before...'

'Before what?'

Mrs Dawes wagged her forefinger at Ellie.

'We've been friends for a long time, you and I, and everyone knows you've been under a great strain what with your husband's illness and death. We can make allowances for you, acting completely out of character like this. But it's got to stop or ... well, I don't like to think what will happen.'

'Why, what could happen?' asked Ellie with false sweetness.

Diana shook her head. 'The neighbours won't like it.'

Mrs Dawes nodded. 'I'm sorry to have to tell you this, Ellie, but someone's got to. There's a lot of talk about you going around. I said, I honestly don't believe that you would stoop to sleeping with that man, but...'

'What?' Ellie set her mug down with a clatter. 'Oh, how could you!'

'That's just it, don't you see?' said Diana. 'People always think the worst and given this man's dreadful reputation...'

'I wouldn't dream of...'

'Of course you wouldn't,' said Mrs Dawes in a soothing tone. 'That's what I said. Ellie wouldn't, not in a thousand years. But that's the word that's going around and there's no denying that since Frank died, you've been keeping company with a number of men who I know you say are just friends, but there's no smoke without a fire and—'

Ellie jerked to her feet. 'Lunch with my solicitor. Doing the church minutes with Archie, our church treasurer. Having the occasional drink or meal with my cousin Roy.

Are these crimes?'

'No, but perhaps a little too rich a diet for a new widow?'

Ellie felt herself redden, because in fact all three of these men had expressed a desire to deepen their relationship with her since Frank died. Of course she had rebuffed them, but ... She wanted to slap the two women's self-satisfied, smirking faces. Both of them. She gripped her hands together. She was trembling.

Diana put her arm around Ellie's shoulders. 'There, now. You see how it happens. We don't want this sort of gossip, do we? Give the little man his bus fare to the hostel or wherever he wants to go and the talk will soon die down.'

Mrs Dawes heaved herself to her feet. 'That's about the size of it. I'll spread the word that you acted foolishly but now realize your mistake. Oh, and by the way, you asked about when you should transplant your snowdrops. Do it while they're still green. Don't wait till the leaves die down or they'll never thrive.'

'We'll let ourselves out,' said Diana, taking out her mobile to check for messages. 'Whoops, I should have been at the flats ten minutes ago...'

'And I still have my shopping to do.'

They went out, closing the door with care behind them. Ellie heard Diana's voice in the hall, telling Gus to get his things together as he was going now, that instant.

What was Ellie to do? She did what she always did in times of trouble. She went to the window overlooking her back garden, so that she could look up the slope to the church. The rain had stopped, but gleaming droplets hung from every leaf and twig. The sun was coming out, picking out a rainbow in the sky. An omen, to those who could read it.

She couldn't read it. She had no idea at all what to do.

Seven

Buying a computer was easy with a gold card. Tod knew exactly what he needed. He wanted a few games, he said, but really he'd grown out of all that stuff and needed to have good Internet access nowadays. He didn't want to go to one of the specialist computer shops, but had heard of a shabby little place out towards the hospital which had good after-sales service, really knew how to build a computer package, and didn't rip you off.

All Ellie had to do was stand back and admire when Tod talked computers with the people in the shop, and produce her card on demand. They would deliver and install the following day. Ellie thought, Oh, I've missed my computer lesson again. Then, But I think the plumber's coming to me tomorrow or have I got in a muddle about who's coming and when? I'll sort it out later.

She dropped her art-nouveau clock into the repairers for a clean and an adjustment. It had been losing about five minutes a day for a while and it was more than due a going-over. Now was as good a time as any.

'Would your mother mind if I got you some new clothes?'

Tod said, 'No, she wouldn't mind. She said last night that I needed them, but she hadn't a clue how she was going to afford them.'

So clothes next. Again Tod was a joy to shop with. A replacement set of school clothes from M&S was easy, though the price of a new pair of black shoes almost stunned Ellie into silence. Then casual gear. Tod knew exactly what he wanted and he was clear that casual gear wasn't to be bought from Marks & Spencer. He knew where to get the best, of course. Jeans, sweatshirt, a couple of T-shirts, new trainers. Tod wouldn't remove his old cap even to try on a new one and Ellie didn't insist. His hair was growing unevenly around the shaved bit. She suggested a new haircut, but he would have none of it.

As they passed the window of the Belgian chocolate shop Tod stopped, looking at the biggest box in the window. For his mother. Ellie produced her card yet again. Well, she could afford it ... She'd always had to watch the pennies when Frank was alive and now she could spend freely, she found she didn't really want to. She'd hardly spent any money at all since Frank died, except for the conservatory. Mind you, today had been expensive. But worth it.

They caught the bus back to the Avenue and had lunch at the Sunflowers Café. Beefburger, beans and chips for Tod. Moussaka for Ellie.

Their favourite waitress was on a trip round the world, and her replacement was a skinny little thing with wispy hair hanging over her eyes and no sense of how to apply lipstick, which was all over her mouth and round the edges. And blurred with it, too.

Ellie asked the new girl if she knew how her predecessor was getting on in Australia. The girl shrugged. Not the talking kind.

Tod finished off his meal and leaned back in his chair. His expression changed. 'Hey, I can reach the floor with my feet.'

Ellie grinned at him. 'That's your new trainers.'

'Can I ask you something?'

'Mm? Cup of tea? Coca-Cola?'

'Coca-Cola. Why don't you drive a car? Everyone else does.'

Ellie blinked. 'I never learned. You see, when I was growing up, there weren't so many cars around and my father didn't have one, even. He could walk to work and I walked to school. My mother didn't work but stayed at home to look after us. Then my father died and we weren't well off and I married Frank but even he didn't have a car at first. Then I got a job near home so I didn't have to have a car and...'

'My mother said it was because you were afraid of the traffic. She says lots of older people are and that they shouldn't be on the roads anyway.'

'That's probably true,' said Ellie, thinking of the hours she'd wasted trying to learn how to drive. Her instructor had made it clear from the start that he didn't expect her ever to pass her test, and that had sapped her confidence. Frank had never thought she'd be able to learn how to drive. Perhaps that was something she would never learn to do. Tod was looking at her with a calm, assessing gaze. As if he were seeing her for the first time.

She returned his look, realizing with a chill that a stranger was sitting across the table to her. The bones of his face had sharpened, his mouth hardened, his chin become stronger. He was no longer a cuddly, mercurial little boy whom she could hug and spoil with chocolate biscuits.

He was distracted by something outside the café and became his old self again. It had been merely a trick of the light, making him look like a teenager.

She remembered that look, though. She must not assume he was the same person as he had been before. She also wondered whether that very clear judgemental gaze meant that he was over his early confusion of mind. There had been knowledge in his eyes, she thought.

If so, it seemed likely that he had remembered – if he had ever forgotten and hadn't just been shying away from the knowledge – everything that had happened to him.

'Can I have a banana split?'

'On top of all those chips? You'll be sick.'

'No, I won't.'

No, he probably wouldn't.

She said, in a very casual tone, looking out

of the window as she spoke, 'Did you see that nice policewoman at the station? I forget her name, but she had long red hair.'

He shrugged, didn't answer.

'Did the police come to your house, then?'

'I can't remember. It's no good their asking.' He was looking at her without panic, without expression. Adult to adult. He wasn't being rude, merely factual. He wasn't going to remember or, if he did remember anything, he wasn't going to talk about it.

She could understand that. She nodded, accepting his position, and he relaxed.

'Raining again,' he said.

'What *am* I going to do about Gus?' She hadn't meant that to come out as adult to adult, but it had.

'I suppose he could live in my shed at the bottom of your garden.'

Now he was back to being a child again. She smiled, agreed, and ordered his banana split.

'You said it was rude to stare,' said Tod, in an injured tone.

Ellie looked where he was pointing. 'It's rude to point, too.'

Ellie knew both of the women, slightly; she didn't know them well enough to remember their names, but they usually said hello when they passed in the street. They saw her looking at them and turned their backs on her. That hurt. She set her teeth and shifted her shopping from one arm to the other.

'Is it because of me?' asked Tod, in a small voice.

'I think it's because of Gus. They don't like having him in the neighbourhood and they think my head needs seeing to because I took him in.'

'Oh. I thought it might have been because of me.'

'That will all have been forgotten about in a couple of days' time.'

She hoped. Glancing down at him, she caught a glimpse of an unchildlike, suffering expression on his face. She said, 'Of course, we *can* give in, if we wish. We can let them see they've hurt us. We *can* turn Gus out and say bad riddance. We *can* lie down in the street and wave our legs in the air and scream for mercy. If we want to.'

He grasped a fold of her coat, but kept his eyes down.

'Do you want to give up?' she asked.

'Would you pay to send me away to boarding school?'

She thought, Ouch. She said, 'I'd have to think about that. I could afford it, I suppose, but would it be the right thing to do? Wouldn't it be running away?'

He sighed, long and deep, but released her coat. 'If I lied down in the road and kicked my arms and legs in the air, I'd look just like an insect. Except I'd need another pair of arms or legs to make up the six. Or eight. Did you know a centipede doesn't really have a hundred legs?'

'Goodness. I was sure it had.'

They came in sight of her front door. Gus was sitting on the doorstep, hands folded into his armpits, looking miserable.

'Do you think,' asked Tod, 'that a grown-up ought to have as many chocolate biscuits as a boy of ten, nearly eleven, who's growing fast?'

'Depends how hungry he is, I suppose.'

'Gus does look hungry. But couldn't he have a sandwich first, to fill him up a bit, so he doesn't need so many chocolate biscuits?'

She laughed. 'I'll see what I can do.'

So obviously she had to let Gus back into the house and prepare tea for them both. It seemed oddly quiet without the builders crashing and banging around the place. On the answerphone were the usual fraught messages from plumbers, central-heating engineers, Diana, Aunt Drusilla, Roy ... and one from the curate, who proposed to call on her later that evening.

There was also one from Kate, who'd picked up Ellie's message on her answerphone. Kate had been at a meeting out of town which had finished early. Rather than go back into the City, she was calling it a day and proposed to pop in to see Ellie at tea time ... and there she was on the doorstep.

Ellie left Tod and Gus to compete for the last chocolate biscuit in the kitchen and took some mugs of Earl Grey tea into the living room. Kate was unlacing some expensive-looking high-heeled boots and easing her toes.

'I think I must have done them up too tightly. Thought I was going to get Business-Class Syndrome if the meeting went on any longer ... oh thanks, wow, that's hot.'

She leaned back in the big chair, throwing one arm up above her head. She was wearing a black trouser suit over a white blouse, rather like Diana. Diana bought from Harvey Nichols and sometimes she went a frill too far. Kate's business clothes looked as if they'd come from a men's tailor in Savile Row.

Ellie also sank down into a big chair and closed her eyes, cupping her hands around the mug, hooking a stool forward to put up her feet. 'I took Tod shopping. Spent a fortune. He wanted to know if I'd stump up to send him to boarding school.'

'You're mad about the boy,' said Kate, closing her eyes and relaxing. 'Diana won't half be jealous.'

'Mm. Don't care.' But the barb struck home. Ellie had to admit, if she was honest with herself, that she was mad about Tod. That she cared for him far more than she cared for her grandson, and possibly more than ... no, of course she loved her only daughter. Of course she did.

But she did feel slightly guilty that she'd spent so much money on Tod when, come to think of it, she hadn't bought anything for Diana or even for little Frank for a long time. Not since Christmas. And birthdays before that. She'd never asked Diana to join her out for a special lunch, or bought her a banana split…

The thought of Diana being faced with a banana split made her laugh.

'Oh dear.'

'Oh-dear-what-in-particular?'

'Just oh-dear-generally. I had a deputation from the Decent Women of this parish this morning, warning me that I was being gossiped about because of Gus. Telling me to get rid of him.'

'I thought I saw him in the—'

'Yes. He was out all day. Sitting on the front doorstep like a drowned rat when we came back from shopping.'

'He *does* look a bit like a rodent, come to think of it.'

'I know.' Ellie flipped her own shoes off and wiggled her toes. 'That's better. Kate, I'm worried about Tod. I was going to see if I could get him some private counselling, but that's no good if he won't co-operate.'

She told Kate how Tod had been reacting, from his early morning refusal to get out of bed, to his shifts of mood, one minute almost adult and the next childlike. And his stolid refusal to admit that he remembered anything.

'Perhaps he really doesn't remember,' said Kate. 'That knock on the head…'

'I know. He knows, too. I think he has remembered but has chosen to put it out of his head. In many ways I can't blame him.'

'Except that it means a dangerous paedophile is still out there, unpunished. Unsuspected. Looking out for another victim.'

Ellie shuddered. 'Yes, and that's what's driving me. From Tod's point of view, it's probably better to forget about what happened. And who'd want to put him through the trauma of a trial, even if we could find the man responsible? I don't think I'd want that, if I were his mother. But then I think that if he's not stopped, the man will go on to harm other children. Perhaps even while we speak, he's planning to rape another child. I just hope the police will catch him.'

There was a long, companionable silence broken only when someone in the kitchen switched the radio on. Someone started to whistle along to the tune. Gus, presumably. Tod was trying to whistle, too.

'I'm amazed at you,' said Kate, in a tone which said precisely the opposite. 'Leaving those two together.'

'Good for them both, I think.'

'The waif and the stray.' Kate jerked herself upright and glanced at her watch. 'We're supposed to be going out this evening. Must keep an eye on the time. You're probably closer to Tod than anyone else. If he won't talk to the police, then maybe you're in a better position to get information out of him? Has he given you any clues at all as to who was responsible? He has, hasn't he? That's why you were asking about Armand and stamps?'

'I could be quite wrong.' Ellie explained

about Tod vandalizing his stamp album and throwing the sheets away. 'You know how he was always pestering us for foreign stamps.'

'Do I not! But how could that be linked to...?'

'I really don't know, but it's the only thing I've noticed that doesn't fit in the picture. Also, he doesn't want to talk about stamps any more. You look tired. Sorry to bother you with my worries. How was your meeting?'

'Ah, interesting. I'd been asked to look at a possible project for some clients of ours to invest in. I did some digging around and found that behind the first company was a string of other companies, most of them offshore. I didn't like the smell of it. It seemed to me that there were too many companies involved to be entirely necessary, if you see what I mean...?'

'Over-egging the pudding?'

'The main reasons for a multiplicity of companies behind any one project are to launder money or get it out of the country to avoid tax, or to hide something. Yet I couldn't fault the figures for the project itself. Today I had to present my report to our clients. The board of directors were all the Old School Tie type. All men.'

She laughed. 'The chairman looked exactly like a tortoise, bald head and all, kept his head down. I thought he'd gone to sleep. Then there was this one chap ... he looked like one of those lids of puff pastry they put on top of pies, when it's risen but not properly cooked. He was Macho Man. He was all for the project. He kept calling me "little lady".' She shuddered.

Ellie grinned. 'He was that stupid?'

'It was clever of him really, because it riled me. He said, "Well, if that's all that the little lady can find to report, I vote we go ahead with the project without any further waste of time." So I said, "All I know is, it smells wrong to me." At that point the chairman woke up and said, "I agree with her. It does smell wrong. I rang up an old friend last night and he gave me the low-down on J.B. ..." Puff Pastry looked as if he were going to have a heart attack, so I knew he'd been hiding something. My guess is he was already on the board of the company that was running the project, hiding behind a nominee. It's the usual way of getting a kickback from that sort of situation.

'The chairman went on to say, "Ms Kate may not have been given all the facts in the case, but her instinct is unerring. The meeting is adjourned." '

Ellie thought that one over. 'You're telling me to trust my instinct.'

'What does your instinct tell you?'

'That Gus is not a paedophile or a really bad man but that he is weak; that Tod does remember but will continue to deny it, and that I'm not going to force him. That it is something to do with stamps.'

'And now you're thinking, Why doesn't Kate want to talk about Armand and stamps?

Well, if you must know, it's a bit of a bone of contention between us. Armand used to collect stamps when he was in his teens. His collection is still sitting at the bottom of the big wardrobe in the spare room and he's supposed to have stopped collecting because we need the money for the house and garden. He promised me he'd stopped collecting. But every now and then I find the odd current catalogue around the house, or there's a letter in the post from one of his old pals in the stamp world. He still goes to the fairs, occasionally. But it's not him.'

'No, of course not,' said Ellie, wondering why Kate had been skirting around the subject for so long that morning. It was absurd to think of Armand abusing children – except for shouting at them. He'd have a mean tongue with a boy who misbehaved at school. But for the rest, a pussy cat. Probably. Even if he had started to hit Kate when they were first married, it didn't mean he'd abuse children. Did it? His hitting Kate had been out of frustration because she'd suddenly begun to earn so much more than he, and it had continued because Kate had put up with it. Once Kate had refused to go on playing the part of victim, he'd stopped doing it and since then husband and wife had been getting on very well.

Did this mean Armand might have turned to hitting children? Or that Kate feared he might have done so? Ellie needed to think about this.

Kate said, 'I'll ask him to talk to you about his stamp collection, shall I?'

The phone and the doorbell rang simultaneously.

Kate said, 'I must go,' and reached for her boots. Ellie opened the door to find Mrs Coppola on the doorstep looking anxious, with the long-haired woman detective behind her. Yes, thought Ellie, that colour hair is definitely out of a bottle.

'You've got him here, haven't you? I've been so worried. The police contacted me at work because I wasn't at home when they went round there and, oh, this is Detective Sergeant...'

'Willis,' she said, giving Ellie's hall the once-over. There was someone speaking on the answerphone but Ellie let them ramble on.

'We met the other day,' said Ellie. 'Yes, Tod's here. I got him out of bed eventually and we went shopping. Would you like a cup of tea?'

The kitchen door opened and Tod came out, wearing his new clothes. And his baseball cap. He closed the door behind him. To make sure Gus wasn't seen?

Mrs Coppola rushed to Tod and hugged him. 'Oh, don't you look grown-up.'

Tod said, 'Oh, Mum!' and pushed her away.

'He's talking, then,' said the detective sergeant.

Ellie met her eyes with a warning. 'Naturally.'

'Perhaps we can have a little chat now?' said

the policewoman to Tod. 'Shall we go back to your place?'

'Well...' said Mrs Coppola. She shot a resentful look at Ellie. 'I'm afraid the central heating's not been fixed yet.'

'No, I know. I did try, but my man's hurt himself and the person he's passed me on to hasn't turned up yet.' Ellie held the sitting-room door open and gestured them inside. 'My friend Kate's just going and I'll make you a cuppa if you like. You can be quiet on your own in here.'

Tod gave Ellie a straight, clear look. Angelic, if you didn't know better. 'I can't remember anything, I'm afraid.' He turned the same clear gaze on the detective sergeant. 'It hurts my head to try to remember.'

'Yes, tea would be good, milk no sugar.' And to Tod, 'Never mind, we'll get at it somehow.' She put her arm round Tod's shoulders and steered him into the sitting room. Mrs Coppola followed, saying, 'Do try, dear.'

Kate came out, holding her boots in her hand. 'Can't squeeze my feet into them again. Have to make the trip next door in my stockinged feet.' She kissed Ellie's cheek. 'Have fun.' And disappeared out into the night.

Ellie found Gus still sitting at the kitchen table; crouching, rather. 'That the police again?'

Ellie nodded. She thought, Why is he keeping his voice down? Why are we trying to hide Gus from everyone? This is madness. He's not doing any harm.

The doorbell rang again. Gus jumped, jarring the table on which she was just laying out tea for the policewoman and Mrs Coppola. Ellie said, 'That might be Kate, always forgetting something, that girl.'

Leaving him in the kitchen, she took the tray into the hall and called out, 'Wait a minute!' to whoever was at the door. As she backed into the sitting room she saw that Tod had sunk down into one of the big armchairs, his eyes lifeless. He had disconnected, as it were. Mrs Coppola was stroking his hand, looking anxious. The policewoman was watching him. Getting nowhere fast.

The doorbell rang again. Ellie dumped the tea tray, muttered an excuse and left, closing the door carefully behind her. It wasn't Kate. Alas, no. It was their curate, Timid Timothy, all ruffled sandy hair and slightly anxious blue eyes behind fashionable glasses. Wearing his cassock, clutching a large golfing umbrella and an impressive new briefcase. Ellie thought, I can't cope – police in the living room and Gus in the kitchen...

'At last I find you at home.' He dumped the umbrella and prepared to step inside but Ellie forestalled him.

'I'm so sorry, I've been out all day and now I've got visitors...'

'Oh.' He took a hasty step back and nearly fell off the porch into the drive.

'So it's not convenient to...?'

'No, I'm afraid it's not. Perhaps later...?'

'Later on this evening? Seven o'clock, say?

That would be best for me. We eat at six and there's a meeting at eight. Right, seven it is.'

He gave a sort of salute, wheeled around and stalked back up the driveway to the road, leaving his umbrella behind him. Ellie eyed the umbrella, considering whether to call him back and deciding not to. She closed the door on the outside world thinking, This is all very reprehensible but Gus could do with an umbrella and dear Timothy didn't exactly pull his weight when asked to help him.

Ellie shook her head at herself. Was she actually aiding and abetting a thief in her old age? Well, not exactly a thief, perhaps, but perhaps not far from it. Gus opened the kitchen door a crack, and whispered, 'All clear? Shall I pop upstairs?'

Ellie nodded and he scuttled up the stairs, carrying his shoes in his hand so as not to make any noise.

How did I get into this madhouse situation? Ellie wondered. She knocked on her own sitting-room door and went in. The tea had been drunk. Tod was in the same position but looked asleep, half buried as he was amongst the cushions. Mrs Coppola had stopped stroking his hand and was sitting back, biting her lip.

Detective Sergeant Willis looked relieved to see Ellie. 'May I have a word?'

'Of course.'

Mrs Coppola got to her feet and coaxed Tod awake, pulling him upright. 'This little one ought to be in bed, I think. Also I must see if I can find someone reliable to deal with the central heating.'

'So sorry,' said Ellie, really meaning it. 'I'll try again tomorrow if you like. Everyone seems to have gone sick all at once. Tod will tell you we bought him a new computer this morning. I hope you don't mind. I promised it him when he was in hospital.'

Mrs Coppola flashed her teeth at Ellie. 'Of course I don't mind. I can't possibly afford to give in to his every whim. Or clothe him in designer wear.'

'Anything I can do, really. Anything.'

The woman hesitated. 'Well, there is one other thing. I'm supposed to go to the school tonight, I'm late already, should have been there at half five, parents' evening, you know.'

'You want me to keep him here till you've been?'

'No, not exactly. The head knows Tod's not fit to go back yet and I'm sure they won't be expecting me or him. But the thing is, he left his best jacket that I gave him for Christmas at school...'

'Jacket?' asked the detective sergeant 'What kind? Was he wearing it when he went to school that morning? Did he wear it to go to the swimming baths? You told me that nothing was missing, apart from his swimming things.'

'Well, yes, I did say that, because it's true. He's left his jacket at school several times before, I don't mind telling you. He says he keeps forgetting it because he doesn't like the colour would you believe. So I asked him if he'd left the jacket at school again and he nodded, so that's where it is. So if Mrs Quicke could ask his form teacher for it that would help, and maybe he could cope with some homework if she can find him some.'

'You want me to go instead of you?' Whatever would the woman ask of her next?

'Oh, I'd be so grateful. So would Tod, wouldn't you, Tod?'

Tod flicked a glance at Ellie and yawned. Unresponsive.

'I suppose I could,' said Ellie. Quarter to six, get there straight away, hang around, talk to the teacher, find his jacket, get back here for seven when the curate comes. I could just about do it, but there'll be no time to eat.

'Bless you,' said Mrs Coppola, torn between her need to thank Ellie, and her dislike of a woman who was so much loved by her only son. She hurried Tod into his ancient anorak and they left. It had started to rain again.

'Just a word, Mrs Quicke,' said the detective sergeant, showing no sign of leaving herself. 'You seem very close to the boy. Before the incident did he say anything to you, anything at all, which might help us?'

'I've been thinking about that but he really didn't. I had the builders in, you see, and they tend to mop up your time. Tod was around and about much as usual, I think, but...' She gestured her helplessness.

'Well, how is he with you since the

incident?'

'Up and down. One minute much more grown-up than he was, the next he regresses to an earlier age. I can see he sometimes feels anger, wants to lash out ... and then he's more or less himself again.'

'He's talking to you, though – which is more than he is to me. What has he said to you about it?'

Ellie shook her head. 'Nothing. He just cuts off. I think he's deliberately burying it. Too painful. I'm not inclined to dig deep.'

The policewoman sighed. 'Meanwhile, the man who did this to him is still out there, maybe targeting another small boy.'

'I know,' said Ellie, feeling the anger burn in her again. 'May I ask...? You've talked to the boys he went swimming with?'

'Our enquiries are continuing.'

Ellie pulled a face. 'I suppose you have to be circumspect but if you want me to help you – and I will if I can...'

The detective sergeant bridled. 'They told me about you at the station, said you liked to dabble in detection. Well, I don't hold with that. The truth is that enquiries are continuing. Everyone who has been known to be in contact with the boy has been questioned or is about to be questioned. That's all I can say.'

Ellie thought about that. 'So I can assume that all his friends at school have been interviewed, and that none of them saw or heard anything. Presumably they don't know why he was late leaving the baths. I can also assume you've checked out the swimming instructor and staff at the baths, and the teachers at school. You have a list of paedophiles in the area? Of course, that's the first thing you'll have checked. Now you don't know which way to turn. Is that about right?'

The detective sergeant didn't like this. 'They told me you'd want to interfere.'

'Oh, no!' said Ellie. 'I know nothing about police procedures and I am sure you are all really thorough. The only thing I can think of that might have a bearing on it is – Tod's stamp collection.'

'Stamps?' Incredulous.

'He used to collect them. I think there was a club run by someone at school. He used to spend a lot of his pocket money on them besides badgering everyone he knew to give him their foreign stamps. Since the attack,' she faltered, but continued. 'He's torn up his stamp album and I can't think why he should do that unless it's connected in some way with what's happened to him.'

The detective sergeant shook her head. 'We haven't come across anything in that direction. I expect he just grew tired of them and chucked them.'

How inadequate and foolish she made Ellie feel! And she'd badgered Kate for information about Armand's stamp collection. Oh, dear. 'I expect you're right.'

'Well, if you think of anything else, or if he starts talking to you about it...'

'I'll let you know straight away.'

Ellie held the door open for the woman to go. The umbrella was still in the porch. It had started to rain again. Sighing, Ellie dumped the tea tray in the kitchen, pulled on her hooded raincoat and shouted upstairs to Gus that she had to go out for half an hour. Out of the back door she went, down the garden path and across the churchyard to the pedestrian crossing opposite the school.

How often she had made this trek when Diana had been a little girl, before she'd gone on to the High School! The school buildings hadn't changed much in the intervening years, except that there was a new block of classrooms on the right where the wet-weather playground used to be.

Luckily it wasn't far to go, though the wind was keen. Yuk. She hated getting her ankles wet. Like a cat, she thought.

The parents' evening was winding down. How well she remembered the big hall with its lofty plasterboard ceiling, its scent of meals served and hastily cleared away, of dust, of hundreds of children passing through. Today it was decked out with displays of children's work, and the door to the new computer suite was open to show how up to date they were.

Two long tables of books had been laid out for parental scrutiny; hopefully the parents would choose to buy a suitable tome or two for the school library. One of the school governors was also a member at church. She pounced on Ellie and dragged her over to the book table. Ellie bought them a couple of large reference books. Well, why not? She'd never had any money to spare when Diana was there, so she could make up for it now.

The head was new since Diana's day. He looked like a rugger blue, surely far too young to be a head. Relaxed, smiling, always smiling, reassuring the last of the straggle of parents now leaving. He didn't know her from Adam, which was all right by Ellie.

Most of the teachers looked jaded, gathering forms and folders together, stretching, looking at the clock. Ellie located Tod's form teacher behind a table at the end of the hall. This one wasn't showing any signs of tiredness. Her glasses flashed, her teeth ditto. Lots of fluffy dark hair, aged about thirty but with a figure inclined to stoutness, clad in something colourful in Lycra, not terribly becoming.

'Ms Thomas?' Ellie explained who she was and why she'd come instead of Mrs Coppola. Ms Thomas gave a hearty laugh which echoed around the hall and said, 'The more, the merrier and better late than never!'

Ellie shuddered. Ms Thomas was not Tod's favourite teacher and now Ellie could understand why. That laugh! Those clichés!

As a teacher she seemed to know what she was doing. She had all Tod's reports in a file before her and expressed a suitable degree of shock and horror at what had happened to him. She said, 'Such a good little boy, no trouble at all, a pleasure to teach, middling in all his exams, not top and not bottom, somewhere around the middle, skates along the surface of life, always happy to help Teacher out.'

Which verdict, given Tod's lowish opinion of her, made Ellie suspect Ms Thomas was not quite as perspicacious as she liked to think.

'Yes, of course. Now about some homework...'

'I'll see to it. Drop something in to him, poor little mite.'

'Splendid. And what about his stamps?'

'Stamps?' Ms Thomas frowned, and then came that hearty laugh again. 'Oh, yes. Of course. I'll tell Ms Parsons – she's our geography expert, runs the stamp club one day a week – that Tod was enquiring after some more stamps. I must say it does give the children an intelligent insight into different worlds. Most helpful. And is there anything else...? Because it is getting rather late...'

'Is Ms Parsons here tonight? Perhaps I might have a word?'

'I think she's just gone. Yes, she has. We share a flat, you know...'

Ellie, whose mind did not normally run on such things, immediately jumped to conclusions. Partners? Are they lesbian?

'But I promise I'll tell her. Now if there's nothing else...'

'I'm afraid there is. Tod has torn up his stamp album, you see.'

'Really? How very odd. But that's boys for

you, isn't it? One minute it's stamps and the next Pokemon cards.' Again the merry laugh rang out, making Ellie wince. 'What a silly little boy he is. Tell him to let me have his old stamps and my friend will be able to recycle them, right?'

Ellie nodded, and asked if she might see if Tod's jacket were still in the cloakroom. Ms Thomas failed to hide her impatience, directing Ellie to the new cloakroom at the end of the hall.

Ellie concluded that this was another dead end. She'd been quite, quite wrong about the stamps being important. Unless Ms Thomas's 'friend' was a transvestite with concealed sadistic tendencies, there was nothing suspicious about the stamps. Oh dear, oh dear. What a fool she'd been making of herself...

She couldn't find the jacket anywhere, either. So Tod must have left it at the ... that place, wherever that was.

It was raining even harder as Ellie plodded back across the Green and up through her garden to the back door. There was a light on in the kitchen, and another upstairs in the room Gus was occupying, but the answerphone light wasn't winking.

Now why was that? Had the stupid thing stopped working, or what?

It was nearly seven o'clock, and she would take a bet on it that Timid Timothy would be on time.

Eight

As Ellie took off her wet things, the front door bell rang and there was Timothy, as happy a little bunny as you wouldn't wish to see on your doorstep when you were tired and hungry and worried about things.

'I could have sworn I'd left my umbrella in your porch,' said Timothy, losing his grin for a moment. 'Ah well, it's probably at home. I'll be forgetting my head next.' A hearty laugh. Ellie flinched. Two hearty laughers in one night was too much.

She ushered him into the sitting room. The tea tray was still there from the policewoman's visit. Ellie asked the curate to make himself at home, and would he like a cup of tea or coffee?

'Coffee would be good, and perhaps one of your delicious little cakes; mustn't tell the little woman at home though, must we?'

Ellie gritted her teeth, and managed to smile. She didn't think there was any cake left in the tin, not after Gus and Tod had been at it, but she'd take her time and make herself a sandwich to eat, keep him waiting if necessary. She hadn't asked for this meeting and she was pretty sure he was on the scrounge for her to do something for the church, so he could jolly well wait for her.

She put the kettle on and rummaged in the fridge. Some cheese and a limp leaf or two of lettuce, half a tomato. She cut thick slices of brown bread, buttered them with a lavish hand, piled on everything she could find and finished with a dollop of mayonnaise. There was hardly a clean cup or mug left in the kitchen, but she ran a tea cloth round a couple of mugs she rarely used, inspected the biscuit tin – empty – and took the tray through to the sitting room.

Timothy had seated himself in the big armchair – Frank's old armchair – and laid out some papers on the coffee table.

'What a splendid sandwich,' he said, reaching for it.

'Yes, I'm afraid I haven't had time to eat today,' she said, removing the plate and pushing a mug towards him. 'I really must go shopping again tomorrow. I'm right out of cake and biscuits.'

So there, she thought, with a childish satisfaction in disappointing him.

'Ah. Well. We busy people...'

She thought, If he wags his finger at me, I'll slosh him one. Then was ashamed of herself. Why was she behaving so badly tonight? The poor man couldn't help his irritating little ways.

It was getting dark and she hadn't drawn the curtains. As he started to talk, she got up to remedy this. She was hardly listening. She was hungry. And something was bothering her. The room looked – not quite itself.

But there, she'd had so many people through it...

'What was that?' she said. 'I'm sorry. It's been a long day.'

'Of course.' He beamed at her. 'We all know how well you rise to the occasion. Just like your dear husband, so greatly missed. Quite an example to us all.'

Ellie took a big mouthful of sandwich and leaned back in her own armchair.

Hmm, she thought. Laying it on with a trowel, isn't he! Aunt Drusilla would say the lad was up to no good.

'So I thought I'd bring round the plans for the new church hall, hotfoot from the architects, I'm sure you'll approve...'

Ellie took another mouthful and leaned forward to see. Their dilapidated church hall had been due for replacement for years. It had been one of Frank's pet projects to get something moving on it. He'd even left them some money in his will towards the rebuilding fund.

'Looks good,' she said. 'Nice big kitchen. One big hall, two smaller rooms for meetings. Big foyer, I like that. An office for the secretary. Very nice indeed.'

'We thought you'd like it. After all, your dear husband was so very much involved in this project, it must be something you have a special interest in seeing through.'

'Yes, indeed,' said Ellie, round the last

mouthful. 'I don't think I put any sugar in your coffee. Would you like me to get some?'

'Oh, don't bother. I'm sweet enough, as they say.' Again he chortled, and again Ellie winced. 'So the parish council feel you should have your say about it, if you want something changed, altered ... you know?'

'Well, that's very kind of you,' said Ellie, distracted by a message that was trying to get through to her from the room. 'But I'm hardly an architect, am I? I wouldn't know how big or small things ought to be or what wood to use, or anything like that.'

'No, but you could head up the building committee, couldn't you? Raise the Profile, etcetera.'

Ellie stared. 'Oh, no. I'm not that sort of person at all. I'm not chairman material, really I'm not. Washing-up rota, that's me.'

His smile wavered. 'You underrate yourself. The parish council are unanimous in agreement that we should call this new building the Frank Quicke Memorial Hall. So you see, you have to be involved.'

'What?' Several messages at once bombarded Ellie's brain. She pushed them out of her head and tried to concentrate on what Timid Timothy was saying.

He was nodding like a china mandarin. 'Pre-cise-ly. We want the Frank Quicke Memorial Hall to be named after the man who has done so much for the parish over the years. A plaque in the foyer or perhaps the large hall will commemorate him and his magnificent gift to the church.'

Ellie understood that if Timothy could swing this, it would help his career enormously. He'd made no secret of his ambition to be the next incumbent of the parish. The parish certainly couldn't afford to rebuild the church hall unless they managed to tap into Heritage or other funding. Frank had been trying for grants for years – as had smarmy Archie Benjamin, church treasurer, erstwhile pal of Frank's, and current admirer of Ellie. Although come to think of it, Archie and his toothy grin hadn't been pestering her so much recently...

She couldn't think straight. If the hall were named after Frank, Ellie would be reminded of him every week. Perhaps oftener. Was that a good thing, or a bad?

She thought that Timothy was quite right. Frank would have been ecstatic to have the church hall named after him. There would have been no bearing with him, he would have been as puffed up with pride as – as Mr Toad of Toad Hall.

If he'd lived, they wouldn't be thinking of naming the hall after him. No.

Another thing. If the hall was to be named after those who had served the church so well, then it should be named after the Sunday-school teachers, the organists, the flower arrangers, those who made the coffee and cleared up and manned the church library and cleaned the brasses, week after week, without any thanks, most of the time.

She wasn't at all sure she wanted the new church hall named after Frank, though it might be difficult for the church council to follow her reasoning.

She thought, I'll have to talk to Bill about increasing the amount Frank left for the rebuilding fund. He'd left them a generous five hundred pounds and perhaps she could double that. She would like to help the church. Perhaps she could do it anonymously, she would hate to be thanked for it in public. Only recently she'd been discussing with her solicitor friend, Bill, how to put a certain percentage of her inheritance into a trust fund for charitable purposes. Bill had thought it a good idea. Something to do with tax, yes. But also to avoid being badgered to give, give, give to all and sundry.

Yes, she would definitely ask Bill about it. She was sure he would agree.

Something that Timothy had said was nagging at her. She set down her mug with care. 'You said *magnificent* gift? He did leave the church something in his will but though it was generous, I'd hardly call it *magnificent*.'

Timothy shook a roguish finger at her. 'You mustn't be coy. He told Archie all about it, of course, and asked him to keep it a secret. Which Archie did. But now that the plans have finally been drawn up and we have to consider how to raise the finance, naturally Archie told us what Frank had promised. I think I may say that although we'd been expecting a little something, we'd hardly thought it would be such a large amount.'

She frowned. 'I don't think I ... How much...?'

'A million pounds!' He sat back in his chair, beaming at her. Like a magician who's just produced the rabbit out of a hat.

Ellie gaped. A million? Almost everything she'd inherited?

She tried to keep her voice even. 'You want me to give you a million pounds?'

His smile became anxious. 'No, no. It was Frank who promised us that, and naturally you will honour his promise. Archie said he knew how pleased you'd be.'

Ellie just stared at him.

Timothy's smile faded. He didn't know where he'd gone wrong, but he knew that something was amiss. 'Of course, you will need to think carefully about ... will have to consult the bank, sell shares, I suppose...'

She nodded. She didn't know what to say.

He stood up, dropping his papers and plans on to the floor. Blushing, he scrabbled for them. Ellie didn't help him. Her eyes were on the mantelpiece, where 'Bargar', a toy rabbit of nondescript appearance, was lying on its side. Little Frank's favourite toy. It had not been there when she had talked to the detective sergeant and Mrs Coppola. Her eyes switched to the dining table. Scrumpled-up paper hankies had been dropped under the table, and on the chair seat was the box of tissues which normally lived in the kitchen. A mobile phone lurked under the box of tissues, mislaid by its owner.

Timothy said, 'Well, I expect this has all been a bit of a surprise, though a pleasant one, I'm sure...' This was obviously from a prepared script, and Ellie was certainly not jumping for joy or pleasure, so he blushed again. 'I think I've managed to take your breath away...' That didn't go down too well, either.

'I'll see you out, shall I?' said Ellie, leading the way to the door.

'I'll just leave these plans here, shall I?'

'No, thank you,' said Ellie. 'I rather think you've given me enough to think about for one day.'

'Yes, of course.' He was bowing and scraping now.

Ellie held the front door open for him. There was still no umbrella in the porch. The answerphone light still wasn't winking. Diana must have been here with baby Frank – and left his Bargar by mistake – and interfered with the answerphone.

Ellie slammed the front door and leaned against it, breathing deeply.

She couldn't think straight. Frank had promised them a million pounds? She couldn't understand it. He hadn't said anything to her about it and...

With an effort of will, she decided to deal with first things first. She went upstairs and tapped on the door of Gus's room.

The window was closed – well, it was raining – and the room stank of cigarettes. Gus was lying on his bed, reading a paperback. One of Frank's paperbacks. Well, she didn't mind that too much. She did mind – a bit – that Midge the cat was lying asleep on Gus's stomach. Fickle cat, she thought. Who feeds you?

She said, 'Gus, someone's been here while I was out this evening?'

'That daughter of yours, plus kid. Screaming he was. I turned off the light, made as if I wasn't here. She yelled for you. Went into your bedroom and all. Screamed at the kid, too, poor blighter.'

'Yes. What else did she do?'

'Listened to the answerphone messages.'

'Then wiped them. Gus, have you any idea who might have been on the phone and left messages for me?'

He bridled. 'I wouldn't stoop to listening to—'

'Of course you wouldn't, but that answerphone plays very loudly. You might have had to hear what was said, whether you wanted to or not. It would help me if I knew who'd been on the phone.'

'That daughter of yours – she don't take after you much, does she?'

'Possibly not.'

He huffed and puffed and looked up at the ceiling. Ellie knew that he'd listened. Of course he'd have listened. Whether he would give her the information she needed or not was another matter.

'That smooth bloke Roy that was here the

other night. Something about wanting to take you out to supper?'

'Roy, my cousin. Good. I'll ring him back.'

'Your daughter, wanting you to ring her back. Twice. The central-heating man, says his thumb's better and he'll be here tomorrow morning. If you ask me, he just took a coupla days off to ... All right, all right. Then there was an older woman, worried about you, didn't say who she was, expected you to know...'

'My aunt Drusilla, probably.'

'Someone called Kate. She sounded upset. And a wrong number.'

'Thank you, Gus. You're a great help. Now what about some supper? Not that I'm exactly feeling like a stint at the stove.'

'Gimme a quid, and I'll go down the chippy. For you an' all, if you like.'

'Tell you what, I'll give you a tenner, and you get fish and chips for both of us.'

Gus did have good ideas, sometimes.

Modern technology was wonderful. In the past, you had needed a lot of equipment and a darkroom in order to record and reproduce those special moments for posterity. Now it was all done by digital and video cameras, and computer.

Only the bloodstained wallpaper remained the same. And the bed.

Downstairs in the study there was no need to black out the windows. The man sat at his all-singing, all-dancing computer, calling up images of children on his shining screen, gazing at each one for long minutes at a time. Playing with himself.

Ellie made a list of those people Gus thought had rung and started with Roy, who picked up the phone with commendable alacrity.

'Are you OK? I've been worried about you. Look, I'll come round now you're back home...'

She wanted to say, No, don't do that, but he'd dropped the phone. Mr Impatience.

She dialled Aunt Drusilla. The line was engaged.

She tried Diana.

'Mother, where have you been? I've been worried sick about you. I got to work and thought, I should never have left you alone with that paedophile...'

'He's not a paedophile. Merely a poor inadequate who drinks too much now and then.'

Diana wasn't listening. 'I checked back on you after work – had to bring little Frank with me – shall I be glad when Stewart's back at the end of the week and can take his share of looking after the child. Anyway, there wasn't anyone in...'

'I know. I had to...'

'The phone was ringing itself silly so I answered it and it was a central-heating engineer, somebody McKeown or something, been recommended by your usual man. Said he'd be round first thing to fix whatever it was. Mother, you should have told me you needed a central-heating man, and I'd have got someone round straight away. With my contacts in the trade...'

'McKeown, did you say? But that's—'

'Anyway, I told him pretty sharply that I'd be checking to see he did a good job, though what it was you wanted done, I can't think, because the house seemed warm enough to me. Oh, and I think Frank left his Bargar toy somewhere, so I'll drop in to see you tomorrow, and pick it up.'

'Diana, please! Let me get a word in edgeways. Did you play back the messages on the answerphone? I seem to have lost some.'

'No, of course I didn't. Well, not meaning to, anyway. You've got such a stupid machine, out of the ark, really Mother you ought to get a new one.'

So it was Diana who had cleared the messages. Probably hadn't wanted Ellie to hear the one from Roy, of whom she'd always been jealous. Poor girl. Ellie stifled a sigh. Perhaps she was rather hard on Diana. Perhaps it was true that she'd paid more attention to Tod, spent more money on him recently, than she had on her own flesh and blood.

'Diana, I've been thinking. How about me treating you to a really good lunch some time later in the week, say? Somewhere on the river, perhaps? It seems a long time since we were able to talk without lots of other people around.'

'Oh. Yes, why not? I'll make a reservation at an exclusive place down by the river that I know. I hear they have a new chef. Twelve thirty all right with you?'

'Fine. But which day—?'

The phone had gone down. Again.

She tried Aunt Drusilla's number once more. Still busy. Ellie had a mental picture of her ancient aunt surfing the Internet. It made her laugh. Good on Aunt Drusilla.

Kate next.

'Ellie, are you OK? I tried ringing you, but...'

'I'm fine, but...'

'Look, I'd better come round. This should not be done over the phone.'

Again the phone went dead. Ellie looked at her receiver, shrugged, replaced it and went to tackle the washing-up.

The doorbell rang. Kate, looking harassed. On her heels came Gus, bearing fish and chips for two. And Roy, smoothing raindrops from his silvery hair.

Everyone stared at everyone else. Ellie sighed. 'Thank you, Gus. Will you have yours in the kitchen, while I take mine into the living room? Roy, a sherry? Kate, you'll have one, too?'

Kate and Roy went into the sitting room, uneasily not looking at one another. They were not enemies precisely, but each was aware of and slightly resented the other's influence on Ellie.

Kate put some magazines down on the table. 'Armand said these stamp magazines of his might help. He's ringing you later about them.'

Roy said, 'You're almost out of sherry. Has that Gus been—'

'No,' said Ellie, cutting him short. 'He hasn't. Finish the bottle, you two. I don't want any. Now, Roy – don't start. Gus is OK as long as he doesn't drink and he hasn't, so far. I know the neighbourhood would like him out of here, but where else is he to go? If he stays sober long enough he can go back to the hostel, and then on to some better lodgings elsewhere. I am not going to turn him out with nowhere to go, is that understood?'

She undid the fish and chips and inhaled the aroma of fresh fish, lightly battered and fried in clean oil ... and succulent chips which broke apart in her fingers.

Roy and Kate seated themselves with a small sherry each.

'Now, Kate. You first.'

Kate pulled a face, glanced at Roy, glanced at Ellie, and away. 'It's not nice. I asked around at the office to see if anyone knew anything about child pornography on the Internet. None of them admitted to it at first. Then one started sniggering, and I got it out of him.

'This man – I've never liked him and now I know why – he said he'd heard of various sites that you could access, where children were shown "having it put to them". That's the way he put it. I said I didn't believe him, and he got angry. So he told me in great detail what he'd seen on one of his friend's laptop.' She shuddered.

'It shows children?' asked Roy.

'Yes. Nasty. Some are very young apparently. I didn't like it at all. He – the man – was thrilled to see me so upset. I was still upset when I got home, so Armand got it out of me. I'm glad I did it. I had to know if...'

'Tod were on it?' Ellie pushed her food aside, half eaten. 'Why did you think he might be?'

'I couldn't get him out of my mind. He was tied up and abused, right? I was thinking what kind of man would do that and yes, I know it could be one man, a loner, satisfying his instincts. But then I thought – perhaps it's because I deal with computers all day long – I thought that paedophiles often know one another, form clubs, exchange information using the Internet. I thought I'd best try. Well, Tod wasn't there, you'll be glad to hear, but I believe there are lots of sites. Every now and then one gets closed down, but they start up again. It's ... it's vile!'

Roy pulled on his ear. 'I've heard about these sites. The police can prosecute you for downloading such pictures from the Internet, but how do we find if Tod is on one?'

Kate took a deep breath. 'Well, if you don't mind, I'm going to opt out of any further searches in that direction. It made me feel sick to ... and anyway, Armand came over all masterful and forbade me to ... Not that his forbidding me to do something would actually stop me from doing it, but...'

Ellie said, 'My dear, of course you can't. You mustn't even think of it. The police asked me to let them know if anything occurred to me, and I'll ask them if they've thought of this. Which I suppose they might well have, but they didn't even hint at it. For which I'm grateful, I suppose. If I'd known about this when he was missing, I'd have gone out of my mind. It was bad enough as it was.'

Kate leaned back in her chair. 'Thanks. I don't normally duck out of unpleasant experiences, but this was one too many for me.'

Ellie said, 'Did you finish the sherry? Because...'

'Have mine.' Roy handed his glass over. Ellie drained it in one.

Kate had finished hers. 'I told Armand what you said about stamp collecting. We had a bit of a row about it, if you must know, because he has still been buying stamps but pretending to me that he wasn't. Actually, I suppose I was being a bit stupid trying to stop him, because it's harmless enough, isn't it? There's plenty worse things men could get up to as a hobby...'

And here she shuddered. 'I told him what you'd said about Tod not wanting anything to do with stamps now and he agreed with me that it was worth looking into. He said he'd have a think about who he knows in that world. When he was growing up he used to buy his stamps at a dark little shop a couple of stops down the tube, but that's gone now. Redeveloped into part of a car showroom. So Tod can't have been getting his stamps there. The stamp fairs are where it's at now.'

'I'm afraid that was a dead end,' said Ellie ruefully. 'Tod bought his stamps from a teacher at school and it's a woman.' She picked at the chips, which had gone cold. Was it worth putting them in the microwave? Probably not.

She said, 'Since you're both here, I wouldn't mind your opinion about something. I'll have to tell Diana about it tomorrow, though I can guess what her reaction will be.

'You know the church needs to rebuild the hall? Well, they want me to head up the committee for the rebuilding and to name the hall the Frank Quicke Memorial Hall. They say Frank promised to give them a million pounds to cover it, and they expect me to honour his promise.'

Kate had a coughing fit, while Roy roared, 'What!' and jumped to his feet.

Ellie slapped Kate on her back, appreciating their reaction. 'I must admit it surprised me, too, because Frank never mentioned it to me at all. Then I thought, how nice for the church council to get their hall rebuilt at no cost to themselves.'

Kate wiped her eyes and blew her nose. 'Hang about, didn't your husband leave some money for the rebuilding fund, anyway?'

'Yes, he did. Five hundred pounds, which I'd thought quite generous till I heard what he'd promised Archie.'

Roy looked anxious. 'They haven't got anything in writing, have they?'

'No, and I shouldn't think they'd want to take the matter to court. It's up to me, isn't it? Do I honour Frank's promise and get the church hall rebuilt? The Lord knows it needs it. Or do I spend the money on myself?'

Roy was striding up and down. 'Why should you beggar yourself for—?'

Kate raised her eyebrows and Roy picked up the message. Reddening, he said, 'Look, don't get me wrong. Of course I care about keeping money within the family, but ... blast it, I do really care about what happens to you, Ellie. I mean, as a person, not just as a cousin. Ellie, you know what I mean.'

'Yes, Roy dear. I understand. So you don't think I should do it?'

'What? No, of course not. Ellie, are you pulling my leg? You are, aren't you? What I meant was that I don't want to see you fleeced out of money that Frank intended to provide for your future.'

'And you don't give tuppence about perpetuating Frank's name, because you never knew him.'

'True.' He leaned over her and took her hand. 'I'm sorry, my dear. That was tactless of me. If you feel that you ought to do it, then you should. I hope you won't, for all sorts of reasons. For one thing, it will mean that your dead husband still means more to you than your own future, and I hope that isn't the case. But if you want to do it and leave yourself short, then go ahead. If the worst comes to the worst, I don't think my mother would let you starve and I wouldn't either ... not that I've got much to offer at the moment apart from my pension, but when the development on the Green gets going, I should be able to help out and—'

'Dear Roy. Thank you.' Ellie felt for her hankie and blew her nose. 'That was most thoughtful of you and I appreciate it, I really do, but...'

'I do hope you've decided against doing it,' said Kate, who knew Ellie better even than Roy did.

'I really don't know. I'll have to think about it when I'm calmer. I loved my husband dearly and I still miss him, all the time I miss him, but I don't want to commit suttee or whatever it was that the Indian widows had to do. There are still lots of good things left in life and I intend to enjoy them.'

Roy hit his forehead with the heel of his hand. 'I completely forgot! Talking of good things – well, actually, you might or might not think it a good thing, but ... Ellie, might we have a word in private? Family affairs.'

Kate opened her eyes wide, and shifted preparatory to getting out of her chair. 'Look at the time. I'd better be off.'

Ellie shook her head. 'Please stay, Kate. You are one of my best friends and I don't have any secrets from you. Go ahead, Roy.'

Roy sighed. 'I really think this ought to be between us two. Oh, all right. My mother wants you to sell this house and move in with her!'

Nine

'What?' Ellie clutched her head in case it fell off.

Kate went very still.

Roy darted a look at Kate and then tried to pretend she wasn't there. He stood in front of the fireplace and prepared to Lay Down the Law. 'That fall shook her up. The house is far too big for her. It's got a garden, garages, lots of space. You could make a guest suite out of the old servants' quarters, come and go as you wish...'

'Nonsense!' It came out as a yelp. 'You can't mean it. I spent twenty-odd years of my life running round after Aunt Drusilla because my dear Frank thought I should repay her for bringing him up. It was "Ellie, do this!" and "Ellie, do that!" from morning to night. "Clean the larder, fetch this from the shops, take me to the dentist."

'I did it because I thought it was what I ought to do. I carried on working after I had several miscarriages even when I was advised by the doctor to stop, because I thought we needed the money to make ends meet. I scrimped and saved to pay her taxi fares and give her little treats. I went without hundreds of times because I thought – we all thought – that she only had her pension to live on, and all the while she was as rich as Croesus and sitting on a goldmine, and I could have saved myself all that bother and had a life of my own. Now you say she wants me to move in with her? Over my dead body.'

Roy said, 'Look, she's old and she needs you.'

'I'm old – well, getting there – and I need me. She needs a housekeeper, a paid companion, someone who doesn't mind being ordered to clean her shoes and investigate a bad smell in the downstairs loo. No!'

'But Ellie...'

'What part of the word no don't you understand? *No!* For the first time in my life I can decide when I get up in the morning, what clothes I wear, what I eat, and whom I invite into my house. I'm not losing that for anyone. There's nothing she can offer which would make me change my mind.'

'It's a much bigger, better house...'

'Last decorated in 1914. The kitchen is appalling, the wiring needs renewing, ditto the plumbing, the bathrooms are unspeakable, the furniture is uncomfortable...'

'The garden's much bigger. Think of the scope for you in that garden, with all that space.'

'The garden is a square of lawn surrounded by a border of incredibly dull shrubs and trees that need a surgeon's attention. Have you forgotten that I'm just building myself a dream conservatory here? *No!*'

'She needs someone who—'

'All right. You move in, then.'

That jolted him, all right. 'Me?' An uneasy laugh. 'I can't even make her a cup of tea and get it right.'

'I know what you mean. Try multiplying that a hundred times a day. *No!*'

Kate shifted in her seat, preparatory to rising. 'It really is getting late...'

Roy was getting desperate. 'Ellie, I thought you were fond of her.'

'I am. But not to that extent,' said Ellie, getting to her feet. 'Thanks for coming, Kate; and thanks for, well, everything. And you, Roy. Thanks for coming over and breaking the bad news. I'll try to pop in to see Aunt Drusilla tomorrow.'

Roy and Kate disappeared into the night, both being very polite about who was to go through the gate on to the pavement first.

Ellie went round the house turning off lights, throwing newspapers into the bin, washing up. Fuming.

The phone rang and she nearly didn't answer it. She was too angry to be polite ... except that it was Armand, wanting to know if she were all right, because Kate was worried about her. So of course Ellie had to pretend to be perfectly calm and in control of herself.

Armand said, 'Well, if it's a bad time to talk...'

'No, talk to me. Distract me, Armand. Tell

me what you know about stamp collecting for boys.'

'Well, if you're sure ... The stamp magazines will give you an overall picture. There are still specialist shops, but not as many as there used to be. Philately doesn't get as high a profile as it deserves, though there's money in it, believe me. Since I got married I'm not really a player any more, but it's one way to amass a fortune if you're serious about it.

'People collect in different ways. A lot is done through the Internet. You can order anything you want there if you can afford it. Then the stamp fairs are held in local venues about once every six weeks or so. They're like a giant swop shop, buying and selling stamps from five pence to five thousand pounds. They're a good way of keeping in touch if you like to deal with people rather than computers.'

Ellie was doubtful. 'I don't think I've ever heard Tod talk about going to a stamp fair. He got his stamps by badgering friends and family, swopping stamps with other boys, and buying from a teacher who used to sell them once a week at school. But, the teacher's a woman.'

'Has this teacher got a boyfriend who's into stamps?'

'No, I think she's the partner of Tod's form teacher.'

'Tod doesn't sound a very serious collector.'

'He wasn't, really ... until ... now you come to mention it, he had got more serious about it recently. I mean, he never used to talk about completing sets or the value of what he was collecting.'

'But recently he did? You think he might have found a new contact, who was supplying him with a slightly better class of stamps? Ellie, do you realize what this might mean? If he wasn't getting better stamps through school, then perhaps he'd become friendly with someone who was, well, grooming him for abuse?'

'I feel sick.'

'If you're right, then we should be looking for someone who knows enough about stamps to entice Tod into his net. Someone who collects stamps himself? Someone in the neighbourhood? Let me think. What we need is to tap an expert's knowledge, someone who knows boys and knows the area. Got it! My predecessor at school used to run a stamp club. When he left, the school wanted me to take it on, but I couldn't do that and run the chess club as well. Can't remember his name, but I could find out for you tomorrow, if you like. He'd be the best man to advise you on this.'

'Dear Armand. Thank you. I'll wait to hear from you, shall I?'

Ellie put the phone down and wondered whether to tell the police about this conversation. Only, she suspected she knew how the police would react. They'd think Armand might fit their profile. They'd say Tod had come home on the bus, crossed the Green by the church, turned into the alley ... and that would place him right by the back gate to Armand's garden. They'd say Armand must have been lying in wait for Tod, knowing that he passed by that way every day after school. They'd take him in for questioning, and search his house and...

Stop it! she said. Armand wouldn't. He loves Kate and though he's got a sharp tongue, he wouldn't physically hurt a child. Well, I suppose he might give him a slap, which no one's supposed to do nowadays, but Armand wouldn't tie a boy up and whip him and abuse him. No. But if the police were to find out he'd been a bit of a wife-beater, they'd automatically think the worst. Ellie couldn't, wouldn't point the police in Armand's direction.

No, it was quite absurd. Her house was a semi, and shared a party wall with Kate and Armand. The party walls were flimsy and she'd have heard if there'd been any nasty things going on next door, just as she'd heard raised voices when Armand and Kate had not been getting on last year. If Tod had been next door and cried out, she'd have heard for sure.

Unless, of course, it had happened after she'd gone over to the church at about half past seven.

No, that wouldn't work either, because what would Tod have been doing from the time he left the baths at just after five, until half past seven?

She wouldn't tell the police.

Of course, he might have intercepted the boy on his way back from the baths, tied him up in Ellie's shed at the bottom of her garden, gagged him and left him there until he had time to attend to him? Ripples of horror ran up and down Ellie's back. It was just about possible. There were some coils of wire in Ellie's shed, which she'd used to tie back some heavy shrubs last year. He'd have needed wire cutters to deal with them ... but she hadn't got any wire cutters, had had to use her kitchen scissors, which had never been any good afterwards, totally blunted. He'd have had to come prepared.

It was no good. She'd have to go and have a look, see if the wire were still in the shed where she'd left it. She got out her torch and went down the garden path, feeling a right prat, trying to pretend she was a detective when she ought to be tucked up in bed with a hot-water bottle.

She couldn't find the wire at all. Remembered that the police had been all over the shed, looking for clues. They must have removed the coil of wire, which meant ... oh dear! Armand couldn't really have done it, could he? This would mean the end of Kate's marriage and she'd probably have to move away and then Ellie would get some horrible next-door neighbours instead.

Ah. A thought. After she'd used the wire to tie the rhododendron back to the fence, she might have left it in the kitchen. On top of the cupboard over the boiler?

Relief! The coil was there, just as she'd left it, with a rather chewed-up end showing where she'd wrestled it into submission with the kitchen scissors.

She began to laugh with relief. How stupid of her to think Armand could have done it! What a fantastic scenario she'd constructed! Some day perhaps she'd tell Kate ... No, she wouldn't. She wouldn't tell anyone, ever.

One good thing: her suspicions of Armand had insulated her against all her stupid family problems and she would now be able to go to bed and sleep.

She walked upstairs, went into her bedroom and began to weep ... and weep...

She was so angry with Frank for dying and leaving her. She wanted to scream with rage. And loss. He'd left a great big black hole in her life. Every now and then she dived into that hole, pulled the covers over her head and let herself go. He should have taken more care of himself. He should have listened to her, had check-ups regularly. It served him right that she wasn't going to build a hall to perpetuate his name.

She sobbed till she got a pounding headache and went to the bathroom for aspirin and water. She showered and got into bed, but the pounding in her head refused to let up. If she'd known he was squirreling away all that money, she'd have suggested they spent some of it on themselves for a change. Perhaps a world cruise. She would quite like to see New Zealand, where she had a cousin.

Bother Frank! Oh, how could he go and leave her?

She didn't care about the money. He would have been proud to have had the hall named after him. He would have worked his socks off on the rebuilding committee to get grants and liaise with the architects and make sure everything was up to standard.

Perhaps they'd still call the hall after him, even if she didn't give them all that money? Frank would like that.

No, they wouldn't do that; the name was tied up with the gift of the money. No gift, no name tag.

At two o'clock, she decided that she would do it. Give them the money. It didn't matter what it cost. She'd been overwhelmed when she first knew Frank had left her over a million and a half. She'd had dreams of using the money to help others and she'd made a start in a small way – gifts to friends, gifts to charities, paying for the church's printing bill, helping a local lad setting up in business, topping up the money the waitress at the Sunflowers Café had needed to go round the world. She'd really enjoyed giving people things. The amount she'd inherited had once seemed so vast that she'd thought she'd never get through it.

She'd been deeply appreciative of her good fortune after years of worrying about making ends meet. She'd been thrilled to think she need never worry about the Community Tax Bill again, or choose a cheap cut of meat if she fancied steak.

Well, let the money go. She'd been brought up to count the pennies and it wouldn't be so very difficult to go back to that. She could always take in a lodger; though not Gus, of course. Or charge Aunt Drusilla rent. After all, the old dear had been sitting in a house owned by Frank – and now owned by Ellie – for years without paying a penny or even maintaining it properly.

She could go back to work part-time. Yes, she would do it. Be shut of the money. Get rid of it. It was more trouble than it was worth. And Frank would love – would have loved – to have the hall named after him.

At five to three she woke with a start. A bomb? Something had crashed into the house, shaking it. Shards of glass falling down? The room was steady around her, so the house hadn't fallen down or been blown up. But what...?

There wasn't a sound from Gus. No noise of cars in the street, not even late-night party-goers returning home. Footsteps in the street, going away?

She sprang to the window and lifted a curtain to see out. Nothing moved outside, not even a cat. Where was Midge, anyway? Had he knocked something over? A chair, perhaps? She was shaking. It must have been a nightmare. She'd make herself a cuppa, take a couple more aspirin and get back to sleep.

She pulled on her dressing gown and crept downstairs. Still no sound from Gus. No sign of Midge.

Hall and kitchen were as usual. Reassuring.

She didn't want to open the living-room door, in case...

She made herself do it. At first sight everything looked normal. Then she noticed the brick on the dining table and the curtains moving in and out, gently, in the breeze.

Oh. The brick had scarred the table, slightly. Shards of glass lay on the stamp magazines Kate had brought her. The curtains had held back most of the broken glass, either holding it in the fabric or letting it tumble to the carpet below. There were great rents in the fabric. The curtains would need replacing.

She thought, I've never liked those curtains, anyway. They'd been Frank's choice. Expensive but boring.

Only, replacing them would mean wiping out a little more of Frank's presence in the house and that was a matter for regret.

She realized she was trembling. Suffering from shock. She could just sit and give way to tears. That would be the easy option. She stiffened her back. She had to see what the damage was. She didn't want to touch the curtains for fear of cutting herself on shards of broken glass, so she fetched a broom from the kitchen cupboard and twitched one curtain back at arm's length.

There was a nice big hole in the window, letting in the rain.

She pushed the curtain back over the hole with the broom and sat down. In the kitchen the kettle began to wheeze.

The brick was a signal to her, wasn't it, that the neighbourhood wanted Gus out. It wasn't just Mrs Dawes and Diana who wanted him out. Neither of them would throw bricks through windows at three in the morning. Ellie knew that when a neighbourhood got worked up about something, all sorts of nastiness came crawling out of the woodwork and attacked the offender. It was the natural reaction, Not In My Backyard.

She must ring the police and tell them. They'd probably suggest she pass Gus on to a hostel. They might even get him rehoused. But he needed to be under someone's eye or he'd slip back into a vicious circle of alcoholism and homelessness.

If she could, she'd keep him.

She rang the police station and told them what had happened. She said there was no point in coming round as she was going back to bed. She'd get the damage seen to in the morning. She made herself a cuppa. She noticed that she was shaking gently as she poured the hot water on to a tea bag. She found some aspirin, took two more.

Carefully she tipped broken glass off the magazines Kate had brought her and went back to bed with them. She hadn't anything else to read and perhaps they'd take her mind off her problems.

Leafing through the magazines was an eye-opener, as Armand had said. She supposed that hobbies did turn into big business if there were enough people – and enough money – involved. Look at the value of stamps being bought and sold on the Internet ... amazing! Yes, and there were official stamp fairs being held all over the country every week, though there didn't seem to be one in her part of London. The articles ... she drifted off to sleep.

At half past four, she woke again. It was no good. Personal problems broke through the aspirin barrier. She pounded the pillow and turned over for the umpteenth time that night. The magazines slipped unnoticed to the floor.

Where was Midge, anyway? He usually slept on her bed with her. She supposed he was out hunting. He'd come back when he felt like it.

It was no good thinking she could ignore the plea from Aunt Drusilla. She'd been brought up by her parents to consider other people before herself. She wondered if Frank had chosen to marry her just because of that. It might be an old-fashioned outlook but if the wife put her husband first, then the husband could act up as King of his Castle to his heart's content. Which is what Frank had done. It made for a quiet family life, and who was to say that the woman didn't get as much out of it as the man? It wasn't a fashionable point of view, of course, but you did earn brownie points that way. And really, was it too difficult to put others first? Hadn't she been doing it all her life, for Frank, for Diana, for Aunt Drusilla? So why stop now?

She couldn't stop now. The pattern had been formed long ago and much as she might resent it in some ways, she couldn't break it.

Ellie wept again. She would tell Aunt Drusilla that yes, she would move in and look after her. Eventually she slept.

The cleaner found Tod's swimming things tucked under a chair in the hall.

'Ugh they stink! I put these in washer, yes?'

'No. Put them with the others in the cloakroom. Boys are so careless, always forgetting things. I know where he lives. I'll drop him in a reminder to collect them.'

'OK.'

She fetched the broom to sweep the prettily tiled floor. Then to wash it down. And finally to buff the tiles to a shine. She liked working in old houses. They reminded her of the days when her grandparents had had a big old house in a pleasant, tree-lined suburb, long ago and in another country.

Ellie woke to someone pounding on the door. Eight o'clock. She never overslept. But she had. The radio was on downstairs. Gus must be up. Her head...!

She stumbled downstairs in the dressing

gown. The kitchen door was shut, the radio turned off. Gus taking cover from whoever might be calling.

It was Mrs Coppola with a sulky-looking Tod. 'Whatever's happened to your window?' She didn't wait for an answer. 'Having a lie-in, were you? I had to bring Tod round, I'll be late for work as it is. Oh yes, and the central-heating man's arrived. It's the same one who gave me a quote for giving me a completely new system. I said you were going to pay for it, but he won't start till he's got your signature on the contract. He's just writing it out now, in rough, of course. Hope that's all right. Be a good boy, Tod.'

She kissed his ear and left.

Tod was wearing his new casual gear with his old baseball hat on back to front. He sidled in, made for the kitchen door, opened it, disappeared inside and closed the door behind him. The radio was turned on again. Ellie wondered whether she should tell Gus about the brick. Couldn't think. Couldn't decide.

She felt like going back to bed. She felt like death warmed up. Death would be rather pleasant, she thought, give her a nice rest – though of course Christians weren't supposed to think like that, weren't supposed to despair or have hangovers or feel like giving up life altogether. She thought, I can't cope. Please, God. Give me strength to cope with the day.

The kitchen door opened to let Midge into

the hall and closed again. Midge made straight for her ankles, banging against her. His fur was cold so he'd definitely been out all night. She winced, feeling too fragile to have even a cat banging against her. He needed to be fed of course, but Gus wouldn't know how and Tod wouldn't remember.

Ellie picked Midge up and cuddled him. He suffered this for a while, purring like a tractor engine in her ear. He even nibbled one of her ears. Reassuring. Ticklish. She laughed. Felt better, put him down and went to feed him. First things first. Food. Then clean clothes. Then...

The doorbell rang. It was Jimbo, her own central-heating engineer, plus his mate; and the man he'd recommended, McKeown or some name like it.

'Mornin', missus.'

'You Mrs Quicke? What's happened to your window? Got to get your name on this ... sign here ... and here ... use my pen...'

'Wait a minute,' said Ellie, trying to work out who was doing what, and why. Workmen didn't usually come in threes like this. It was unheard of. Usually you had to wait weeks for one to arrive – and now three had come at once.

Jimbo knew her of old, knew when to take his time. 'Make a start on extending your central heating into the conservatory, right?'

McKeown was impatient. 'Tear out the old central heating, it's knackered, down the road, the woman said you was paying, right?'

Down the path came her plumber. 'Mornin', Mrs Quicke. Looks like it might clear up, right? Make a start on the water feature for you, right?'

Four workmen?

Jimbo asked Mr McKeown, 'Is that the Coppola house that I passed on to you? I looked at it the other day, it needs a new pump, right?'

'The whole lot's got to go, take me four days, maybe five.'

'Stop!' cried Ellie, holding her head in her hands. 'Gentlemen, please. Jimbo, if you say the Coppola house only needs a new pump, that's fine by me. I'll pay for that, but not for a complete new system. Mr McKeown...'

'I tell you that system's knackered.'

Jimbo looked worried. 'I'm pretty sure that...'

'I can't afford to pay for a new system,' said Ellie, thinking that if she were going to fund the rebuilding of the hall, she wouldn't be able to afford lots of things she'd been buying lately. Tod's computer, and all his new clothes, for instance. The plumber put down his toolkit and stood, arms akimbo, taking everything in.

Ellie said, 'Look, let's try a new pump first. I think I can run to that.'

McKeown went a dull red. 'You can't just call me out and then say you've changed your mind.'

'How much for just replacing the pump?'

He mentioned a figure which made Ellie

open her eyes wide. Jimbo looked at the floor. The plumber whistled. 'You're too expensive for me,' said Ellie. 'I'm sorry, but you've just lost the job.'

'There's a call-out charge, you know. Sixty pounds. Cash preferred, but credit cards accepted.'

Jimbo took the man aside but Ellie could hear what he said. 'Don't you think that's a bit of a rip-off? Look, I know this old dear of old. She's not made of money. Lost her husband only a while back. She can't afford to go paying for someone else's new system when all it needs is a new pump.'

'What about my call-out fee?'

'Forget it, mate. You shouldna tried it on.'

'I know my rights,' yelled McKeown. But he backed off up the drive and got into his van, slamming the door after him. Ellie felt thankful that at least some people didn't know how much money she'd been left. And was shortly about to give away.

'Make a start, shall I?' said the plumber.

'I'm so sorry,' said Ellie. 'I can't think what day of the week it is and who should be working where. You weren't both booked for today, were you? Can you work around one another?'

'Don't you worry about a thing,' said Jimbo, doing his Old Retainer act. 'I'll go have a look at that pump first, and get on with my bits after. Or shall I put a bit of hardboard over that window for you first, while you – er – tidy up?'

Ellie realized she was still in her dressing gown at nearly nine o'clock. Whatever would the neighbours think! 'Bless you, Jimbo. If you could do the pump first, I'll ring the replacement window people. Here's Mrs Coppola's key.' And to the plumber, 'Is that all right with you? I'll show you just where I want the water feature...'

Yellow pages were very helpful. Yes, they'd be round that morning. The bill would probably be ... ouch! Why did everything need replacing as soon as money was short?

She went upstairs to shower, dress and try to make herself look presentable.

She found herself thanking God for Jimbo and the nice plumber. And for Tod's recovery – which she realized with a start she had neglected to do. And for good friends. She finished with a plea for Him to be with her as she had some rather nasty jobs to do that day. She must push herself into doing some sums. She had yet to pay for the conservatory and the extension of the central heating into it. Tiling it, installing a water feature. She'd tentatively made some plans for a holiday abroad and new clothes ... oh dear, she'd better forget about those.

The plumber took no time at all to install his piping and left after telling her all about his little boy's piano lessons and how they were hoping the next one would be a girl. Jimbo returned shortly after to say the new pump was in and the central heating at Mrs Coppola's was now on. Then he and his mate started unloading piping and radiators and humping them through the house to the conservatory. More noise. Ellie's head ached.

A glazier came round to replace the window. Ellie swept up most of the glass but left the curtains as they were. Ripped to pieces. The police called to say they'd be round to inspect the damage soon. They said a patrol car had gone round the streets in her neighbourhood after she reported the 'incident' but had not spotted anyone behaving suspiciously. Dead end.

Gus and Tod accompanied Midge to see what Ellie was doing in the sitting room. Midge sneezed at the glass and retreated. He didn't want glass splinters in his paws. Neither Gus nor Tod commented on the broken window.

Diana rang to say she'd booked a table at a most exclusive restaurant by the river for that very day and would Ellie please remember to wear something decent for a change. Diana rang off before Ellie could explain that she couldn't come that day because she was looking after Tod. Oh well. She could find someone else to look after him, perhaps, and it was really rather important for her to talk to Diana.

Ellie mentally reviewed her wardrobe and decided that last year's dark-blue two-piece, perhaps with a light floral scarf at the neck, would have to do.

Gus went off somewhere – to the luncheon club, she supposed. Jimbo had brought his transistor radio and turned it on full blast. He and his mate didn't believe in communicating at anything less than a bellow. Ellie took some more aspirin.

Tod was whiny. His wrists had healed well enough but his hair was a mess and he refused to go with her to the barber's. She suggested he stay in her house with Jimbo and his mate for company while she went out to lunch with Diana, but then Tod's new computer arrived and they had to rush down to his house to take it in, unpack it, and exclaim over it. Of course, he didn't want to leave it for a minute, which meant that she must either cancel her lunch date or find someone to babysit him at his house while she went off for lunch with Diana.

The phone rang for this and that. Two nicely dressed young men came to the door asking if she believed in life after death – which she did, but by that time she was so muddled in her mind that she told them she was a Catholic, when she'd really meant to say she attended the church across the Green. Luckily they didn't stay to cross-question her about it. Kate and Aunt Drusilla both rang while she was at Tod's, asking her to ring them back.

Ellie tried to raise Diana on her mobile to cancel lunch but couldn't get through ... and then realized that of course she couldn't because Diana had left her mobile at Ellie's. She darted backwards and forwards between the two houses, making tea for Jimbo and his mate, checking what she'd got in the freezer that would do for Tod's lunch, phoning Kate and Aunt Drusilla to say she'd ring again later.

Who could look after Tod? She offered him an early lunch of cauliflower cheese, which he turned down with sick noises. She said that if he was going to be like that, he'd be better off at school. That shut him up for a bit.

Ellie was so wound up by this time that she even considered doing a little housework for Mrs Coppola, and started getting the vacuum cleaner out – a blessing that the house was warm now as it was raining yet again. She did the ground floor but couldn't face carrying the vacuum up the stairs. However, she did a sweep round the bedrooms to empty the waste-paper baskets. Only to find that they were all empty. Including Tod's. Was it dustbin day today? She couldn't think. If it was, then she'd forgotten to put her own bag out and it would have to wait a week and...

'Tod, where are those old stamps of yours? Your teacher said that if you didn't want them any more, to let her have them so she could re-sell.'

Tod just shrugged and turned his shoulder on her. Ellie sat down on his bed to contemplate the back of his head. Couldn't he even bear to look at the torn-up remains of his stamp collection? She said, 'Tod, we need to talk about this.'

Tod hit his table. 'I need to get on to the Internet.'

There were all those nasty porn sites on the Internet. 'You'll have to ask your mother about that.'

'You promised to pay the subscription for me.'

'Tod, I'm not made of money, you know.'

'Everyone knows you're so rich you could afford to buy up the street. Why are you so mean to me? It's not fair!'

Ten

Ellie tried to keep calm. 'No, Tod. I'm not so rich any more.'

'You're only saying that to upset me and I shouldn't be upset, you know I shouldn't.'

Ellie sighed. 'Tod, listen to me...'

He stormed out of the room and threw himself on the sofa down below. Before Ellie could follow, he had the television turned on, full blast.

Ellie covered her ears and retreated to the phone in the hall. Perhaps dear Rose could spare a couple of hours to look after him? Unfortunately Rose was working at the charity shop and though happy to oblige at any other time, couldn't help that day, but was *so* pleased to hear that dear Ellie was going to do something about the church hall, which, as everyone knew, was threatening to fall down about their ears.

Which news made Ellie wince. How did the gossip get around so quickly? Dear Rose put the phone down before Ellie remembered that her old friend had mentioned a problem she'd been having. Something to do with her daughter's wedding? Whatever it was, it could wait. Rose hadn't brought the subject up again so it couldn't have been important.

The phone rang. It was Armand, in a tearing hurry between lessons or lessons and a meeting or some such. 'This is the name of the man who used to run the stamp club at school here ... have you got a pencil? He'll be able to give you the low-down on who collects stamps locally. I've got to run, so ... the name's Pearsall. Lives locally, they say. You can look him up in the phone book ... What's that?' To someone in the room with him? 'Oh. Coming ... All right, Ellie? Got to dash...'

Pearsall. Ellie wrote the name down. It didn't mean anything to her. Should she try it on Tod? But more importantly, who could she find to look after Tod while she went out with Diana?

After a search through the bits of paper in her handbag she found Roy's mobile phone number and tried him. In a meeting, would ring her back.

As a last resort she tried Betty, the delightful girl who looked after young Frank while Diana was out at work. If Ellie paid her double – here Ellie winced – would Betty bring young Frank over and look after him and Tod in Mrs Coppola's house? She would. Blessings and thanks.

She told Tod what was going to happen and he covered his ears with his hands. She said, 'What you need, my boy, is...' Then she sighed. A good spanking was not going to help and was against the law anyway. He needed a cuddle, she supposed. But when she tried to give it him, he pushed her away and called her a dirty name.

She'd had enough, and more than enough.

Betty arrived with little Frank, who was grizzling in his pushchair. Ellie turned over her charge with thankfulness, pointing out that she'd left some frozen meals in Mrs Coppola's freezer for lunch.

Diana had chosen one of the most exclusive and expensive places to eat in the whole of London. The dining room overlooked the river. The decor was all metal, the waiters had shaven heads and wore black, and the clientele – both men and women – were power-dressed.

Ellie felt dull and inadequate as the maître d' led her to where Diana was sitting, hoovering up crudités. Diana was also wearing black, of course. Diana looked her mother up and down and Ellie knew what was coming.

'Oh, mother, really! Couldn't you have found something a little smarter to wear than that old thing? One of these days I must take you shopping for some good clothes, although you'll have to lose a good stone in weight first.'

'I'm on an economy drive, I'm afraid. No, I won't have anything to drink before we go in.'

Diana laughed as if Ellie had said something witty, and Ellie wondered whether it would be better to look at the prices on the menu and worry about them all through the meal, or ignore them and worry later.

Their table was not by the window, which annoyed Diana. But as she explained to Ellie, you usually had to reserve a fortnight ahead to get a table anywhere at this restaurant, so she had been lucky enough to get even this one, which she'd only been able to do by using someone else's name.

Ellie smiled and tried to relax. It really was not her sort of place. To her mind the decor was too harsh, the food too rich and the staff too contemptuous.

'Lovely to get you on your own, dear,' said Ellie, wondering how to start.

'About time.'

A mobile trilled nearby and Diana sought in her bag to check if it were hers, but of course it wasn't. 'Can't think where I've put it.'

'You left it at my house, dear. I put it on the mantelpiece for you, with Bargar.'

'Oh, did I leave it there? I feel undressed without it.'

'Well, this is very pleasant,' said Ellie, ordering asparagus soup and goujons of sole wrapped around smoked salmon, all done in some kind of weird and wonderful sauce. She would have liked something really plain, but there wasn't anything like that here. Well, at least she could have some food she wouldn't normally eat at home.

'Oysters ... and then the lobster for me. We'll have a good white wine with it. Yes, a full bottle, of course. Mother, there's a great deal to discuss, especially now that Stewart will be joining me next week ... and what we'll do then, in that cramped little place...'

'Yes, I wanted to talk to you about that, dear.'

'You agree it would make sense for us to swop?'

'Well actually, Aunt Drusilla wants me to move in with her...'

'She ought to be in a home.'

'She's very far from wanting to go into a home.'

Diana frowned. 'I must think what we can do about that. Perhaps if we were to install a carer – someone of our own choosing...'

Diana making plans for other people was bad news. Diana would come out on top, of course, but everyone else would lose. Ellie hastened to say, 'I suppose I could be her carer. So, if I do move in with her it would free up my house, and then it would make sense for you to buy me out.'

'What? Why? That's ridiculous. Why should I? I already own half...'

'Well, not exactly, dear. You know perfectly well that I own half outright, and I have a life interest in half, which only reverts to you on my death.'

'Well, yes. But naturally you'll leave your half to me and ... why should I have to buy you out, and what with, may I ask?'

'A mortgage, of course. Just like everyone else.'

Diana laughed. 'Oh, mother, you are so droll.'

'I think,' said Ellie, with care, 'I should tell you that the church council has decided to name the rebuilt church hall – The Frank Quicke Memorial Hall.'

Diana clashed her glass down on the table. 'But ... that's ... why, that's brilliant. He earned it, I'll say that for him. I used to joke to Stewart that he put in so many hours for that church, he should have set up a bed there.'

'There's a snag. He promised to give them the money for it and they expect me to honour that promise.'

Diana's voice was sharp. 'What? How much?'

'Nearly everything I've got.'

Diana gasped. 'What? But that's ridiculous!'

'Yes.' Ellie waited for it...

'That's family money, isn't it? Money that would normally be passed on down through the generations, to little Frank, say, or ... or...'

'Or you? Yes.'

Diana looked at her oysters and Ellie looked at her soup. Ellie was hungry. She picked up her spoon and made a start. Delicious! She gestured to the oysters. 'Eat up.'

Diana took one, swallowed and choked.

'Of course,' said Ellie, 'I'm delighted to do as they ask. Your dear father deserved the best. But I must admit I do worry about my future now. I've been looking at the money situation. If I move in with Aunt Drusilla and you buy me out, then I could probably invest in an annuity...'

'But an annuity dies with your death. What about Dad's insurance money?'

'That's what I'm living on now. It's paying for the new conservatory and general living expenses till probate is granted and the rest of the money comes through. I could have got a bank loan "against my expectations" as they say, but I was always brought up to avoid debt, so ... eat up. This meal is on me, remember.'

'So the house is your only asset?'

Ellie sighed. 'I hate to part with it, but I can't think how else I can manage. I don't think I can go on paying your childminder's fees, and you'll have to find the rent for the flat you're living in when the lease is up at the end of the six months. I was really getting upset about that until I remembered you've sold your house up north, so you can use that money as downpayment on a smaller house or flat here.'

'But I was going to get rid of my old car and buy myself a new one.'

Ellie thought, That 'old car' was my car that I was going to learn how to drive till you pinched it. But she didn't say anything. She finished her soup. 'Perhaps this will be the last time I shall be able to afford such a meal. Let's make the most of it, shall we?'

'Mother, don't be in such a rush to throw everything away. It's good news, of course, that the church wants to name the hall after Dad, but...'

Ellie lifted her hand. 'I can't possibly refuse. What would people think?'

Ellie sat back and watched Diana writhe a pathway between pride and cupidity. Not a pretty sight.

Ellie had done her sums that morning, and although she'd never regarded herself as a Great Brain financially and would have to get the figures checked out with her solicitor and/or Kate, she thought she'd be able to manage even if she did make that enormous donation to the church. If Diana were off her back financially and she got Aunt Drusilla to stump up some rent, she'd be all right. Not rich, of course, but comfortably able to afford little treats if not a diamond ring every year.

She was not going to share her thought processes with Diana. For one thing, after having decided in the night to give the money away and move in with Aunt Drusilla, this morning she was having second and third thoughts. One part of her said that of course she must be unselfish and Christian and do it, while the rest went screaming bananas at the thought.

Ellie lifted her glass of wine to her lips and wondered if she were playing games with Diana. If Diana were to think of anyone but herself for a change, she might back Ellie in giving the money away and moving in with Aunt Drusilla. And then, Ellie thought, she just might be able to go through with it. Give the money away. Live for others. It was, with gritted teeth, just about possible.

But if Diana were greedy, then she'd find some reason why her mother should keep the money.

Cupidity finally won, as Ellie had half feared and half hoped that it might. Diana worked her way through astonishment that the church could possibly think Ellie was worth that much, to outrage that they would expect her to beggar herself for them. Ellie heard her out with mixed feelings. Perhaps relief was dominant?

'Oh no, dear,' said Ellie. 'I won't be beggared if you buy the house from me. At a fair price. Considering all the alterations I'm having done.'

She ran a piece of bread roll – nice and hot, fresh from the oven – round her plate to collect the last of the herb and cheese sauce that had surrounded her fish. There was no doubt about it, the restaurant deserved its popularity.

Diana wasn't doing as well with her meal. Diana in a temper wasn't at her best with a lobster and the wine was probably turning sour as she drank it.

Ellie was touched with pity for her poor, unhappy daughter. Ellie didn't know how the girl had got to be so self-centred, but there it was. She was sorry for her.

Then Ellie remembered how Roy had reacted to the news, offering her financial support even though his own future as a developer was a trifle dicey and he only had his pension to live on.

Ellie lifted her glass in a toast to Diana. 'Here's to you, Diana. I'm so proud of you, my dear, holding down such an important job, doing so well. One day perhaps, when you're on the council or standing for parliament or something, it'll be your poor old mother looking to you for support.'

Diana looked as if she'd sat on a pin. Ellie thought, That was naughty of me, but thoroughly deserved, I feel.

She relished the last drops of her single glass of wine, and considered the sweets menu. Would it be gilding the lily to have a sweet? Fresh strawberries? Or cheese?

Diana pushed her plate away. 'Just coffee for me.'

'Whatever you say, dear.'

'I must talk to Stewart. I can't believe you'd let them bully you like this.'

'Well, you know, dear, it is for your father.'

'But he's dead.'

Yes, thought Ellie. He's dead and until now I don't think you've missed him, whereas I miss him every day in every way. Though I must admit to experiencing just a trace of enjoyment in this situation. I know I shouldn't. It's probably very unkind of me, but there it is. I'm learning how to play dirty. Woe is me.

'Are you sure you don't want a sweet, dear?'

In one final burst of extravagance, Ellie took a taxi back to Mrs Coppola's, guiltily aware she must relieve Betty as quickly as possible.

Besides, she was feeling the effects of drinking wine on top of a bad night.

As she let herself in, she heard Frank wailing. Oh dear.

'What's happened?' The living room had been wrecked. Cushions were on the floor, chairs overturned, magazines torn and scattered, china ornaments from the mantelpiece shattered.

Betty was crying, too. She was holding little Frank in her arms, jiggling him up and down, trying to soothe him. It looked as if she were in need of soothing as well. Ellie dropped her handbag and put her arms round Betty, who turned her face into Ellie's shoulder and howled. As did little Frank.

'Hush, shush, my dear. It's all right.'

'It isn't! Oh, do be quiet, Frank!'

'There, there. Let's sit down in comfort.' Ellie let go of Betty long enough to replace the cushions on the settee and urge her to sit down. But where was Tod? 'Tod...?'

'I don't know where he's gone,' sobbed Betty, trying to reach for her handkerchief and at the same time calm Frank. 'He got this envelope through the door, tore it open and went mad. I'd just got Frank up from his nap and he was crotchety and the next thing I knew Tod was trashing the place and then ... and then Tod ran out of the back door and I tried to run after him, but Frank started crying really hard and Tod went down the garden path and I didn't know what to do.'

'Shush, dear. You did the right thing. You

looked after Frank. There, now.'

Betty's sobs were subsiding but she was shivering. Ellie took off her own jacket and put it round Betty's shoulders. Frank was wailing, his right cheek bright red. Teething. As if they didn't have enough to cope with. Ellie took him from Betty and joggled him in her arms, trying to assess the damage in the room.

There were torn pieces of paper everywhere. Mostly glossy paper from magazines.

Betty struggled to her feet. She was still shaking but enough in control now to try to help Frank. She scrabbled in her big tote bag, produced some soothing gel and managed to smooth some on to Frank's gums while Ellie fought to hold him still. The relief was instantaneous. Frank stopped wailing.

Silence.

Betty smiled through her tears. Sought for a tissue and mopped Frank up. And then herself. Ellie lowered herself on to the settee with Frank, who started playing with the gold chain she wore round her neck. Who's a lovely little boy, then...?

Betty looked around her and winced. 'I'm so sorry. I let you down. Tod was fine at first. He was on his computer for a while. Then he came down and played with Frank. We had lunch, and then ... he's so big! I'm not used to handling boys that big. Almost as tall as I am. I must admit, I was frightened.'

Ellie hadn't thought of it that way but of

course Betty couldn't be expected to look after a half-grown lad like Tod. Ellie blamed herself. Mrs Coppola had asked Ellie to look after Tod and she'd agreed to do so. That ought to have been her first priority, but she had ducked out of it. She ought to have cancelled the lunch with Diana, no matter how important it seemed at the time.

Betty sniffed. 'Where do you think he's gone?'

'My shed, probably. Or else he'll be annoying the central heating engineers working at my place. I don't think he'll go far.'

'You didn't see him. He was in a terrible state, shouting, swearing, smashing...'

'I'll go and look for him in a minute, when I'm sure you're all right.'

Betty blew her nose again. She was not a pretty girl, too plump, too badly dressed, mousy hair drawn back in an elastic band, nondescript skin. But she looked kind and kids adored her. Even now Frank was abandoning Ellie to move on to Betty's lap.

'I'm all right now,' said Betty, trying to smile. 'Stupid me. Can't even look after two kids at once, right? I knew he'd been hurt bad. I told him, you go back to school looking like that, and everyone'll think you tried to give yourself a Beckham. He laughed. He was just fine ... I blame myself. I wasn't quick enough. The envelope came through the door and I never thought. I said, "Will you get it?" and he did.

'You know when they fall and hurt themselves? If they yell straight away, there's nothing much wrong, usually. But if there's a horrible silence for a coupla seconds, you know something really awful's happened, that they've hurt themselves bad. Well, it was like that. I was just getting Frank up from his rest on the settee here and I thought, Tod's been quiet too long. Then all hell broke loose.

'I'd got Frank in my arms luckily. Tod came in, tearing up this envelope. Then he took a swipe at the pushchair, which was in his way. That went over. Then the cushions flew off the settee and the magazines and then he swept all the china bits and pieces off the mantel ... and he stamped and tore and shouted...

'I didn't know what to do. I was frightened he'd start on me next. Frank was upset. I needed to put him down to try to calm Tod but I couldn't, with the pushchair on its side. So I got behind the settee and sort of crouched down and the next thing Tod tore out to the kitchen and down the garden. Then you came.'

Ellie patted her shoulder. 'I couldn't have done any better if I'd been here. Whatever it was that upset him ... you think the pieces are by the door here?'

'I suppose so.'

'Well, I'll look for them later. The first thing is to call a taxi to take you home. Then I'll go and look for Tod. Right?'

Betty shook herself. 'I need to know he's all right. I'd never forgive myself, otherwise. You go and look for him. I'll stay here. Perhaps he'll come back of his own accord.'

'Are you sure? Because if I can't find him...'

'We've got to phone the police.'

Ellie picked her way through the mess that Tod had made in the living room. Nothing had been disturbed in the kitchen. The back door was open. She went down the steps into the garden, which was mostly under concrete and very dull indeed. She knew Tod hated it. There was no garden shed here. Nowhere for him to hide.

At the bottom there was a gate – broken – leading into the alley which divided the bottom of the gardens from the church grounds. Ellie lifted her eyes to the church. The sun had come out and lit up the spire with its gilded weathervane on top.

Ellie thought, Dear Lord, what a mess I've made of things. Please, please, don't let anything else bad happen to Tod.

Three houses along she turned into her own garden through a gate which was trim and neat. The shed door stood open but there was no Tod inside.

Jimbo and his mate were still entertaining the neighbourhood with a selection of pop music, courtesy of their transistor radio. And whistling along to it. Perhaps a third person was joining in?

Ellie found Jimbo showing Tod how to use a spirit level.

'Getting on nicely now we've some help,' said Jimbo, grinning.

Ellie's first impulse was to smack Tod round the head or put him over her knee. She felt she could understand parents who went over the top and hit their children. He was ignoring her.

'Fine,' she said. 'But Tod's got some clearing up to do at home today. Come on, Tod. Betty's got to get off home with little Frank.'

Judging by the mutinous set of his shoulders, Ellie suspected he might not obey her, but he did. Slowly. She didn't speak to him on the way back and he didn't say anything, either.

In Ellie's absence, Betty had righted the furniture and found a plastic bag to stuff all the torn magazines in. She was now on her hands and knees with a dustpan and brush, sweeping up the fragments of china.

Tod walked past her without a word, went through the hall and upstairs to his room, where he banged the door shut on the world.

Betty pointed. 'I left the pieces of the envelope where they were. I didn't touch them. Fingerprints, maybe?'

Ellie bent over them. If you made a sort of jigsaw puzzle out of the pieces, they looked as if they might make up into a plain white envelope, such as you could buy anywhere. Although it had been torn across, someone had written TOD on it in capital letters. There didn't seem to be any enclosure.

Nothing. Except, possibly...

Betty and Ellie bent lower.

A book of second-class stamps, unused. It had been crumpled up, but was still identifiable.

Stamps. Oh dear, oh dear.

Eleven

Betty was puzzled. 'Someone sent him some stamps?' Frank managed to tumble off the settee and set up a roar. This upset Betty all over again. 'Oh, my little pet, I should never have left you on your own. Who's Betty's brave little man, then?' She picked him up and gave him a cuddle.

'I'm afraid,' said Ellie, 'that this is a message for Tod to keep quiet about what's happened. We have to get the police on this. Can you hold Frank for a few minutes?'

'Yes, but it's getting late. I have to pick my kids up from school soon and...'

'I know. Put him in his pushchair. You get off and I'll cope here.'

'If you're sure?'

Ellie paid Betty for the extra trouble and added a tenner for good measure. There was no sound from Tod upstairs.

Detective Sergeant Willis was not at the police station, but a voice at the other end of the phone took a message and said she'd be along straight away.

Ellie looked around. Apart from the magazines and the china, the room now looked much as it should. There wasn't anything she could do about replacing the china. Ellie rather hoped Mrs Coppola wouldn't expect her to pay for it, but ... sigh ... she probably would. After all, Ellie had been left in charge of Tod and had opted out. Very bad.

Ellie went upstairs, tapped on Tod's door and went in. He was playing a game on his new computer and didn't turn round.

'Tod, I've called the police, told them what's happened. This is all to do with someone who sold you stamps, isn't it?'

Tod didn't move as much as a muscle.

'Was it a warning to you to say nothing?'

No reaction.

Ellie was getting angry. 'Well, all I can say is, I hope your mother doesn't hock your new computer, to pay for the things you've broken.'

He reached for something to throw at her, so she made herself scarce.

This is hopeless, she told herself. I'm no good at this. I'm getting upset when I should be calm. I'm not qualified to deal with a boy in such a state. I don't know whether I'm doing or saying the right things or making matters worse. We can't go on like this and I'll tell Mrs Coppola so.

She went downstairs and tried to raise her dear friend Liz, the counsellor, on the phone. Predictably, Liz was out.

'I could weep,' said Ellie. So made herself a cup of tea instead.

Jimbo came to the door, saying he was off now, but would be back tomorrow early and would then want to drain the tank so would she make sure she'd got the kettle filled and the washing-up done before he started.

Detective Sergeant Willis arrived, looking harassed. Her hair was loose around her shoulders and her eyebrows needed plucking, but she was as businesslike as ever. 'I tried your house but no one was there. In future if you call the police don't waste our time trying to guess where we might find you, but please tell us exactly where you are. You reported a brick through the window?'

Ellie swallowed a disclaimer. She was sure she'd told the policeman on the phone that she was at Mrs Coppola's, and it wasn't her fault if the message hadn't been passed on. But it was childish to play the game of *You did, I didn't*, under the circumstances.

'Come in. I've got the brick still and the curtains are ruined, but I had to get someone to replace the glass. I expect the damage was done by someone who disapproves of my taking Gus in. However, you're one incident behind the times.'

As Ellie let the policewoman into the house, another car drew up and Mrs Coppola got out of the passenger seat, making kiss-kiss noises to the driver. When she saw the policewoman Mrs Coppola screamed, 'Oh, no!' which brought the driver out of his car, too.

'What's happened? My baby, where's my baby?'

Some baby! 'He's all right now,' Ellie said. 'He just threw a wobbly and beat the place up a bit.'

'What's that?' said the driver. No tie, black suit, sharp haircut. The office Romeo?

'What? How? My precious little china figurines...!'

Mrs Coppola clasped her hands together in anguish and closed her eyes, while her friend put his arm about her and said, 'There, now, Luce.'

Ellie told them what had happened. She didn't try to disguise the fact that she'd left Tod with someone else that afternoon.

'You did ... what?' shrieked Mrs Coppola.

'I'm sorry. I had an important appointment and I found a trustworthy person to look after him during that time – whom I paid out of my own purse.'

Mrs Coppola flounced. 'You can afford it.'

Ellie wasn't going to be drawn on that. 'I got back to find the place wrecked and Betty in tears. Tod had run off but I got him back and he's upstairs playing with his new computer again. He won't talk. Betty righted the furniture and put the torn magazines into that plastic bag over there. She left the envelope – the message – whatever it is, on the floor for you to see.'

Mrs Coppola stirred the fragments with the point of her shoe.

'Don't do that,' said the policewoman. 'Evidence.' She got down on her hands and knees and with tweezers carefully put the torn scraps into a plastic bag. 'I'd better take the bag of magazines, too. There may be something that's been overlooked. Some written message, perhaps.'

'The message was the book of stamps,' said Ellie.

Mrs Coppola pounced on it. 'That's mine. I've been looking everywhere for it.'

'I think it came in the envelope,' said Ellie. 'Look how it's twisted and torn. Tod did that.'

'Nonsense, it's mine,' said Mrs Coppola, putting it in her handbag.

Ellie said, 'Are you sure? I thought it was a message, especially since he's dumped his collection of stamps.'

'I put them in the bin this morning,' said Mrs Coppola, defiantly. 'The dustmen will have collected them by now.' She picked up a tiny fragment of china which Betty had overlooked and broke into noisy tears. 'My little shepherdess? I got her on holiday in the Lakes.' She turned on Ellie. 'This is all your fault! If you'd looked after him properly, none of this would have happened.'

'I don't think I could have stopped it...'

The man puffed out his chest. 'You should sue her, Luce.'

A mean look came into Mrs Coppola's eyes. 'Yes, I will. I'll take you for every penny I can. Oh, my lovely collection, my pride and joy!'

The policewoman raised her eyebrows. 'Apparently it was your son who—'

'She was supposed to be looking after him, wasn't she?'

Ellie sighed. Once she might have let all this pass, but she was beginning to learn that if you didn't fight back when you were down and out, you didn't get helped back on to your feet. You got your ribs kicked in, instead.

She said, 'As you will have noticed, your central heating's working again. It was only the pump that needed to be replaced. I'll send you the bill for that when I get it. As for the new computer that was delivered to Tod today, please regard that as a gift from me to him. I don't want anything for that, nor for his new clothes, nor payment for the time that Betty kindly gave to look after him, nor for feeding him this last couple of days. And now, I must be going.'

'Good riddance!' cried Mrs Coppola and threw the fragment of china at Ellie's retreating back.

Ellie thought, There's no point my throwing it back. I shall rise above it. I've had more than enough excitement for one day. As she turned to leave the room, the policewoman followed her. 'Betty's address...?'

Ellie gave it. And then, 'I think I'm right about the stamps, you know. I've got the name of a man who might know people in this area who collect stamps.'

The detective sergeant dismissed the information with a wave of her hand. 'We're following a different line of enquiry now and hope to have some news soon. I'm sorry about the brick ... the patrol car kept an eye out afterwards, but didn't see anyone.' She hesitated. 'You and Mrs Coppola...?'

'Don't get on. I think she resents it that Tod

spends so much time at my house. Or rather, used to spend so much time at my house. He's changed.'

Mrs Coppola came out to the hall and yelled up the stairs, 'Tod, the police are here. You're wanted.' She touched the radiator. 'Far too hot. Burning gas. What my bill will be like...!'

Ellie closed her eyes for a minute. No, she was too tired to fight any more.

She went out into the drizzling rain. Would the sun never give them a chance this spring? She remembered the brick through her window and her nerve almost failed her. Suppose the brick had been thrown at her? A full head of hair would be no protection. Suppose someone had thrown another brick, perhaps through her bedroom window, while she was out? She slept in the bedroom overlooking the road, and a brick thrown through that window might well land on her in bed and...

Roy was sitting in his car outside her house. He got out when he saw her coming. She felt intense relief, even joy, at seeing him. Now she needn't go into her house alone.

'Ellie, my dear. Sorry, I was locked into a meeting when you rang. Are you all right? Have you any plans for the evening? I've got some good news to share with you.'

'Lovely to see you, Roy.' She allowed him to kiss her cheek and put his arm around her for a moment, although she was thinking all the while that if the neighbours saw, they wouldn't half talk. 'Yes, it's been a busy day. Come on in for a moment.'

Then she remembered her lodger and called out, 'Hello? I'm home. Gus? Are you there?' He was lurking in the kitchen, looking somehow rather grubbier than he had been. He didn't reply to her greeting but slunk out of the door into the conservatory when she came in. Yes, he did slink. Furtive, very.

She thought of going after him, reassuring him that she wasn't going to turn him out in spite of the brick. She tried to put herself into his shoes. He must feel hunted. Afraid. She didn't know how to deal with the situation. She thought, I'd better do some praying about it, get some guidance, but not now. Now I've got to talk to Roy.

She made tea for herself and Roy and took it into the living room, leaving a mug on the table for Gus. If Gus wanted to be antisocial, then so be it.

The answerphone was blinking. There was a pile of letters on the chair in the hall – mostly bills by the look of them. She pushed the living-room curtains to with the broom handle, to shut out the light. Everything else could wait. Sinking down into her chair, she put her feet up. That was a mistake, because her eyelids decided to close on her.

Roy hadn't noticed anything wrong with the curtains. He was doing his Man of the House act, standing in front of the fireplace. 'I've just heard that the plans have been passed for the redevelopment of that derelict house on the Green. Isn't that splendid? I met the builders today – they're the people my mother recommends and certainly gave the most sensible quote of the three who tendered for the job. I've accepted it and they'll start as soon as the site's been cleared.'

Ellie congratulated him. 'In a way though, I'll be sorry to see that old house go. It's been part of the scenery for ever. I know it's past redemption...'

'Yes, it's hopeless, disintegrating more every day. You can't even walk up the stairs now and the ceilings are falling in one by one. What we're going to provide instead will buck the neighbourhood up no end. Town houses with patio gardens, integral garages, landscaped surroundings ... just the thing. They should sell like hot cakes. I've been on to the demolition people. I wanted them to start on Monday next, putting up hoardings round the site, making it secure, but they may not be able to start for a couple of weeks, they're ringing me back on that. They reckon four weeks maybe to clear the site. Then the builders move in and we'll really see something happen.' He rubbed his hands together, enjoying the prospect.

'Good for you,' said Ellie, sliding into a doze. She jerked awake. 'Aunt Drusilla. I must get round to see her.'

'About time. She's been on to me twice today, asked me to stay overnight, which I might have to do, if you won't. I'll give you a lift and then perhaps we can have a bite to eat together.'

'There's Gus to consider.'

'Give him a tenner to send out for a pizza or something. Come on, Ellie, we haven't got all evening.'

The sun was setting, a red ball glimpsed between the bare branches of the lime trees down the street. 'Red sky at night, shepherd's delight,' said Ellie, hoping it was true.

'What? Mind that puddle as you get out of the car.'

Ellie looked up at the great gabled front of the Quicke family house, and suffered the usual feeling of depression. A while back Aunt Drusilla had promised to do some repairs to the house but nothing seemed to have been done as yet. Paint was peeling off the portico. The steps to the porch were greening over with moss. The laurels and hollies that crowded around the semicircular drive had been cut back hard not so long ago and failed to soften the harsh exterior.

Was the house really depressing, or was it all in her mind, a legacy of Aunt Drusilla's critical attitude to her through the years? Was it really a very pleasant late-Victorian house which merely needed a softening touch here and there? It had been built with the intention of housing a large family and servants. One elderly lady plus itinerant cleaners did not give it the same ambience.

There were no lights on inside. Roy switched on all the hall lights and made for the stairs.

Aunt Drusilla's bedroom was chilly and huge. She was sitting up in her great carved walnut bed, huddled into what looked like a black velvet evening coat, with only a glow worm of a small bedside light on. The bedside table held a Teasmade, a mobile phone, a digital radio, an alarm clock and an interesting array of pills and potions.

Ancient and Modern, thought Ellie, dutifully kissing her aunt's cheek and enquiring how she felt today.

'My blood pressure's way up and I'm likely to dehydrate unless someone sees fit to bring me something to drink,' snapped Aunt Drusilla. 'The cleaner forgot to fill up the Teasmade – again – and the water from the bathroom tap tastes foul. You've taken your time. Thought I'd pop off and save you the trouble of a visit, did you?'

Once Ellie would have winced and denied it, but she'd learned the hard way that giving in to bullies doesn't pay. So she just laughed. 'Roy, your mother requires tea, Earl Grey, in the silver teapot with a good china cup and saucer, no milk, no sugar. Extra hot water in the silver jug. And a slice of lemon. Can you manage that?'

Aunt Drusilla's face split into a nutcracker grin. 'I've heard this new generation of women make the men do all the work. Well, Ellie? What have you been doing with yourself? Gadding about, spending money? How's the boy?'

Ellie drew up a chair, took the old lady's hand in hers and began the sorry tale. Ellie wasn't quite sure how it had come about, but over the past few months Aunt Drusilla had almost become a friend. Certainly, with her razor-sharp mind, it was never a waste of time for Ellie to try out theories on her.

'Now this Armand,' said Aunt Drusilla. 'You're absolutely sure he didn't have anything to do with it?'

'Yes, I am. For one thing, he didn't get back from school till about five and took me out straight away to B&Q to look at tiles. We got back about six fifteen. Tod left the swimming baths about five and if he'd come straight home as he usually did, then he'd have got back while we were out. We've got to allow time for him to have been abducted and abused, and I don't reckon that could be done in under an hour – do you? More likely two. Or more. By which time Kate would have got home.'

'The lad could have dallied on the way back ... gone home with a friend ... spent some time in the Avenue ... bought himself some sweets. Then when he reached the alley, this Armand could have pounced on him...'

Ellie shook her head. 'You think Armand would have been prowling about his back garden, waiting for Tod to come back home, on the off-chance? That man doesn't go into the garden at all. As far as he's concerned, gardens are for looking at out of windows. He'd be perfectly happy with a concrete wilderness, provided it looked as if it were modern. Their garden at the moment is a muddy slope, awaiting the attentions of a bulldozer and landscape gardener. I assure you, nothing less than a full-scale emergency would get Armand stepping out of his back door.

'And why would he want a boy like Tod? He could lay his hands on half a dozen boys at school, if he had that sort of urge – which he hasn't, believe me. He's very very heterosexual. And then, even if he were that way inclined, he wouldn't go out looking for a boy at half past six in the evening, with Kate due home any minute. And supposing he did, where would he have hidden Tod until he could abuse him? In the airing cupboard till Kate had gone to bed? And then had his wicked way with him? In what room of that small house could he possibly have held the boy? There was a lot of blood, remember. The boy had been whipped...'

Her voice failed her, remembering Tod's injuries. She cleared her throat. 'I did wonder if the boy had been abused in my garden shed where we found him, but it won't do. There was no blood spattered there, so it's not the crime scene.'

Aunt Drusilla nodded. 'You've convinced me. It's not Armand. But you say that Armand's given you the name of a man who might help you?'

'Someone called Pearsall. I'll go to see him tomorrow.'

Roy came clattering in carrying an old wooden tray which had seen better days. On it rested a stained tray cloth, the silver teapot, a cracked mug and a milk bottle. No hot water, no lemon. The two women regarded this in silence.

'Thank you, Roy,' said his mother, eventually. 'Now please go and see what that inefficient cleaning woman has left me for supper, will you?'

Roy grinned. 'I know when I'm not wanted. Has Ellie told you yet about the church wanting all her money?'

Aunt Drusilla sipped at her mug of tea, watching her niece with hooded eyes.

Ellie lifted her hands and let them fall with a sigh. 'They say Frank promised them a million pounds to rebuild the church hall. They'll name it the Frank Quicke Memorial Hall.'

Aunt Drusilla looked bland. She was probably working out bank charges on the proposed gift, taking into account interest rates and charity status.

'No comment?' asked Ellie.

'None. I trust your judgement.'

'I don't,' said Ellie ruefully. 'One minute I think I should do it, and the next I think not. I'm taking a straw poll. Everyone at the church will want me to do it because it saves them the trouble of raising the money in the usual way. There's also – this is embarrassing, but I don't think I'm imagining it – there's a sort of groundswell of envy there. You know?

They think, why should I have been so fortunate to come into so much money when others are scratching around on a limited pension? I think they'd be not unhappy if I lost my money and was reduced to their level again.'

'That's human nature for you.'

'Yes. I asked my neighbour Kate for her opinion. She didn't actually put it in so many words, but I could tell she thinks they've got a nerve asking for so much money. Diana expressed shock horror. She's going to be against it, for selfish reasons ... which perhaps I ought to discount. Roy was sweet. He thinks I'll do it and leave myself penniless. He'd have offered me his hand and his heart again, if Kate hadn't been there to cramp his style.'

'He's not a bad lad.'

'No, not once he'd abandoned his original plan to live off his rich long-lost mother and cousin.'

'You wouldn't consider...?'

'Marrying him?' Ellie shook her head. 'Too like my dear Frank. As far as he's concerned, a woman's place is in the kitchen first, and then in bed. Oh, and she'd better not have any ideas of her own. It's no wonder his marriage to a younger woman broke down. He'd make a good husband and father if we could, perhaps, find him a sensible divorcee who's got a couple of children from a first marriage and doesn't hope for too much in a second.'

'You astonish me, Ellie. Though you're

probably right.' Miss Quicke laid down the mug. 'I asked him to stay here overnight but I'm rapidly reconsidering my invitation. This tea is disgusting.'

Ellie peered into the teapot. 'He's put three teabags in. Shall I make you some fresh?'

'In a minute. Do you want my opinion about the money or not?'

'I think I know what you'll say. No matter what verbal promises he may or may not have made, when he made his will Frank decided what he thought he should give the church, and that's that. On the other hand, you're also going to point out that this might be a good opportunity to start a rumour that I'm not as well off as I was.'

'It saves a lot of trouble. When people think you have money to burn, they reach for the matches. Did Roy tell you I want you to move in with me?'

Ellie opened her mouth to say that yes, she'd do it. But found she couldn't. She simply could not give away her liberty like that. So she fudged the issue.

'I'm flattered and I'm thinking it over. Surely what you need is a housekeeper.'

'If you're planning to throw away all your money and pass your house over to Diana, you'll need a job.'

'Not if you pay me a proper rent for this house.'

'The very idea!' Miss Quicke dwindled into a little old lady. How on earth did she manage to shrink herself like that? On demand.

Once Ellie would have hastened to reassure Miss Quicke. Now, very much amused, Ellie said, 'Remember the story of Little Red Riding Hood? You remind me of the wolf in bed in granny's nightclothes.'

Aunt Drusilla cackled with laughter and returned to her normal size. 'Listen, my girl, I'm not leaving this house to go into any retirement home, is that clear? They'll carry me out in a box and not before. No nonsense about cremation, either. Into the family vault, if you please. No flowers, by request.'

'Have you made a note of what hymns you want sung at your funeral?'

'Of course. The instructions are in the top drawer of my bureau. You and Roy are joint executors. He gets a third of everything, you get two-thirds. Nothing to the cleaning woman. I had to sack her today. She wanted to move in and act as my official carer. You'll have to get me someone else.'

'Roy could move in permanently.'

'Yes, and pigs might fly. Ham-fisted. Can read a plan for a building, but can't find a china cup to save his life. I'm putting a considerable sum of money into this development of his. Should be foolproof, and he's no fool.'

'I suppose there's always Diana. If she moved in...'

'She'd want to get me sectioned so she could take over the house herself. She thinks that just because she's family, I'll leave her well provided for. She's trying to be pleasant to me at the moment, agreeing with everything I say. Stupid girl. As if I can't see through that. It's about time she grew up and stood on her own two feet, instead of relying on handouts from other people.'

'She might change, start pulling her weight, now she thinks I'm giving all my money away.'

'You aren't going to do it, then?'

'I don't know what I'm going to do. My brain's made of tissue paper at the moment and I can't think straight. I'll get on to the employment agencies in the morning, see if I can find you a good housekeeper and another cleaner.'

'I'm perfectly capable of doing that for myself.'

Ellie applauded her. 'Of course you are. You do it, then. But I still don't like your living all alone in the house at the moment. Not till you feel strong enough to skim up and down those stairs and do your own cooking again. Can't you put up with Roy for more than one night?'

'Certainly not. This is an emergency measure, for one night only. What about you? No, I suppose you're still buzzing around after that boy Tod. What about that other lame duck of yours – Gustavus or some such ridiculous name.'

'Yes, to both, but I rather think Tod's beyond my help. A professional would—'

'Give him the love and support he needs? What about his mother?'

'His mother's got a lover, unless I'm mistaken. The police think I'm barking mad suggesting the stamps are at the bottom of it. They've got another lead. I don't know what.'

Aunt Drusilla patted Ellie's hand. 'Go home and get some sleep. You look as if you need it.'

Roy appeared, carrying a tea towel. 'Finished with the tea things? I've found a frozen shepherd's pie on the table, but it's almost completely defrosted already. Will it be safe to eat, do you think? Shall I shove it in the oven?'

Aunt Drusilla shuddered and Ellie shook her head. 'I'll see to it, shall I? Unless – Aunt Drusilla, would you like to put some clothes on and come out for a light supper with us?'

'Am I made of money? You only say that because you think I'll foot the bill.'

Both Ellie and Roy laughed.

'We know you better than that.'

'Get away with you both. Roy, please see to drawing the curtains and putting some security lights on. Ellie, see what else there is in the freezer – it should be stocked with frozen meals – and make me another cup of tea. Then you can both go out and enjoy yourselves.'

Twelve

Roy never asked Ellie where she'd like to eat, but assumed she'd be happy and grateful to go along with his wishes. This usually annoyed her but tonight she couldn't have cared less where they went so long as the seats were comfortable and the food tasty and hot. She knew that after that cream-laden lunch she ought to be content with a salad – Diana's remark about Ellie needing to lose a stone had rankled – but it had been a long and tiring day and yes, the Carvery was just right.

Roy happily talked away about his new project, which was all right by her as it meant she could just nod and smile every now and then. And eat. And try not to fall asleep at the table. Until he asked her a question which she had to get him to repeat.

He said, 'I can see you're tired, but this is important. I've been worrying about you being short of money. My mother and I have formed a company to redevelop the site on the Green and we're the sole directors. How about us employing you as a secretary, just to do the odd letter now and then, not a full-time job or anything?

'I know you've been taking a computer-training course, and you used to work as a secretary years ago, didn't you? Not that we'd ask you to do much – just the occasional letter now and then, perhaps? It would mean we could put you on the payroll. I'm sure I can swing it with my mother, and maybe I can even get her to agree that you be a director as well. I couldn't offer much at first, but if all goes well and the units are sold quickly – well, it could give you some sort of income.'

Ellie found her handkerchief and blew her nose. Obviously Roy had no idea that Ellie owned the house Aunt Drusilla lived in. He really was rather a dear. Not much of a financier but then, he could leave all that to Aunt Drusilla, who was. Ellie said she was most touched and that she'd think about his proposition seriously.

It was, of course, quite dark by the time he took her back home. There were no lights on in the house, so maybe Gus was in and maybe he wasn't. The road was lit well enough to show that all the windows on this side of the house were intact. But suppose someone had thrown another brick through a window at the back?

Suddenly she was afraid. 'Roy, I know I'm being silly but do you think you could come in with me, look under the beds to see if there are any burglars or anything…?'

'Reds under the beds?' A hearty laugh. Of course he didn't mind. Big men like Roy like to show off in front of weak little women like Ellie.

He took her key and opened the front door to let her in. She stayed in the porch. Pointed. Roy hadn't seen it.

'…s perve out …t !' Someone had spray-painted the message across the front door.

'What the…!' He touched the paint with his finger. 'Dry. It must have been done after we left.'

She switched on the lights in the hall.

'Gus? Gus, are you there? Are you all right?'

No answer. A sort of listening silence. Only, it was the house that was listening and not a scrawny little wino.

Roy picked up the phone – the answer-phone light was still winking. 'I'll ring the police.'

Ellie felt a bit swimmy. Told herself she was not going to faint. She went into the living room and turned on the lights. Checked.

Frank's silver christening cup was gone and the little silver vase that she used for single blooms. And the video, though not the television. Diana's mobile phone was missing, but the china in the glass cabinet was still there.

Nothing had been touched in the study.

While Roy was getting through to the police station, she went up the stairs and switched on more lights.

Gus had gone, of course. His bed was unmade. All his clothes and belongings had disappeared, along with – she checked the top of the wardrobe – Frank's best suitcase, the one with the wheels and the handle which pulled out. It had always been too heavy for her to use. The room still stank of cigarettes.

With the calm of foreknowledge, she went into her own bedroom. The pretty mosaic-covered box which contained her bits and pieces of jewellery had gone.

She'd gambled that he'd stay honest if she treated him well and she'd lost. Everyone would say what a fool she'd been. But what else could she have done?

She called downstairs to Roy. 'Tell the police he's taken the video, a large suitcase, Diana's mobile phone, my silver cup and vase, and some of my jewellery.'

'What? What!' Roy dropped the phone on to its hook. 'You mean, you've been burgled?'

'No, not burgled. I invited him in, remember. Theft, I suppose they'll call it. Personally, I'd say the poor little rabbit was frightened out of his wits by the brick and the message on the door, took what he could lay his hands on to exchange for cash, and ran.'

Roy swelled with anger. 'When I catch him, I'll...' He turned back to the phone and relayed the message. Ellie went into the kitchen and looked around. Everything was as she'd left it. Dirty cups and mugs in the sink. No sign of Gus having had supper there. He must have taken the money Roy had given him for supper, lifted the items he could sell with ease, and gone. Thank God she'd had the sense to take her parents' clock in for repair.

'You really can't blame him,' said Ellie. She put the kettle on for a cup of tea.

Roy came off the phone, fuming. 'They'll be round when they can, they say.'

'Could be a lot worse,' said Ellie. 'I've been keeping my pearls and my mother's diamond ring in my handbag ever since he came, and wearing my good rings and watch. The rest of my jewellery was pretty, but mostly costume quality. The video is easily replaced. I never really liked Frank's christening mug, anyway. An ugly shape. I'm sorry about the vase, though. It was pretty. And Diana will be furious about her mobile.'

Roy gaped. 'You mean, you guessed this might happen? You took precautions?'

'Of course.' She poured out some tea, offered him some. He didn't seem to want it but she did. 'I hoped it wouldn't happen but I realized it might. I never let him have a key. If I bolt all the doors tonight, no one can get in. The news will be all round the neighbourhood in the morning and they'll be calling in to commiserate with me while thinking it serves me right.'

'I don't understand you, Ellie. I really don't.'

She sighed. She knew he didn't and she couldn't possibly explain. Far too tired. She wished she could just go to bed and forget about everything. If someone did throw a brick through her bedroom window tonight, the curtains would catch most of the damage and she didn't care, anyway. She needed to lie down and sleep.

The police arrived. Not the detective sergeant, but two large men. Strangers.

It took another hour to get rid of them, and Roy. Then she went around the house, checking locks and bolts.

She was actually – somewhat to her surprise – pleased that Gus had gone, though it stung to think he'd taken so many of her precious things with him. Sentimental value, those bits and pieces of jewellery. Presents for anniversaries. Birthdays. Some bits of Victoriana. Some art nouveau. Some holiday bits and pieces bought abroad.

She wished now that she'd locked the whole lot away somewhere safe. But no, she'd had to leave out just enough for him to imagine they were all she had. If he'd known about the pearls and the diamond ring, he'd have torn the place apart looking for them and done who knew what amount of damage. As it was, he'd been a neat thief. She mourned for her mother's lapis lazuli beads, which were the wrong length for today's fashions, but a beautiful blue.

Midge leaped on to her bed, gave himself a lick and a promise, and fell asleep. So did she.

The morning was all things bright and beautiful. She'd woken once or twice in the night but heard nothing to alarm her. No brick through the window.

At seven Ellie wandered downstairs in her dressing gown accompanied by Midge, fed him, made herself a cuppa in her favourite china mug with the forget-me-nots on it and went to stand in the unfinished conservatory. With glass panes all around her and above her, she could imagine she was really standing in the garden itself.

When it was finished, this would be her favourite room in the house. She would have a table and chair just there ... with a lamp on a bracket on the wall behind her just there ... and the water feature would provide a gentle burbling sound. Soothing.

She would eat her meals here.

Midge leaped on to the packs of floor tiles which had still to be fitted, and began a thorough wash. Hind leg up, investigate rear end. Hind leg stretched out in front, investigate between the paws. Scratch behind ear. Wash mask. Wash under chin. A ray of sun touched his back and he stretched his neck in ecstasy. Then got down to the serious business of finding the best place for a nap.

Midge liked the conservatory, too.

Midge had quite liked Gus, which had misled Ellie into thinking him trustworthy. She thought, But Gus was trustworthy, at first. Perhaps he would have gone on being trustworthy if the neighbourhood yobs hadn't frightened him away.

Oh well. She had to face it; she'd made a right mess of things.

She looked down the garden, sparkling with overnight rain but greening over fast in the morning sun. The forsythia was a stunning, burning yellow, and the deeper yellow balls of the kerria were just beginning to show off their true colour. There were gleams of yellow, too, under the leafless lilac where celandines had spread themselves. One or two of the wallflowers were showing red. They looked bedraggled after all that rain, but their scent would be delicious if she cut some and brought them inside – though not to put in the missing silver vase. An early rose – it was really far too early for roses, but everything seemed to be early this spring – showed pink, climbing a post at the edge of the lawn.

At the bottom of the garden, the shed door was still hanging open. She hoped last night's rain hadn't spoiled anything inside. She would investigate when she'd got her outdoor shoes on. And refill the bird feeder, which the tits had emptied again.

She looked beyond the garden to the Church Green and the spire of the church rising up to the incredibly blue sky. Cloudless. Almost a dark blue.

She wished that the church were open so that she could go in and talk to God, but there, it was a rare building that could be left unlocked nowadays.

But I am always here, waiting for you to turn to me...

She closed her eyes for a moment. Yes, it was true. He was always there, waiting for her to turn to him. He knew everything that had happened. How she'd tried to do what she thought was right, taking Gus in. He knew how she'd tried to help Tod. He knew how she'd failed. He knew her limits and he wasn't going to scold her for failing.

She let herself rest on his strength. She laid bare to him all her feelings of inadequacy, all the mistakes she'd made, all the misery that had resulted. She offered up to him the times she'd lost her temper with Tod and Mrs Coppola. Her impatience with Gus. Her doubletalk with Diana. Her cowardice about refusing to move in with Aunt Drusilla. Her uncertainties about giving away her money to the church.

She offered them up unreservedly. She felt his great love settle around her shoulders, calming her, bringing her peace of mind. She asked for strength and wisdom to deal with the problems in her life.

No particular new ideas dropped into her head, but she felt as if she could now cope with the day.

Someone knocked on the front door and rang the bell. Half past seven. What a time to call!

It was Armand from next door with Kate behind him, both looking perturbed.

Kate said, 'I've got to fly, but ... Ellie, have you seen...?'

Armand was angry, but it had to be admitted he got angry very easily. 'They ought to be strung up...!'

The message on the door looked even uglier in daylight, but Armand was pointing to the low wall that divided her front garden from the road. 'Someone's spray-painted a message out there. Not the same person, I think. It's in a different colour from that on the door. I could murder them!'

'Your garden,' wailed Kate. All the shrubs within the wall had been trampled down and broken. Ellie's pride and joy – a lovely fragile magnolia stellata – had been ruined. The early daffodil bulbs, which had just begun to break into colour, had been smashed by heavy boots.

Ellie let out a long breath, holding on to the peace of mind which she'd so recently been given. She would not let herself be disturbed. Kate, however, was almost in tears. 'Look, we'll go to the garden centre this weekend, shall we? And perhaps your builder can paint over...'

'I haven't got any meetings after school today,' said Armand. 'If you wait around for builders, in my experience you could be waiting for Godot. What say I get a pot of paint at Homebase and make a start on it this evening?'

'Poor Gus must be terrified,' said Kate, almost wringing her hands.

'He's gone,' said Ellie. 'Last night. With some bits and pieces. I'm amazed you didn't see the police here.'

'We were out last night. What do you mean, "he's gone"? Look, I'll have to catch you later. I'm going to be late.' She looked at her watch, shrieked, kissed Ellie and dashed out to her car.

'I might not be able to match the paint exactly,' said Armand.

Ellie had never liked him so well. How absurd to have suspected him of harming Tod, even for a minute. 'You're a dear man. I don't want to take up your time – I know how much marking and preparation you have to do. Give me a ring later on this morning. I'll see if I can get my builder back to attend to it.'

'Bastards!' said Armand, getting into his own car. 'Ought to be...' The rest was lost as he drove off, crashing gears.

Ellie thought, I'm shaken but not stirred. I'll live. This too will pass.

Another car drew up and Mrs Coppola got out, her pretty face set in spiteful lines. The driver was her friend from the night before. He was pointing at the graffiti and laughing. Mrs Coppola looked, too. And also laughed.

She said to Ellie, 'It's no more than you deserve. I came to tell you that you're not to have anything more to do with Tod. Last night a neighbour saw that paedophile taking in a pizza delivery as calm as you please. How you have the nerve to shelter him when you know what he's done to poor Tod...'

'He didn't touch Tod.'

Mrs Coppola laughed again, and rolled her eyes. 'I pity you, I really do...'

'No need. He's gone.'

The woman's eyes narrowed, as she calculated what this might mean. Then she shrugged. 'Whatever. Tod's going back to school today, and my neighbour will see to him after school till I get back. I've told him, he's not to go anywhere near you in future. Is that understood?'

Ellie clenched her hands within the pockets of her gown. She nodded. She was so angry she was afraid she'd say something unforgivable. Interested faces were appearing at other front doors around her. A neighbour on his way to his car stopped to eavesdrop.

Mrs Coppola made as if to get back in the car, but then remembered one last thing. 'Oh yes, and Tod says you're paying for him to go on the Internet. I'm holding you to that.'

She ducked back into the car before Ellie could speak. Her friend drove off, spitting gravel and Ellie slowly went back into the house, closed the front door and set her back to it.

She would not cry. No.

Oh, Tod!

She drew in a deep breath. Lord, have mercy on me ... and on Tod ... and on that – woman. One door opens as another one closes. Sometimes God closes one door before He opens another. That's to make sure that you know which direction you ought to be going in. It can be very painful.

Very.

The doorbell rang and someone shouted, 'Yoohoo!' It was the central-heating engineer, Jimbo, with his mate. She opened the door to them.

'What's been going on here?' asked Jimbo, cheerful as always. 'Offended the local mafia, have we?'

'Something like that.'

'If you've got a pot of paint to spare, I daresay we could fit in a quick dip and splash when we've finished today, OK?'

'Bless you, Jimbo. I'd appreciate it.'

'You've remembered to fill the kettle, have you? I've got to drain the tank in a minute.'

No, she'd forgotten.

Clattering and clanging, he and his mate went through to the conservatory to continue their work, while Ellie filled various receptacles with water and slowly went upstairs to wash, dress and get ready for what the rest of the day might hold.

Jimbo had turned on his radio. Of course. Ellie remembered the peace and calm in the conservatory early that morning and the feeling that she was being upheld in God's love. Only the tattered remnants of that peace remained.

Oh, Tod.

Coming downstairs to the workmen's racket, she realized how much she'd come to relish her privacy. Solitude.

Until Frank died, she'd hardly ever been alone in the house and it had been one of the worst things she'd had to bear in the aftermath of his death. But she'd become accustomed to it in the months since and now she wished, fiercely, to be alone and quiet again.

Fat chance.

Another lot of post had arrived. The blinking of the answerphone beckoned to her. She made herself a bowl of cereal and took it into the study to get up to date. She switched on the computer with a feeling that she could at least control one thing in her life ... if it wasn't in a mood, which sometimes it was. But no, the screen flashed up the usual information and she got down to answering some letters.

Another ring on the doorbell. This time it was Detective Sergeant Willis, looking slightly unkempt as usual. Why didn't the girl get a good haircut? Because it would do a lot for her grooming. She wore no rings, didn't have the look of one who liked shopping for clothes. A pity. She could be stunning, if she took a little trouble. She was accompanied by a youngish man, also in plain clothes.

'It seems you've made yourself unpopular.'

'Indeed. I expect the insurance will pay for the brick through the window, but I don't think they're interested in graffiti. Are you looking for Tod? He's gone to school, I believe.'

'No, I was looking for Gus. This is PC Watts.'

'He's gone. Didn't you know? You'd better come in.' Ellie led the way to the living room.

'Where's he gone?'

'I've no idea. He got the message that the neighbourhood wanted him out. Two of them even came round to tell him to clear off. Tuesday night there was that brick through the window here – you can see how it tore the curtains. I went out last night with a friend to have something to eat and a neighbour says she saw Gus taking delivery of a pizza. When we got back, he'd gone. With some of my bits and pieces and the video recorder.'

'Damn.' DS Willis turned to the PC. 'Will you phone in and let them know?' The man nodded and went out to the hall, closing the door behind him.

The detective sergeant said, 'We should have been told.'

'I don't suppose the police who came last night would know about Tod's case. I suppose you'll say I was stupid to take Gus in. I'm not trained to look after recovering alcoholics. I'm not even a very good landlady. But I was sorry for him. I still am. I'm angry, too, of course, but mainly, I'm sorry for him.'

The policewoman sighed. 'You weren't to know, but late last night his alibi fell to pieces and there's a warrant out for his arrest. I thought I could pick him up here nice and easy, but as he's done a runner we'll have to put out an all-points bulletin for him.'

'His alibi fell through?'

'Yes. You knew there were four of them, all winos, dossing down in that garage? When we brought them in, they swore they'd been together all the time and we couldn't break them, so we had to let them go.

'Then yesterday evening one of them – his name's Mick – was caught shoplifting from an off-licence. He's done it before, many times. He's not very bright. Never learns about the video cameras trained on the shelves. Always thinks he can talk his way out of trouble. So he talked. He thought that if he dumped Gus in it, he might get off the shoplifting. Well, he won't.'

'How did he dump Gus in it?'

The PC came quietly back into the room and sat down.

'He said that late on Tuesday afternoon they ran out of hooch so they sent Gus off to buy some more. Mick says Gus was away for hours. So you see, Gus has no alibi for the time Tod was attacked.'

Ellie blinked. 'I don't believe it. For instance, why would Mick lie and say they were all together in the first place, when they weren't?'

'Because the money they'd been using for their binge had come from a woman's handbag that Mick and one of his mates had pinched that afternoon in the Broadway. They were sober enough at that point to realize they mustn't attract attention by spending too much of the cash at one go. They bought a couple of bottles each and were just dumping the stolen handbag in the bushes by the church when—'

'Gus, who was sleeping off his first binge nearby, woke up and challenged them.'

'We've found the handbag, by the way, just where Mick said it would be. They cut Gus in to keep him quiet, picked up another of their mates and decided to go off together for a quiet drinks session. But now there were four of them, and the four bottles they'd bought didn't last them very long. So they elected Gus to go out and buy some more drink. They chose him because he hadn't bought any earlier, so it wouldn't arouse suspicion if he bought some then. This was early Tuesday evening about the time that Tod was attacked.'

'I still don't believe it,' said Ellie. 'Oh, I believe the bit about the handbag and them cutting Gus in. If I understand these things, once an alcoholic falls off the wagon, he craves more and more drink. Yes, I can see him agreeing to go along with his "friends" and agreeing to get more drink for them but I can't see him abandoning his quest for liquor in order to search out a suitable boy, take him to a safe place, tie him up, abuse him and still get back to his mates before they started out to look for him. It doesn't make sense. An alcoholic wouldn't be diverted so easily, would he?'

'You forget the boys who were taunting Gus on Monday afternoon. If Tod strayed across Gus's path when he was by himself and Gus was tanked up – well, anything could have happened.'

Ellie got to her feet. 'It still doesn't feel right. Where is Gus supposed to have taken Tod? And what did he tie him up with?'

'We think he made use of another of the abandoned garages by the park. They've been searched and in one we found evidence that it's been used as a den by boys going there to smoke. We also found a jacket which we think belongs to Tod.'

His jacket was missing. Ellie knew that. 'Tod wasn't wearing that jacket when he left school on Tuesday. His mother says she asked Tod and he said he wasn't. He left it at school by mistake. Any of the other boys could have taken it. No, I can't believe this of Gus. You should have seen Tod and him together. Tod wasn't frightened of Gus. Gus liked the lad. Said he was sorry for him. Taught him to whistle.'

The sergeant got to her feet, smiling slightly. 'Believe me, we know what we're doing. So, if you hear anything or see Gus, just let us know. We'll see ourselves out.'

Thirteen

Ellie felt stunned. She looked around her restful green living room, the room in which she had passed so much of her married life. Now with the removal of the clock, the silver vase and the christening mug, it seemed to have gone out of focus. It was no longer her refuge in times of trouble. She thought, Perhaps it was bringing Gus in which altered everything? If I could go back in time, would I do it again?

She didn't know the answer to that, so she set about some housework. Making her bed, dusting, putting the stamp magazines out to be returned to Armand. Tidying, washing up, making shopping lists. Making tea for Jimbo and his mate. Cutting some forsythia, hammering the stems, putting them in a glass vase on the mantelpiece. They'd have looked better in the silver vase, but it was no use snivelling about that.

And all the time she felt anger building up inside her. She'd been pushed around, her opinion ignored, been forbidden to contact Tod and...

She just knew the police were wrong about Gus. But how to prove it? Well, there was one thing she could do. She could ask this Mr Parsley, or whatever his name was, for help in locating other people who collected stamps in the area. She pulled the telephone book towards her and looked up Parsley. And then hit her head. Silly me. Not Parsley. Persleigh? No, Pearsall.

There was one living not far away. She made a note of the address.

She didn't often go that way to the shops, because it took slightly longer to walk round by the park. But what did she have to lose? She might as well call on him and ask his advice.

She sat down at Frank's big old desk in the study to pay bills, chuck junk mail in the waste-paper basket, return phone calls. Dear Rose was in, sounding very subdued, not working at the charity shop that day. Ellie recalled with an effort that Rose had had some problem she'd intended to share with Ellie some time ago, before all the trouble with Tod. Perhaps Rose would join her for lunch at the Sunflowers Café, yes? Ellie thought, I must get back to normalcy. Food. Clean clothes. Contact friends. Pick up my life again from the point where everything went haywire. Not think about Gus, or Tod or anything.

She couldn't think what day of the week it was. Looking at the calendar, she saw she'd got an appointment with her nice solicitor friend Bill later that morning – a good thing she'd looked, because she'd forgotten entirely about that. It was supposed to be about arrangements for Stewart's new job with Aunt Drusilla, but Ellie rather thought she'd ask him what he felt about her giving so much of her inheritance away to the church.

She also saw that she'd been due to go to a talk at church the previous evening. This was Thursday, so soon Mrs Dawes would be plodding across the Green to the church hall to take her weekly flower-arranging class. She'd be well wrapped up in her Burberry against the wind with a thick scarf around her head, and carrying an enormous bag which Ellie knew from experience would be filled with the tools of the trade: secateurs, tape, lengths of wire in different thicknesses.

The front door bell rang and there was Mrs Dawes, even larger than life in her Burberry and scarf, carrying her tote bag bulging with equipment.

She gestured at the door and the wrecked plants. 'My dear Ellie, words fail me! Someone told me that you'd had a spot of trouble, but this is...'

'Come in, do.'

'Not if...?'

'He's gone.'

'Well, only for a minute. I'm on my way to my class, you know. The cornus and the viburnum might be saved if you cut them down to the roots, but I'm not so sure about the magnolia. What a thing to happen.'

'I thought you'd say I brought it on myself.'

'I'm told that graffiti can be cleaned off or

painted over, but wrecking plants...'

Ellie hid a smile. 'Yes, it's beneath contempt, isn't it?'

'Perhaps you were foolish to take the man in, but...'

'Perhaps I was.'

'But I'm sure you did it with the best of motives. Truly Christian.'

'Mm.' Ellie thought, Is she working round to talking about my giving money for the church hall? 'I'm afraid I'm out of sherry. Would you care for a coffee?'

'No, no dear. I just popped in to say that they were all talking about it last night at the meeting – a very good speaker, from the hospice, you know, a pity you missed her – but there, you had enough on your plate. We saw the police car here as we were walking back. A burglary, was it?'

'Gus did a runner with some bits and pieces of mine. They've broken his alibi and are looking for him now for Tod's case.'

The older woman's pencilled eyebrows rose and rose. 'So I was right and he did do it.'

'No, I don't think he did,' said Ellie, keeping her voice steady. 'But the police certainly think so.'

'Ah. Well ... everyone will feel better when they catch him. And of course we now have something else to think about, thanks to you. They were unanimous, you know, saying that the hall should be called after your dear Frank. Not a murmur about anything else...'

'Anything else? Such as?'

Mrs Dawes reddened. 'Well, dear, you have perhaps been a little indiscreet now and then since dear Frank died, but your generous gesture makes up for everything, all quite forgotten as it were. Such a relief to know that Gustave has gone. I'm sure I shall sleep better tonight.'

'About the money,' Ellie began. 'Nothing has been decided yet, you know.'

'Oh yes, dear, it has. Quite decided. Everyone's so thrilled, you can't imagine.'

'It's true that a suggestion has been put to me about raising the amount my husband left to the rebuilding fund...'

Mrs Dawes patted her arm. 'No need to be discreet with me, my dear. I *know* how generous your offer was. Naturally, it couldn't be kept from the church council. But I do know you don't like to be thanked. Now, I must go, or my dear class will be wondering what's happened to me.'

Ellie shut the door on her with controlled violence. Dreadful woman!

Jimbo appeared, holding a spanner and looking preoccupied. 'Airlock somewhere...' He wandered upstairs with his spanner.

The house was cold because the central heating had been turned off. Ellie huddled into a jacket, collected umbrella, shopping basket and list, and checked to see how much cash she had in her purse. On the verge of going out, she hesitated. The stamp magazines were still in the hall, waiting to be returned to Armand. She'd drop them in to him later. She'd have to hurry now if she wanted to call on Mr Pearsall before she met Bill.

She called up to Jimbo that she was going out and left by the back door because it was too painful to look at her poor massacred plants. Truth to tell, she felt the same way as Mrs Dawes about them. That magnolia had been just about to bloom ... well, no good thinking about that.

Oh dear, Mr Pearsall lived in yet another looming Victorian red-brick pile with a gravelled front driveway. This time there were holly bushes instead of laurel in the front garden. Ellie didn't think holly an improvement on laurel, although there wasn't much in it. There were turrets on this house and bay windows, neither of which Aunt Drusilla's house possessed. Also the windows on the ground floor were blandly shut off from curious eyes with Venetian blinds, all lowered to shut out the sun. It must be very dark inside. She could hear the faint rumble of a train. The tube line must pass close by. There was an expensive-looking silvery car in the driveway – no garage, obviously.

Sighing, Ellie rang the doorbell. Twice. Eventually a solid looking girl wearing a sweatshirt, jeans and slippers opened the door, still holding a mop in one hand. The tiled floor behind her was wet and slippery. A cleaner?

'Yes, who is it?' came a voice from within.

'Is woman, Mr Pearsall. You want?' Polish origin? Spanish?

Footsteps. A tidy, rather cadaverous man came into sight, holding reading glasses in one hand. Grey all over, trousers, sweater, shirt, hair, eyes. The cleaner turned away to pick up her pail.

'Mr Pearsall? I got your name from the teacher at the High School who took over from you. I wonder – could you spare me a minute?'

'I'm retired, didn't he tell you? I'm afraid I can't help you.'

Ellie flushed. He was almost, but not quite, rude. She realized she must be as irrelevant to him as a door-to-door salesman. What could she say to interest him? The cleaner opened a door on the left and went in to flush away her pail of water. The scent of a strong antiseptic wafted into Ellie's nostrils.

'I know this is a great imposition on a busy man, but...' She had been going to confide in him about Tod, but he didn't look as if an appeal to his softer feelings would work. In fact, he didn't look as if he had any softer feelings at all. She sought for an excuse. 'They're looking for someone to start up a stamp club at another school and they wondered whether you might be able to give me some ideas as to who might—'

'No, I'm afraid not,' he said. He moved to close the front door.

Short of putting her foot in the door, she couldn't stop him closing it in her face. She'd never been any good at doorstepping. The door closed, and she hadn't even got as far as the hall.

What's more, he'd made her feel thoroughly intrusive. What right had she to knock on people's doors and demand their help? None.

She would give up this business for good. She mopped her eyes and blew her nose. Fat lot of use she was. She remembered her fantasy about becoming a private enquiry agent and blushed. How embarrassing!

Even a month ago, Ellie might have given up at that point. But now anger drove her on. She'd been given the run around by Mr Pearsall? Well, he wasn't the only pebble on the beach and there was a public telephone box in the Lane which by some chance was in working order. She dug out the stamp magazines and leafed through them.

There were no stamp fairs held in the immediate vicinity, but they were put on regularly not far away, and the magazine helpfully gave a contact number for the organizer. She even had the right amount of change in her purse to make a phone call. Wonders would never cease.

Telling herself that she was asking for another snub, she located the telephone number and rang the man. He would probably be out. Of course. And even if he were in, he wouldn't be able to help her. Would he?

Amazingly, he was in. She gave him the same excuse that she had given that horrid Mr Pearsall. A local school was thinking of starting up a stamp club – would the organizer be able to give her some names of people who might be able to help with advice?

To her amazement, he gave her some names straight away. She wrote them down, checking the spellings as she did so. How trusting he was! She couldn't believe it had been so easy to get the information. She could have been anyone, ringing out of the blue like that.

She looked at the names, none of which meant anything to her. What on earth was she doing, busybodying around like this? It was ridiculous. She wasn't going to do anything about any of them, was she? She nearly tore the paper up, but instead tucked it into her purse. She was much too busy to go chasing rabbits – or was it hares? – like this.

Bill's office was at the far end of the parade of shops nearby and she was shown in straight away and plied with coffee by his secretary.

'You look a picture, as always,' said Bill, smiling. He was an old friend and meant well but she didn't feel she deserved the compliment.

He had had the paperwork done on Stewart's new job, so that affair was quickly disposed of. 'And now...?' he said, with a rising inflection.

Ellie sighed. 'You've heard about the rebuilding fund?'

He steepled his fingers. 'Gossip, merely. I was waiting to hear from you before I took it seriously. When probate is granted – which won't be long now – the money will be yours. We had talked about investing most of your inheritance in such a way as to give you a settled income. We'd also discussed setting aside the rest of it – about a quarter you thought – which we would set up in a trust fund on which you could draw for charitable purposes. That way there'd be a sort of bulwark for you, so that you wouldn't be pestered for handouts by charities and everyone who knew you'd inherited money.'

'I'm afraid that it's got a bit out of hand,' said Ellie. 'From the moment Frank's insurance cheque came through I had more money to spend than I've ever had before. I did spend some on myself, of course – the new conservatory and all that that needs – but I was able to help all sorts of people, just in small ways, nothing more than a thousand pounds at a time. I enjoyed being able to help them.'

Bill smiled. 'I know you did and I've also heard that you've made a lot of difference to the lives of those you've helped.'

'No one was supposed to know.'

'Word gets around. Don't get me wrong, Ellie. You must do what you like with your own money. I only hope they're grateful.'

'Some are,' said Ellie. 'Though some seem to resent me for helping them out.' She thought of Mrs Coppola, and one or two others who had made it very clear that nowadays they expected her to help them out whenever they got into difficulty.

'But this matter of the church hall is different, isn't it?'

'They say that in a private conversation Frank promised to give them enough to rebuild – about a million pounds...'

'What!'

'Yes. That's roughly what it's going to cost to rebuild. They want me to honour that promise and say they'll name the hall after my husband. There's nothing in writing but if that's what Frank promised them, how can I refuse? Wouldn't that be very selfish of me? They need the money, and I expect I can manage without it. I've even been offered a job – though I think it was invented – which would bring in a little. Then I can make Aunt Drusilla pay me rent for her house. Also, she wants me to go to live with her and if I do, then I could sell off my house to Diana.'

'What!' said Bill again.

Ellie tried to laugh. 'Yes, I know. I can't, can I? I've been kidding myself that I could, but I can't.'

'Do you want my opinion?'

'I may not take your advice,' said Ellie, somewhat wildly. 'To tell you the truth, I can't think straight on this one.'

Bill smiled at her. 'Ellie, dear...'

She sniffed and scrabbled for a hanky. He pushed his box of tissues towards her. She said, 'Does everyone cry when they come to see you?'

He laughed. And waited.

'All right,' she said. 'Tell me.'

'Frank discussed the provisions in his will with me. He was very clear what he wanted and what he didn't want. He knew exactly how much he wanted to leave the church for the rebuilding fund and that was five hundred pounds. His instructions for the will were given to me within weeks of his death. He was clear in his mind right up to the end and if he had wished to alter his will, to increase the amount he left to the church, he could have done, but he didn't. His overriding wish was that you were never to have to scrimp and save ever again. He knew your soft heart might lead you to giving a lot of it away but he thought that if he made me your executor, I'd see that you didn't beggar yourself.'

Ellie stared at the sepia photograph of Old Ealing on the wall behind Bill. Then she looked at her shoes. They needed cleaning, drat it. She moved the rings around on the third finger of her left hand. At least Gus didn't get those.

Bill was waiting for her to comment.

'You're right, of course. Frank did know what he was doing. But it's going to be very difficult to make the church council believe that I'm not the answer to their prayers. They're all so pleased about it. If I don't go along with it, I'll be the most unpopular person in the parish. I might even have to leave that church and go somewhere else. Even move house. Can I cope with the unpopularity? Wouldn't it be the Christian thing to do, to give them the money?'

'Don't ask me to split theological hairs, I'm only your solicitor. All I know is that you have used your money so far to make a difference in lots of people's lives. Giving little treats, setting that grandson of Mrs Dawes' up in business, ensuring that little waitress had enough money for her world tour, helping your family and friends out of difficulties time and again. Ask yourself if you could continue to do good in those ways, if you give away the bulk of your money? Ask yourself if the church people aren't being a trifle selfish themselves, expecting you to do for them what they should be doing for themselves? Stick to our original plan; tell them that they must apply to your trust fund. That should get you off the hook.'

'I could still give them what they want and not bother with a trust fund?'

'Yes, you could. You needn't bother with a trust fund if you don't wish, although as your husband's executor I would strongly advise it. The money is yours, to give away or spend or keep. But if you spend it all on the church hall, there won't be anything to spare for other charitable impulses, will there? What happens the next time you want to rescue someone in distress?'

Ellie pulled a face. Put like that…

'A thought,' said Bill. 'Have you asked your old vicar about it? The one who moved to the other side of London? What's his name? Nice chap, looks like a Lowry stick man, tall and thin, popular round here, great pity we lost him.'

'Gilbert Adams. Yes, I could ask him. I will. Thanks, Bill. For everything.'

He glanced at the clock on his desk. 'Keep in touch...?'

He kissed her cheek and showed her out.

It wasn't raining for once.

Dear Rose was late, so Ellie went into the café and secured a table at the back. The new waitress brought the menu and looked sulky when Ellie said she would order when her friend came. Ellie found the two stamp magazines were still in her shopping basket. She really must remember to pop them through Armand's letterbox on her way back.

She leafed through the first one, marvelling at the enormous number of categories of stamps to collect. At first glance, most of the selling seemed to be done through email orders.

One of these days she supposed she must be brave and get on the Internet and try email. Kate was always urging her to do so. And apparently Aunt Drusilla used it all the time. Amazing woman, Aunt Drusilla.

'Am I late? Sorry.'

Rose had been crying. She slid into the seat beside Ellie and started disentangling herself from her coat.

'Rose? Whatever's the matter?'

'Oh, nothing. Just a bit of a cold. Sorry to keep you waiting, but Madam called me in to the charity shop just after you rang and ... oh dear! You're bound to hear sooner or later. You know dear John, who was always so good at the charity shop, such great friends we three were, weren't we? Well, you know that his wife Sue isn't exactly, I don't know how to put it...'

'Is on medication to keep her stable?' said Ellie, who'd had an unpleasant experience with Sue.

'She tried to commit suicide last night.'

'Oh, no.'

'Nobody's supposed to know, but of course you can't keep a thing like that secret. John found her and took her to hospital and they pumped her out, but of course he couldn't get into the shop this morning, so he rang Madam and told her that she'd have to do without him for maybe a couple of weeks and she went ballistic because we were short-handed, of course, always have been since you left us, dear Ellie. So she rang me to come in, which I did, and that's when she told me she wanted me to do extra, but what with the wedding coming up and all...'

'Of course.'

'...so I suggested she tried to see if she could get you to come back, which she took very badly because as you know, dear, she's always been jealous of you being so popular with the customers. She said ... no, I'm not going to repeat what she said, but I'm afraid I lost my temper and said something rude and the long and the short of it is, that she told me to clear out and not come back.'

'My dear Rose, that's awful. The misery that woman causes.'

Rose sniffed, couldn't find a tissue, so took a paper serviette from the table and blew into it. 'It's quite all right. I've been meaning to leave for ages, ever since you went. That woman is a – a – cockroach!'

The waitress was shoving a menu into Rose's hand. Her attitude seemed to say that if old women chose to make an exhibition of themselves in public, then let them, but don't expect her to show sympathy, because she had her work to do.

Ellie thought, How unlike her predecessor, who had taken an interest in her customers and was always ready with advice about what was best on the menu.

They ordered a steak-and-kidney pie each, with a pot of tea to follow.

'Now dear Rose,' said Ellie, making an effort to disengage herself from her own troubles. 'I know there's been something else upsetting you for quite a while. I'd have had it out of you long ago if I hadn't got so tied up with Tod and his problems – and yes, he's gone back to school today. He is better though not quite himself again yet. So tell me All.'

'It's all so silly, not worth complaining about, really...'

'Rose!'

'Well, then. You'll smile, really. Such a tragedy it seems at the moment, though we'll probably all laugh about it in future...'

'Rose!'

'All right. You know the wedding's fixed for the end of next month. Nothing but the best for my daughter. She'd booked the golf club for the reception, with outside caterers and everything. Now they say they've double-booked and we've got to find somewhere else, but at this short notice ... I've tried everything, the hotel by the tube station, the pubs ... but of course my daughter doesn't want a pub, but it's the best I could do and well, she's not best pleased.'

Ellie refused to let herself smile. Rose was a sweetie, but her daughter Joyce wasn't. Joyce was almost as haughty and difficult as Diana. Ellie could well imagine how Diana would have reacted if her wedding reception arrangements had come unstuck.

Rose tackled her steak pie. 'I've told myself – and her – that it will all be the same in a hundred years time, which was what our dear Gilbert used to tell us, didn't he? Such good sermons he used to give us. Lively, but short. I do miss him still, I must say. Ah well. Joyce can't sulk for ever, I tell myself.'

Ellie didn't share her friend's optimism. Joyce could hold a grudge longer than anyone else she knew. 'I feel for you.'

'Think nothing of it. The pub's all right in its way and beggars can't be choosers. Anyway, how are you getting on with Gus? I've been meaning to say that I think you were very brave there and that you did the right thing, even if it did cause a lot of gossip.'

'He's gone.'

Rose stared at her.

'With some bits and pieces of jewellery and silver. There was some graffiti, some damage done to the garden. He took fright and scarpered. I don't really blame him.'

'Oh, the poor creature!' said Rose. 'I don't blame him, either. If he's heard half the things people have been saying behind his back ... Are your potatoes all right? Mine don't seem to be quite cooked. I don't like to make a fuss, because the food here is usually so good...'

Rose took a gulp of tea, coughed, choked. Used another paper serviette. Looked Ellie in the eye.

'It's none of my business what you do with your money but I want to say, just once and then we'll forget all about it, that I don't like the way they've got all that money out of you for the church hall.'

Fourteen

Ellie pushed her own plate away. The pie was tasteless and the vegetables overcooked except for the potatoes, which were raw. Perhaps it was the cook's day off? Ellie poured tea for them both.

Rose had gone crimson. 'I'm not on the church council. How could I be? Not clever or anything. But I can go to the meetings though I can't vote.'

'So you were there when Timothy suggested I pay for the church hall?'

'It wasn't his idea. It was Archie's. You know? Our church treasurer, who was so keen on you and you kept refusing to go out with him. I don't blame you, mind. I knew his wife, poor dear, and it was no wonder she ran off with someone else, more power to her elbow, I say. I wouldn't like him pawing me about, either.'

'I had heard that Archie suggested it but I don't know why.'

'A woman scorned, dear. Or rather a man scorned. You wouldn't give him the time of day and then you started seeing Roy, who seems perfectly nice to me, but there's no denying there's some talk even though he's your husband's cousin. So a couple of weeks ago Archie started seeing this pretty little blonde thing, only she's neither true blonde nor as young as she'd like to pretend. It turns out he met her chatting on the Internet.'

'In a chatroom?'

'Is that what they call it? Anyway, she's got pound signs in both eyes and a liking for gin. Short-sighted as well, though she wouldn't dream of spoiling her looks by wearing spectacles and her contact lenses keep dropping out ... well, we all have our little problems, don't we? She's got her hooks into Archie so firmly that he takes her everywhere. My guess is that's why he started being bitchy about you. Showing off, I suppose. Trying to make out he ditched you because...'

'It makes him feel better?'

'At the church council, they were worrying away about rebuilding the hall and Archie said Frank had left you over three million pounds...'

'What? But that's not true.'

'That's what he said. He also said that Frank had promised him a very large donation for the rebuild. At least a million. Everyone was most surprised and impressed.'

'Yes, they would be. How dare he!'

'Archie said that as you'd undoubtedly want to honour your husband's promise, we should name the hall after him.'

'Archie is a spiteful little...'

'Yes, but clever with it. Everyone believed him. I did, too, at first. Then I got to thinking and I remembered that one day you'd told me how much Frank was leaving the church in his will. Five hundred, wasn't it? Also, if you'd had three million, I don't suppose you'd still be wearing that old jacket.'

'So that's how it all started.'

The new waitress totalled their bill, ripped it off and slapped it down on the table in front of Ellie. 'If you've quite finished, I'm waiting to clear.'

Ellie paid and added only a small tip.

They stood outside the café, trying to work out whether or not it was going to rain again.

Rose said, 'Sorry I moaned. You've got enough on your plate without that.'

'I'm glad you did. That meal wasn't very good, was it? Would you like to come over for supper? Maybe we can think of somewhere better than a pub for the wedding reception.'

'I'd love to, if it's not too much trouble. I'll bring something from the bakery for a sweet, shall I?'

'Delicious. By the way, Rose; did you ever collect stamps?'

'My father did, but his collection went when our house got bombed in the war. Ah me, how long ago that seems. I used to help separate the little stamp hinges for him. Do you remember stamp hinges? Do they still use them, or have they something very clever instead?'

'Where did he get his stamps?'

'There was a shop here in the Avenue where

the sandwich bar is now. He used to correspond with people all over the world. It was exciting, looking through the post for a foreign stamp. We got a prefab after we were bombed but he was never the same after that. He said he couldn't breathe in those small rooms and he died soon after. My mother liked the prefab, though. Do you remember prefabs? They pulled them all down when they built the flats and we moved into one of them. I liked it at first, so high up in the air, seeing everything, with nice neighbours. I'd still like it if ... ah well, young people will play their music too loudly, in my opinion they're all deaf. About half past five, then?'

'Lovely. Here's some money for a taxi. You mustn't walk if it's raining.'

'I can manage, dear. You know I can.'

'Take it just in case.'

As Ellie did a little shopping in the Lane and walked home she reflected that Bill had had a point. Sometimes being able to give someone even a few pounds could make all the difference to their quality of life. The thought of Rose trying to struggle with an umbrella, her handbag and a box of goodies from the cake shop made Ellie shake her head and sigh, and then laugh. Dear Rose got through more umbrellas than anyone Ellie knew. Either they turned inside out on her or someone would bang into her with their umbrella and hers would be ripped open. Or she'd forget it and arrive drenched to the skin.

Rose's friends always worried about her in bad weather. Giving her the taxi fare was the easiest solution.

And Rose appreciated it.

Ellie turned the corner and halted. Retraced her steps to the corner. The name of this street rang a bell. Wasn't it here that one of the stamp collectors lived? What was his name? Ellie got out her list. Yes, there it was.

Logan, number five. That was two houses along. Mr Logan wouldn't be at home now, would he? Early afternoon, Thursday. But Mr Pearsall had been at home and this man might be retired, too.

She forced herself to walk along. The houses here were largish, probably four-bedroomed, semi-detached but with small gardens. Number five had children's stickers on the inside of the windows and the curtains upstairs were half drawn. The garden was a bit of a wreck, a double pushchair was half tipped over in the porch, and Ellie fancied there was an air of quiet desperation about the place.

Ellie pressed the doorbell and waited. She used the door knocker, thinking that she'd give it one minute and then leave. A woman in her thirties opened the door, a sleepy toddler in her arms. The woman looked worn out. Behind her was a muddle of coats, jackets, toys and tricycles. Ellie took a step back.

'Yes?' The woman swept hair off her forehead. Her fringe needed cutting.

'Mrs Logan? Is your husband in, by any chance?'

'He'll be back just after seven. Wait a minute; don't I know you from somewhere? Didn't you used to work in the charity shop? That's right, you know my mother, don't you? Sonia? Helps out in the shop now and then?'

A rhythmic banging from the rear of the house was interrupted by howls of outrage and a cry of pain. The woman was distracted, trying to be in two places at once. 'I'm afraid I must ... the twins are ... come in, do.' She was leading the way to the back of the house, to a kitchen-cum-playroom. 'Rory, stop that! Emma, how many times have I told you not to hit him...?'

Ellie whisked herself into the hall. 'Just for a moment, then.'

A howl interrupted them from upstairs. That made three children yelling.

Mrs Logan started for the stairs, then looked around for somewhere to park the toddler, who was beginning to grizzle.

'Let me,' said Ellie, taking the toddler. 'You fetch the baby and I'll take this one through to the back and see what the twins are up to, right?'

Ellie jiggled the toddler, who gazed at her with round eyes. The kitchen and playroom were in chaos with plastic toys all over the floor and two red-faced children attacking one another with plastic spades. 'Stop that!' commanded Ellie and to her amazement, they did. Identical twins, by the look of them, dressed in identical blue outfits. Now there were three children gazing at her with round eyes and open mouths.

'Which is Rory, and which is Emma?' Ellie pulled out a chair, checked it for spilt food and sat with the toddler on her knee. Mrs Logan reappeared with a red-faced baby on her arm, while all three older children continued to gaze at Ellie.

'That's quite a gift you have,' said Mrs Logan, pulling up her sweater and freeing a breast to feed the baby.

'I wish I had it for my grandson,' said Ellie. 'I can't do anything with him at the moment. Teething, you know.'

'Tell me about it. I don't suppose you remember, but my mother introduced us one day at the charity shop. I'm so sorry, I can't remember names. Mrs ... Thick?'

Ellie winced. That was about right. 'Quicke,' she said. 'However do you manage, with four such young children?'

'Five. Mother helps. She'll be collecting the eldest from school soon. Yes, it's tricky. There's nursery and Toddlers' Club in the mornings but the afternoons can be difficult. Roll on September when the twins go up to big school and the baby sleeps through the night.'

'Does your husband help?'

'Yes, but he doesn't get back till late, works in the City, you know. He's marvellous with them, but sometimes he's too tired to do much. Except for Monday nights. That's his night out, when he goes to choir practice at the town hall, they're doing another Messiah, would you believe. My turn comes on Tuesdays, when I go to art classes. That gives us each a few hours off each week. There's a dummy on the table. Shove that in her gob if she yells. She would *not* go down to sleep this afternoon, and she's almost dead with tiredness.'

Ellie shoved. The twins went back to battering their toys. The baby sucked. Mrs Logan relaxed into her chair. She must have been pretty once, and would be so again when she wasn't so tired. Every line in her body showed fatigue, but she was a nice girl and remembered her manners.

'Can I give my husband a message?'

Ellie began rocking the toddler, who relaxed in her arms, eyelids flickering. 'I don't think you need bother. One of the schools was thinking of starting up a stamp club and I was asking around, seeing if I could find someone to run it. Obviously, your husband wouldn't have the time.'

'It's a good idea, though. If he didn't have so much on, I expect he'd have been interested. Collecting stamps used to be his passion in life. Stamps with butterflies on. He used to collect quite seriously but all that's had to go by the board for the time being. I expect he'll pick it up again later.'

The dummy fell out of the toddler's mouth, she half clenched her fists and then relaxed completely. She was asleep. The baby fell off the breast, was burped, and put on the other side. Ellie remembered that little Frank had been just as sweet when he was little, before he began teething. Perhaps he'd be like that again soon.

There was a ring at the door, a key turned in the lock, and a woman called out, 'Yoohoo, we're back!' A stolid five-year-old boy stumped into the kitchen, followed by a matronly figure whom Ellie recognized as Sonia, an occasional helper at the charity shop. Presumably this was Mrs Logan's mother.

'Well, fancy bumping into you again, Ellie. We miss you something awful at the shop nowadays. Did you hear about John and poor Sue trying to harm herself? Some people do have bad luck, don't they? And did you know Madam's gone and given Rose the push? You've heard? Word gets around, doesn't it? Let me take the little one off you. There, my pretty, let's go up to beddy-byes, shall we?'

Relieved of her burden, Ellie brushed down her lap – was it faintly damp? – and said she must be going. The five-year-old was helping himself to a biscuit and the twins were clamouring for some, too. The five-year-old was wearing the uniform of the Catholic school a couple of streets away. Catholic equals big families equals no opportunity for Mr Logan to have come across Tod, even if he'd had the energy to do anything about it. And if he'd been looking after five children on Tuesday evening he wouldn't have had time for an encounter with Tod.

Scratch his name off the list.

Pearsall, Logan and what was the other name? Cunningham. Two down, one to go.

The trees were coming into leaf, some more quickly than others. Soon the grass would need cutting.

Ellie took the shortcut across the alley and opened the gate to her back garden. Midge appeared from nowhere and wound around her ankles. The shed door was still open so she looked in. Empty, of course. It made her shiver to think of Tod hiding there. She closed the door but it sprang open again. No padlock. Wonder where that went?

The house was unaccountably silent. No workmen.

She unlocked the conservatory door and went in.

Warmth. She touched the radiator, which was on. Good for Jimbo. He'd left a note on the kitchen table saying that the builder had called to see if she was ready for the tiler, and Jimbo had said she was. He'd done his best to clean up the front door for her, he hoped that was all right. It was very much all right. The front door looked as good as new, almost.

She fed Midge, whose stomach appeared to be elastic; whenever she appeared, whether it was nine in the morning, three in the afternoon or six at night, that was feeding time for Midge. She put away her shopping and went upstairs to turn out the back bedroom where Gus had slept. She couldn't put it off for ever.

The room stank of cigarettes. The duvet and pillows might have to be dry-cleaned. She opened the windows wide even though there was a wind getting up. She'd forgotten to get new bags for the hoover, but used the carpet sweeper instead. Stripping the bed, she heard something drop to the floor. A small mobile phone. It was Diana's, she was pretty sure of it.

She tried to turn it on, to see if she recognized any of the numbers in the memory bank but she'd always been hopeless at gadgets and couldn't get any sense out of it.

She would have to get Diana to look at it and advise the police it had been found. She wondered how Gus had come to overlook it. She imagined him getting the big suitcase down and opening it on his bed, throwing in all his possessions and the bits and pieces he'd picked up from round the house. He'd be in a hurry, ears stretched to hear Roy and Ellie returning from their supper. In his haste he must have thrown the mobile phone wide and it had got tangled up with the duvet on the unmade bed. He'd closed the suitcase, dragged it downstairs, collected the video machine and legged it. She wondered if he'd packed the pizza as well. Yes, pillows and duvet would need dry-cleaning. Bother.

Now she'd started, she'd finish cleaning out the room, which certainly needed it. Junk-food wrappers, tissues, a dirty black sock with a hole in it ... would Gus try to sue her for the loss of this sock? That made her smile.

By the time she'd finished and the room was clean and wholesome again, it was tea time.

As she closed the window against the gathering wind, she looked down the garden path. In the dusk she saw a lad cross the Green, walk through the gate into the alley and hesitate. Tod. By himself. Normally he'd look up at her window and if there were a light on in the house, he'd come on up the garden path, let himself in through the back door and expect to have tea waiting for him.

This time he didn't look up. That hurt. He turned and went along the alley to the gate leading into his own garden. He walked slowly, heavily. There would be no one at home to look after him, but at least his house would be warm again.

Ellie squeezed her eyes shut. Lord, help me ... I can't bear it. Be with him, Lord. Help him through this difficult time, and don't mind me if I have a moan now and again. She went downstairs to draw the curtains in the sitting room. The ones at the window overlooking the road looked dreadful. She really must get round to replacing them.

It was getting dark now, which veiled the ghastly wreck of her garden, but someone was out there, working on her front wall. She opened the front door and peered out. Armand waved his paintbrush at her. 'Nearly finished one coat. It's grey undercoat, and all you have to do is give it a quick once over with white or cream later, OK?'

'Bless you. A cuppa? Tea or coffee?'
'Five minutes. Coffee. Kate'll be late tonight. Another meeting.'
A good neighbour.
The answerphone was blinking again. Ellie pressed replay.
Aunt Drusilla. 'Where are you, girl? Diana's left a message on the answerphone saying she's coming round to see me at six o'clock, bringing some woman she wants to set up as my carer. I'd like you to be there.' End of message.
Oh no, whatever next? I ought to have taken Diana's plans more seriously. If she really has got someone of her own choosing to move in with Aunt Drusilla, then Aunt Drusilla needs armour-plated protection.
The phone messages kept coming. Next was Liz Adams. 'Are you all right, Ellie? Been thinking and praying so much for you and Tod. And Gilbert has, too. He sends his love. I've got it in my mind that we're coming over to you for lunch soon. Have we got a date fixed? Let me know.' End of message.
Heavy breathing, a man's voice. 'It's the tiler here, Ms Quicke. Start tomorrow at eight, OK?' End of message.
Diana. 'Mother, are you there? Stewart will be home tomorrow and I beg you not to do anything rash until we've had a family conference. Oh yes, and I've found someone suitable to look after Aunt Drusilla, which will be a great relief all round. If she won't leave that big house, we need to know she's being cared

for properly.' End of messages.

Ellie scooped up the post, found the claim form from the insurance people and reflected that she now needed a second one to cover the damage done to the garden. She could have sent them a request by email – if she'd been on email, which she wasn't. She really must get herself up to date and on to the Internet, though not for looking into chat-rooms.

She rang Aunt Drusilla to say that she'd be round as soon as she could. Rose was coming to supper. What would they have to eat? And Armand was due to arrive any minute now.

In the past, Kate had been Ellie's great friend and she'd been a trifle wary of Armand, but that situation was now changing.

She pushed coffee and the biscuit tin over the kitchen table to him, thinking that it should have been Tod sitting opposite her after a hard day at school. She wondered how he'd got on...

Armand stirred sugar into his coffee. 'Thanks, Ellie. Appreciated. I'm tied up all day at school tomorrow and in the evening or I'd do the top coat for you. The undercoat hides the graffiti, but doesn't look wonderful.'

'I've got the tiler coming round. Perhaps I can get him to do it.' She pushed the stamp magazines back towards him. 'Thanks for letting me have a look at these. I went round to see Mr Pearsall but he was most unforth-coming, almost rude. No help there, I'm afraid. Then I rang the secretary of the local stamp fair association and got some names from him. Three names, in fact. The first was Pearsall, of course. Logan, and then Cunningham. I went to see the Logans, but he's got five young children, they're Catholic and he babysits on Tuesday evenings. It's not him. I've got one more on the list to see, and if he's no good...' She shrugged. 'But I was thinking, do you know where Mr Pearsall got his stamps from when he ran the stamp club at school?'

Armand turned the pages in idle fashion. 'No idea. One of these smaller businesses that stock stamps costing anything from ten pence to twenty pounds? Or he might have been one of those small dealers working from home. They get their stock at trade fairs.'

'I saw there are lots of trade fairs all over the place.'

Armand took a biscuit, dunked it and sucked, while studying the pages. Then he sat back with a frown. 'I go occasionally to one up at Harrow. Is that the one where you rang the secretary? It was? There's something at the back of my mind about Pearsall. I might be able to dig up some gossip if I ask around. Mind if I use your phone?'

He went into the hall and tapped in a number he got from his filofax. Ellie looked at the clock. A quarter to five. She began to peel potatoes and scrape carrots for supper. Rose should be here soon.

Armand seemed to be on good terms with

whoever it was he was calling. Another teacher at his school? Armand said he'd heard from an old pupil, from before his time, who wanted to contact the previous teacher in that job ... no? Ah? Oh. Yes, perhaps that did explain it and ... really, like that, was it? Well, well. He'd have to pass the message on ... yes, see you tomorrow, then.

Armand rang off. 'Pearsall left to nurse his wife, who'd become seriously ill with cancer. She died but he was coming up to retirement age, so he didn't come back to teaching. He was left quite well off, apparently. There's no suggestion that he was ever involved in anything untoward.'

'Only one more name to go. I'm beginning to think I was completely wrong about this.'

'Maybe, maybe not. Give us a hold of that top magazine. I've got an idea.'

He went back to the phone with it. Ellie sautéed some onions, threw in some chicken drumsticks, a tin of chopped tomatoes, some herbs, half a chicken stock cube, and topped off with hot water. There, that could go in the oven on medium till they were ready to eat. Armand seemed to be a long time on the phone. She went through into the sitting room, checking for dirty mugs and glasses. Still Armand was on the phone, making notes on her pad.

She tidied the sitting room. The forsythia on the mantelpiece was perky enough. Good. Sometimes it flopped though she never knew why. When Armand got off the phone she must ring the police about the mobile phone she'd found. It probably was Diana's. She'd ask her tonight. To remind herself, she popped it into her handbag.

Armand was still on the phone. He turned the pad over and was making more notes. Half past five. Rose was usually punctual. What was keeping her? Well, it could be anything from a button lost off her coat to ... real trouble. Ellie wished Armand would get off the phone so she could contact Rose. Or maybe Rose was trying to contact her?

Armand finally got off the phone. He looked pleased with himself.

'There, now. I phoned someone I used to know quite well in the old days, doesn't live locally now but I still meet him sometimes at the stamp fairs. He mentioned Pearsall too, but obviously we don't need to concern ourselves with him. Way above suspicion. However, my friend mentioned another couple of names and I've jotted them down for you.'

'Bless you, dear Armand.' Somewhat to her own surprise, she found herself reaching up to kiss him. Armand blinked, too. He hadn't expected it, either.

The phone rang and they both jumped.

'I'll be off then,' said Armand, looking at his watch and letting himself out.

It was Rose. 'Ellie, dear, I've been trying and trying to get hold of you. Why don't you get that call back thingy or caller waiting or something? The thing is that I'm going to be a little late, I'm afraid. I've had Joyce on the phone in tears, because she and her fiancé have been round to see the pub and apparently the place is one vast barn and most unsuitable, and I really don't know what we're going to do...'

'Hang on, Rose. Look, I'll get a cab and pick you up in ten minutes. And if you don't mind, we'll call round on my aunt on the way back. I've had a phone call from her saying she's in a spot of bother and wants me round there at six. I'll leave the supper on a low light here and if we're a few minutes late, it won't hurt. All right?'

The cab driver was late and the traffic was terrible. Ellie kept glancing at her watch. She didn't like to think of Aunt Drusilla being railroaded into taking on a carer whom she didn't want. There was nothing much wrong with Aunt Drusilla that a little tender loving care for a few days wouldn't put right. Of course, in the long term she could do with a housekeeper or companion or somebody, but she must choose that person for herself. She must retain her independence, or...

Ellie let an idea grow and blossom in her mind. Somewhere to hold a wedding reception. Rose being thrown out of her job at the charity shop. The charity shop hadn't paid Rose anything but it had lent structure to her life. Ellie knew all about needing a structure in your life. She'd floundered around like anything when Frank had died. Rose wouldn't leave her little flat, of course. But if she could just move in with Aunt

Drusilla for a couple of days...?

But no, Aunt Drusilla wouldn't put up with Rose's twittering for a minute, would she?

No, it was a bad idea. Ellie thought she'd been having one bad idea after the other recently. This one would no doubt come to nothing, as the others had.

They picked up Rose, who was unfortunately not looking her best in the oldest of her winter coats. It had started to rain again, so Rose had clapped her pink and white tea-cosy hat on her head. Slightly lopsided. Ellie sighed. No way would Aunt Drusilla take to dear Rose, who had a heart of gold but a taste for the garish in clothes.

No way.

Fifteen

Ellie gave the driver Aunt Drusilla's address, thinking they wouldn't make it for six but would be there soon after.

'Dear Rose, I hope you don't mind our calling on Aunt Drusilla, but she had a nasty fall some days ago and her cleaner has left. She really oughtn't to be on her own in that big house while she's recovering from her accident, so my daughter's arranged to take round someone this evening to see if they'd like to stay there – just temporarily, you know.'

'I do admire Miss Quicke. Such a grande dame. She didn't break any bones when she fell, did she? Old people often do. HRT helps, they say, though personally I've no experience of it ... and oh dear! I've just remembered that I didn't have time to get anything from the bakery for our tea and they'll be shut by now, won't they...?'

Ellie let the gentle flow wash over her, wondering if she were doing the right thing or not.

'What a magnificent house,' breathed Rose, as they drew up in the driveway. Diana's car was already there, as was a stout little Smart

Car with a dented front bumper. Someone had been a little too hasty at traffic lights, perhaps.

Ellie signed the driver's chit. 'We may be a good half hour or so, so I'll order another minicab when we're ready to go on home.'

'They don't build houses like this nowadays,' said Rose, taking in all the gloomy grandeur of the hall. 'Look at that stained-glass window on the stairs. A real parquet floor. And the twisty balusters on the stairs...'

Ellie led the way to the big sitting room at the back of the house, but Rose hung back to run her finger along a mahogany side table.

Aunt Drusilla was fully dressed and sitting in her big chair by the fireplace, with a rug over her knees and her stick close to hand. The harsh centre light was on but not the softer side lamps, and the long velvet curtains hadn't been drawn against the darkness outside.

Ellie bent to kiss the old lady, who took her hand and held on to it. 'I'm very glad to see you, Ellie. I did ask Roy to come too, but he hasn't seen fit to appear yet. Something to do with the golf club, I believe.'

'Aunt Drusilla, this is my dear friend Mrs Rose McNally. You may have met her before at my house? I hope you don't mind my bringing her but she's coming to supper with me later on.'

Rose beamed. 'How are you, Miss Quicke? I hear you've not been too good. What a splendid house,' said Rose, meaning it. 'If I'd known I was coming to visit you, I'd have brought you some flowers. That's all this room needs, a bunch of flowers.'

Aunt Drusilla held on to Ellie's hand, steering her to sit on a low stool beside her. 'Yes,' she said to Rose. 'We always used to have flowers in here when my mother was alive, but I'm afraid I'm not very good at arranging them.'

'It's something I've missed, being so far up in the air in those flats, but I always have my pot plants to remind me. Now a big bowl of tulips just there,' said Rose, indicating a pie-crust Victorian tea table. 'And perhaps a bunch of narcissi on the mantelpiece – shall I draw the curtains? It's getting quite nasty outside...'

'You have good taste,' said Aunt Drusilla, relaxing a trifle. 'I'd offer you a cup of tea, but unfortunately I can't get as far as the kitchen today.'

Rose glowed. 'May I make you a cup? Ellie and I had a truly nasty lunch today, though I really shouldn't say it as it was dear Ellie who paid for it, but nasty it was and I could just do with a good cuppa. How do you like it?'

'Earl Grey, weak with extra hot water. The silver teapot and jug. No milk, no sugar. And a slice of lemon. The kitchen's across the hall and through the door in the middle.'

'I'm off, tra-la!' cried Rose and out she went, shutting the door carefully behind her.

Aunt Drusilla tightened her hold on Ellie's hand. 'Roy stayed here last night but he sleeps so heavily that even when I called to him, he didn't wake up. He said he'd stay till I felt better and that's very good of him, of course, but he's absolutely hopeless around the house. Diana's brought in a woman built like a battleship and with a prison warder's mentality. I tried to say I didn't need a live-in carer and neither of them listened to a word I said. They treated me as if I were a child. Diana said that if I wasn't prepared to have this woman living in and looking after me, I'd have to go into a home. They're upstairs now, assessing the prison warder's new quarters. She's already said I've got to sleep in a small room downstairs, that the kitchen will have to be torn out, and she must have her own quarters, television and video, and of course telephone. Oh yes, and a new car, as she seems to have had an accident with hers.'

Ellie said, 'Who does she think is going to pay her wages?'

'That's simple. Diana says she's going to get a power of attorney so that she can pay all the bills in future.'

'That's ridiculous. You must stand up to her.'

'Easier said than done. If I could tell her you were moving in...'

'Yes, dear. I know you want that and I've thought and thought about it. If you'd asked me just after dear Frank died, I'd probably have done it. But I've been all these months now by myself, learning how to take my own decisions and really rather relishing being on my own. I couldn't move in with you now. But if it helps you to get rid of Diana, then by all means say that I'm considering it.'

The harsh overhead light made Aunt Drusilla look even more sallow and shrunken than usual. Ellie turned on the side lamps and turned off the main light. At once the room looked more welcoming.

'That friend of yours,' said Aunt Drusilla. 'A nice little woman. All alone in the world, is she?'

Ellie laughed. 'She has a daughter rather like Diana. Joyce would like everyone to think they were descended from the nobility. I believe Rose's husband was a butcher and she worked in the primary school here as a cook for years. She's a widow, her daughter has left home and she lives in a council flat.'

'She doesn't work, then?'

'She's been working at the charity shop for a couple of days a week, but she's got to give even that up now. I know what you're thinking, but it won't do, not even for a few days. Rose twitters!'

Aunt Drusilla nodded. 'I think I can cope with that. Let's see what she does with the tea tray.'

The door opened and Rose carried in an old rosewood tea tray, covered with a neat white cloth. On it in splendour were the silver teapot and jug and Aunt Drusilla's Crown Derby tea set, resplendent in red and black and gold. Also three cups and saucers, matching plates, a milk jug, biscuits arranged on a dessert plate and three wafer thin slices of lemon on a saucer.

'Sorry I was so long. Your gas stove is a bit temperamental though I've dealt with worse in my time. I know Ellie doesn't take sugar and I don't, either. I'm afraid I couldn't find the silvercloth, because the teapot could do with a polish, but there ... a strange kitchen is like a desert island, you never know what you'll come across when you start opening drawers...'

Talking the while, she poured out and handed round cups of tea exactly how Aunt Drusilla and Ellie liked them.

The door banged open and a bulky woman thrust her way into the room, followed by Diana.

'What's this, eh?' A falsely genial voice, hands like hams, a footstep to shake the floor-boards and a pair of nasty twinkling eyes without any humour in them. 'We can't have our patient upset with all these visitors, can we? Beddy-byes for sleepy heads.'

Rose looked at her in amazement. 'I'm so sorry, I didn't know there were other visitors. I'm afraid I didn't put out a cup and saucer for you, but I can easily fetch—'

'Tea's very bad for my patient,' pronounced the wardress from hell. 'As is coffee, chocolate and cream. Also cheese. We can't have our little tummies being upset like this, can we?'

Aunt Drusilla said, 'Would you kindly leave...?'

'Now, now,' said the wardress, in ferociously playful tones. 'Who's in charge here, may I ask?'

'Actually,' said Ellie. 'I was going to ask that myself. My aunt—'

Diana interrupted. 'Mother, please. If Miss Wickham is so good as to take on the care of Great-Aunt, then it's up to us to back her up.'

Miss Wickham stretched her mouth in a smile to terrify. 'Dependent on my terms being met, of course.'

'Of course,' said Diana. 'Great-Aunt to move her bed downstairs, a new kitchen, new television, video and car for you.'

'Something will have to be done about the bathrooms, too. We shall have to have a little shower room put in downstairs for my patient, of course, and—'

Ellie said, 'Was that the doorbell?' She hurried out into the hall. Roy was just letting himself in.

'Sorry I'm late. Couldn't get away from the golf club. What's up?'

Ellie hurriedly explained.

'We'll see about that,' said Roy, putting on his Master of the House face.

He strode into the sitting room, kissed his mother on her cheek, acknowledged Rose with a smile and a duck of the head, and Diana with a nod. Taking up his position with his back to the fireplace as usual, he said, 'So what seems to be the problem here?'

Aunt Drusilla, Rose and Ellie picked up their cups and sipped tea with downcast eyes, allowing the dominant male to deal with the situation.

'And who might this be?' demanded the wardress, in slightly less powerful tones.

Roy raised his eyebrows. 'I'm Miss Quicke's son. And you are?'

'I have been employed to care for your—'

'Who has employed you?' Roy's eyebrows did their ironical jerk up and down.

'I have,' said Diana, with some defiance still in her voice.

'And who asked you to interfere?'

Diana went red. 'She can't possibly stay on here on her own, as you very well know. It is essential that someone qualified moves in with her and Miss Wickham comes highly recommended.'

Aunt Drusilla said, 'My dear Diana, if you had only asked I could have told you that I am already in the process of asking a delightful woman to come to stay. Her own quarters, of course. The kitchen will be re-structured according to her wishes and there will be a generous monthly salary. That's right, isn't it, Rose?'

Rose sighed with rapture. 'The perfect position for someone who appreciates a lovely house like this. I was just thinking; we've been let down over the venue for my daughter's wedding at the end of next month. Don't you think this room and the hall would be a magnificent venue for the reception?'

Ellie considered Rose's innocent expression and wondered how quickly her old friend had worked out the possible benefit to herself in this situation.

Roy laughed. 'Do you have someone to give her away, Rose? Or shall I do it?'

'Oh, that's perfectly all right, Mr Bartrick. Dear John from the charity shop will be giving her away and our old vicar is coming back to take the service, but all we could get for the reception is the pub in the Avenue, which is not at all satisfactory.'

Diana and the wardress both had their mouths open, conscious that they'd lost the initiative.

Ellie explained to Aunt Drusilla. 'They'd planned to have the reception at the golf club but it was double-booked.'

'We must have banks of flowers,' said Aunt Drusilla, enjoying herself. 'White flowers, I assume? Ellie dear, is that clever Mrs Dawes doing the flowers for the wedding? I don't attend your church of course, but I've heard she does that sort of thing rather well. Outside caterers, naturally.' Aunt Drusilla set her cup down and inched forward on her chair. 'Do you know, I think I have a drawer-ful of damask tablecloths somewhere. Rose, you can help me look them out afterwards.'

'I do love beautiful things,' said Rose, and everyone heard the longing in her voice. Ellie heard it, and was ashamed that she hadn't recognized this in her old friend before. Diana heard it, and knew the game was over. The wardress heard it and flushed an un-becoming red.

'Well, I've never in all my born days...!'

Roy said, 'I'll see you out, shall I?' Somehow he wafted her from the room.

Diana was so angry she almost spat. 'You'll be sorry for this! I mean,' remembering perhaps that Aunt Drusilla paid her salary, 'I don't think you quite realize how much you need someone to look after you. Miss Wickham was a highly qualified—'

'Bully,' said Ellie. 'Give it a rest, Diana. By the way, what have you done with young Frank while all this has been going on?'

'The childminder agreed to have him till half six.' She looked at the clock, bit her lip and said, 'Well, I suppose I must be going. I only hope, Great-Aunt, that you don't live to regret this.'

'I shan't, dear. Drive carefully.'

Diana made a cross 'Tchah!' sound and swept out.

'Now,' said Ellie. 'Aunt Drusilla, Rose. That was a spot of quick thinking on your part, both of you. But I can't think you were really serious...'

She crossed her fingers behind her back, because she really did hope that they meant it, both of them.

Aunt Drusilla smiled at Rose. 'I think we'd suit rather well, don't you, Rose? Come for a week, see how you get on. I'll pay you, of course. And yes, it is about time I had the kitchen and the bathrooms brought up to date. Perhaps you'd be so kind as to help me organize that. As for the wedding reception, well, why not have it here? So long as I don't have to lift a finger...'

Rose grinned. 'I'll take you up on that. But you know I'm not at all clever at dealing with builders and money and so on. I wouldn't know what was the latest thing in shower curtains or bidets and I've never even known what you use one of them for, anyway.'

'But you'll come and stay with me for a few days, won't you?'

Rose looked at Ellie. 'Is it all right, Ellie? I don't want to upset any of your arrangements...'

Roy came back into the room, rubbing his hands. 'Mrs Rose, you are a blessing sent from heaven.' He kissed her hand, which made Rose blush and Aunt Drusilla laugh. Ellie gathered the tea things together.

'Well, if you've finished with your mutual congratulations, I'll carry these out to the kitchen for the cleaner to wash up.'

'No, you don't.' Rose was shocked. 'You'll never trust that fine china to a cleaner. Let me.' She hit her forehead. 'Bless me, I'll forget my own head next. Miss Quicke, what are you having for supper, then?'

'Ellie will get me something out of the freezer and put it in the microwave for me. In the morning we can discuss what food you'd like to get in for the two of us. I'll expect you about ten, shall I?'

Rose punched the air. Laughing, Ellie said, 'I'd better show you your rooms, Rose. There's a sitting room on the ground floor –

the door to the right of the kitchen. And stairs up from there to a flat, two bedrooms and a bathroom of your own. They need redecorating but I'm sure that can be arranged.'

'Anything you want, Rose. Just ask,' said Aunt Drusilla. 'I'm so glad Ellie found you and brought you to see me.'

Rose said, 'I don't know whether I'm on my head or my heels, I really don't.' And burst into tears.

Ellie shepherded her out into the hall. Aunt Drusilla didn't approve of such weaknesses as tears.

'She doesn't really want me to stay, does she?' asked Rose.

'Yes, she does. I warn you, she's a difficult woman...'

'She's old, that's all. And hates having to ask for help.' Rose looked around her. 'I'll stay till after the wedding reception if she can put up with me till then, but that's six weeks ... do you think that would be all right, Ellie?'

'You'd want to stay on in this house even without a wage, is that right?'

Rose blushed. 'Oh, I don't want money for looking after her, I mean, it wouldn't be right, would it? Did Diana have her wedding reception here?'

'No, she never thought of it and I would never have dreamed of asking Aunt Drusilla in those days.'

'It'll make Diana mad, won't it? Joyce having it here?'

'It will amuse Aunt Drusilla no end. It'll be

as good as a tonic to her. Dear Rose, you understand my aunt even better than I do. You'll be doing us all a great favour if you stay.'

The two women washed up, deplored the unimaginative contents of the freezer cabinet and explored the quarters which were to be Rose's home. Ellie was dismayed. The rooms didn't look as if they'd been cleaned in a decade. The furniture was solid enough, mostly pine. The bathroom fitments – like those in the kitchen – had originally been good, but you couldn't see what colour they'd originally been for years of undisturbed grime. And spiders.

'You can't stay here,' said Ellie, sneezing as she disturbed the dust on the lumpy mattress in the main bedroom. She switched on the bedside light and it fused. There were only two-pin sockets for electricity, and there was a nasty smell of damp in the lavatory.

Ellie was ashamed of herself. Although the house had belonged to her since her husband's death, she'd never really pushed Aunt Drusilla to maintain it properly. There had been a verbal agreement that Aunt Drusilla would have it on a repairing lease, but it was clear that nothing whatever had been done for years ... and doubtless nothing would be done in the future unless Ellie did something about it. Until recently Ellie had been too frightened of her aunt to cross her. Now, grimly, Ellie had to face the fact that thousands needed to be spent on the house.

Of course, Aunt Drusilla was loaded, but she was also a bit of a miser. Ellie foresaw a struggle to get the house put into proper order.

Just think what the gutters must be like! If they were dicey – as Ellie suspected they must be, then soon that damp patch in the old lavatory would be spreading all over the house. And the electrics were definitely unsafe.

The main reception and bedrooms were better, though only Aunt Drusilla's bedroom and bathroom upstairs were as clean as they should be. There was a guest bedroom, with a bed already in use. Roy must have been sleeping in this room, for a man's toiletries were laid out there. That room was shabby but not unclean.

'Roy must move out and you move in here,' declared Ellie.

'Agreed,' said Roy, coming up behind them. 'If you like, Mrs Rose, I can run you back to fetch a few things for tonight. It won't take a couple of minutes for me to clear my stuff out.'

Ellie opened her mouth to say that they'd planned for Rose to have supper with her and closed it again, for Rose was looking more than interested.

'If you don't mind, dear Ellie, I think we'll do as Mr Bartrick...'

Roy treated her to one of his ladykilling smiles. 'Roy, please.'

'Well, then ... Roy ... I think that would be

a good idea. If we make the changeover now, then I can cook Miss Quicke something nice but light for her supper – I've a couple of things in my fridge which would be a lot better for her than all that frozen muck in the freezer. Then I'd be here in the night if Miss Quicke needs me, and I'm sure Mr Roy has something planned for this evening.'

Ellie thought, And who is going to share my supper? Not Roy. Oh, no. Not even if he asks. I'm pretty sure he wants to get back to the golf club, which, come to think of it, is exactly the right setting for him – moneyed men and women, drinks in the bar, good hearty food at the table and lots of business contacts to be explored.

I'll eat by myself, thought Ellie, and what's over I'll put in the fridge to be heated up again for tomorrow night's supper. A widow's bite.

It was quite dark by now and she didn't want to walk home by herself so she rang for a minicab. On the way home she realized she didn't want to face going into her quiet house and eating supper all by herself.

Perhaps there'd be something good on television? She sighed. She'd had enough excitement for one day, and a murder on television really did not appeal. Besides she had a nagging feeling that Tod was in danger. That book of stamps had been a message, definitely. A threatening one? The more she thought about it, the more worried she became. Should she try to speak to Mrs

Coppola again? And be humiliated again?

No, it would be better to go doggedly on, checking through her list of people who might be able to help her about stamp collecting. She fished out the scrap of paper Armand had given her and asked the cab driver if he would drop her at the end of the shops ... just past her solicitor's office. He wasn't too happy about leaving her there, pointing out that there was a group of young lads hanging around the chippy a little way along, and was she sure she'd be all right?

'Perfectly,' she said, and watched him drive away. She turned into a side road and counted off the numbers. A Mr Fenwick lived just along here. She halted, somewhat bemused. A respectable stamp dealer wouldn't live in a house like this, would he?

Sixteen

This was a street of upmarket Edwardian terraced houses. Most had loft conversions, new paint and new windows. Nearly all had made an effort in their front gardens, planting up with winter pansies, cyclamens and variegated ivies, or evergreen shrubs. It was a keeping-up-with-the-Joneses sort of street.

But Mr Fenwick's – and here Ellie checked her list – was a bedraggled, run-down house with dirty grey curtains hanging askew at the windows, a broken gate, peeling paintwork and an air of neglect.

She shrugged. Obviously, she had the wrong address. She would ask at the house for the right number. She rang the bell and noticed there was an entryphone. And two locks on the door. Odd.

A querulous male voice. 'Who is it?'

'My name is Mrs Quicke, but you won't know me. I'm looking for a Mr Fenwick, who might be able to help me about some stamps.'

Quiet breathing. 'How did you get my address?'

Was this Mr Fenwick himself? 'Through the stamp fair people.'

Keys turned in locks. Proper mortice locks, not Yale. A bolt was withdrawn. The door opened a couple of inches on a chain.

'What's it about?'

'I was told you were a serious collector and I need some advice.'

The chain was taken off, and the door opened. The hall inside was bare but clean, lit by a low-wattage bulb. Mr Fenwick was a neat-looking little man with hardly any hair, wearing a beige cardigan over grey slacks. And half-moon glasses. An old-fashioned little man.

Mr Fenwick re-locked the door, put the chain back on and led the way past two closed doors to a room fitted out as an all-purpose living room. The furniture was dark oak and probably dated back to the thirties, but there was a large television and a computer set up on a modern desk. A computer? Ellie suppressed a shudder, remembering what Kate had had to say about child pornography on the Internet. She wondered uneasily if she had been wise to come here, to a strange house. No one knew she was there. Yes, she was definitely uneasy.

He sat on an upright chair, and pulled another one out for her. 'Now, what do you want to know? Have you something to sell me? You collect yourself, perhaps?'

'No, no. I'm afraid not...'

'Your husband...?'

'He died last year.'

'And left you a collection, and you don't

know how to dispose of it? Well, I'm sure I can help you there.'

'No, it's not that.' She plunged into her story about starting up a stamp club in a local school. He was shaking his head before she'd finished.

'I don't have time for all that trivial nonsense, grubby little boys with half a set here and half a set there, and nothing much to spend. I'm afraid you've been misinformed, Mrs ... Quicke, did you say? Any relation of Frank Quicke? I used to go to school with a man of that name. Lived in a big house the other end of the shops, lived with an aunt, what an old dragon she was...'

'That would have been my husband, but he died last year.'

'Sorry to hear it. Not that he was interested in stamps, either. But it makes all the difference, knowing who you are. I have to be careful, you know. People come to the door with all sorts of excuses, wasting my time, wanting to pick my brains. I tell them, read my articles and they'll learn something, but they don't want to pay out the price of the magazine, do they?'

'Magazine? Ah, you write some of those really good articles for the stamp magazines, do you? I thought I recognized the name.' She hadn't, but saying this pleased him.

He rubbed his hands. 'All the top stamp magazines come to me for articles, of course they do, and what's more I review the new stamps as they come out. Would you like to see some of my treasures? Stay here and I'll fetch some for you to look at.'

Without waiting for her to reply, he went out, shutting the door behind him. With her ears on the stretch, Ellie fancied he'd gone into a room at the back of the house, perhaps a kitchen? Did he have a safe there?

He came back with a large cardboard box, labelled Christmas cards. Donning latex gloves, Mr Fenwick took off the lid to reveal a veritable treasure trove. Delving into the box, he selected various pages of stamps for her to look at, giving her a running commentary as he did so.

Ellie's brain went into orbit as he detailed how he had acquired this, and what it cost then, and what he could sell it for now ... and this one here was ... and this page was ... figures rolled through her head and out again...

He was quite animated now. Ellie suddenly realized that he was a modern miser, gloating over treasures which only he had access to.

Eventually he tidied everything away and put the lid back on his box. As he took off his latex gloves, his face resumed its normal dull expression.

Ellie said, 'I'm amazed. I'd never have thought you would keep so many valuable stamps in an ordinary house. Oughtn't they to be in a bank vault? Aren't you afraid of being burgled?'

'They look at the house and think there can't be anything worth stealing here. I've never had any trouble. In any case, I've taken the precaution of having the doors and windows alarmed and the alarm is connected to the police station. If anyone tried to force their way in, the police would know straight away. I'm much safer here than living in an expensive-looking place. There's safety in anonymity, you know.'

Ellie's head was still whirling with all the figures he'd given her. The man was worth more than she was! It took some thinking about.

'Thank you for showing me,' she said. 'An amazing experience.'

He grinned, displaying a stained set of dentures. And showed her out; chain, two locks, bolt.

Once in the street again, Ellie looked up at the house with renewed interest. She presumed he never even bothered to draw back the curtains in that front room. The house looked as if it were derelict, almost. A good disguise.

But, strike Fenwick off her list. He wasn't interested in children, he had a computer only for professional articles, and his eyes didn't light up for any stamp worth less than five hundred pounds. She was getting nowhere and the danger to Tod was still there.

When she got home she looked at the phone for a long time before picking it up. This could be a difficult conversation.

'Hello, is the Reverend Gilbert Adams there by any chance? I need to speak to him rather urgently on a church matter.'

The man hated dirt and dust, but he couldn't allow his cleaner up into the nursery, which he always kept locked. So he had to clean it himself. He donned an apron and rubber gloves. He seemed to remember his mother saying something about dried breadcrumbs to clean stains off wallpaper. He didn't know if they would work on bloodstains.

Really, the boy had been too tiresome. He needn't have got hurt, if he'd only been sensible. The next time he came, things would be different. It wouldn't be long now. He smiled.

Friday morning. A bright and cheerful sky, possibly a little too bright too early? But a good start to the day. The tiler was only half an hour late and said he'd finish within the day, if all went well.

Ellie tidied, swept and dusted, cleaned the bathroom. From the back bedroom window she watched Tod plodding off to school. He still hadn't had his hair cut and he didn't look up. Or look happy. She tried to pray for him, found herself crying. Told herself not to be silly. Mopped up. Attacked the stairs with a brush. Wondered how Rose had got on. Shoved Armand's notes in the waste-paper basket.

The phone went. It was a policeman – no one she knew. They'd found a silver christening cup and a silver vase in a down-at-heel jeweller's shop in West Ealing – would she like to confirm that they were hers?

'None of my jewellery? My jewel box?'

No, none of that, but they had a line on the thief, they thought. Keep in touch. Would she like to drop in to see if she could identify her pieces? Yes, she would.

The phone went again. This time it was Timid Timothy, now sounding not timid at all. He proposed to set up a meeting with her and the architects. Would that afternoon about four o'clock be convenient?

She replied firmly that no, she did not wish to see the architects but she would like to see him and Archie by themselves, at three p.m.

He said that he didn't know if Archie would be free to come at that time, but the architects could probably make it. No, she said. Just him and Archie. No architects. She added that he should not, repeat not, take any donation from her for granted.

'What do you mean? It's all cut and dried, isn't it?'

She put the phone down with a clonk, terminating the conversation. She felt guilty that she hadn't been straight with him but she was not feeling brave enough yet to tell him the truth. He rang back, so she took the phone off the hook and left it on her desk till he'd finished quacking.

She filled in one insurance form and requested another, tried to sort out the mess in the front garden, decided it was going to need a large man and a skip to do it, and sat down for a cuppa.

The tiler was cheerful. Noisy. Too noisy. She needed peace and quiet if she were going to sort out exactly what she needed to say to Timothy and Archie ... and what she could do about the stamps. Only, of course she wasn't going to do anything more about the stamps, was she? There were only two more to visit on her list and she would lay a bet on it – not that she was a betting woman – that neither of them would be able to help her.

She decided to go out. She would look in on Aunt Drusilla and see how Rose was getting on, perhaps get them started on new wiring and plumbing. On the way she would call on just one more person on Armand's list.

She was beginning to think that there was really nothing in her fanciful notion that stamps were in some way connected to what had happened to Tod. It was just that she hadn't anything better to do. Well, she did have lots of things to do, but didn't particularly fancy doing them.

Jacket, umbrella, shopping basket. At the last minute she rescued Armand's notes from the waste-paper basket.

Just as she was about to leave, the phone rang and it was Diana. 'Mother, I've been thinking, perhaps we were at cross-purposes yesterday. Miss Wickham had been so highly recommended to me that I thought ... but then when we got there, I saw that Great-Aunt was getting on much better than I'd thought, and in a way I can quite understand her not wanting to have a carer as yet. Though, of course, how long that will last is anybody's guess.'

'I agree, dear.'

'So although Miss Wickham was extremely, well, disconcerted at her reception, we did agree eventually that the time was not yet ripe for her to move in.'

'Graciously put, dear.'

'So I assume all that about Rose Whatsit moving in was just a joke, wasn't it? After all, we really don't want someone taking care of Aunt Drusilla who might, well, have a bad effect on her.'

'You mean, influence her to leave her some money in her will? Oh, I don't think Rose would do that although I'd be very pleased for her if it did happen. She's had a rotten life to date, you know.'

Diana let out a restrained yelp. 'You've got to stop her!'

'I couldn't, dear. Besides, she already has moved in. I think they'll be very good for one another, especially since Rose's daughter is going to have her wedding reception there.'

A strangled cough at the other end. Ellie smiled, enjoying the moment. 'Well, if that's all, dear, I have to...'

'Wait, mother. You know Stewart gets home today. I want your firm promise that you won't try to deal with the church about money until we've had a chance to talk it over. There's more at stake here than just having the family name on the church hall...'

'I quite agree, dear, and I've taken professional advice on the matter. Now if that's all...?' Ellie rang off, smiling to herself.

Out she sallied into the blustery but fine morning sun. The front door was nearly as good as ever and the grey undercoat had covered the graffiti on the front wall. On to Aunt Drusilla's, with a tiny diversion on the way. The man would probably be out. Or turn out to be in hospital, or dead.

Fronting on to the park at the end of her road was another church and in the vicarage next to it lived the Reverend Howard Greenway, who was not an Anglican minister but a Methodist. Ellie seemed to remember having gone to a meeting once which the Reverend Greenway had chaired and he'd been extremely approachable and had made everyone laugh. He wouldn't remember her, of course.

After having been metaphorically bruised by Mr Pearsall, the Reverend Greenway might provide an antidote.

The vicarage – or did they call them 'manses'? – was in an ordinary though spacious semi. The garden was that of a typical rented house; the lawn had been cut and the bushes trimmed, but there were hardly any flowers. There were two children's bicycles in the front porch and a child's plastic windmill had been tied with string to the gatepost – which also boasted three limp deflated balloons. Some child's birthday party in the not too distant past?

The doorbell was answered by the man himself. Beard, dog-collar, blue sweater, jeans, brogues.

'You've just caught me ... Mrs...?'

'Ellie Quicke. You won't remember me, but...'

'Have I heard about you! My parishioners are all dead envious of your church – doing great things for them, aren't you? Come on in. What can I do for you?'

'You were just going out?' She stepped inside the tiny hall to be confronted with a child's scooter, a skateboard and a dog of indeterminate ancestry enquiring what scent it was on her clothes.

'Only to fetch some groceries. It can wait. Come on in. The place is a mess, but with both me and my wife working ... take that chair, it's the most comfortable. Do you fancy a coffee? Only instant, I'm afraid.'

His study was cluttered but there were businesslike computers and filing cabinets amid the jumble.

'Thank you, no. Please, let me explain...'

She knew this man by reputation and from having watched him while he gave a talk. If she were any judge of character – and she had to believe she was – then this man was no child abuser. So she told him the truth, not fudging the issue with her story about wanting to start up a stamp club. He was the sort of man you did tell the truth to. He propped his head on one hand, elbow on desk and listened with all his attention. She could imagine him drawing secrets out of the most reclusive of parishioners.

He was also a compulsive fidgeter with pencils or pens. And a doodler. His notepad was covered with doodles, as were the covers of various files. Everything within reach.

When she'd finished he thought for a while, leaning back in his chair, stroking his beard. 'How is the boy doing? He's in my elder son's class. Jojo told us Tod was back at school. Jojo hasn't had much to do with Tod, although they're in the same class. Jojo's not academic, you see. He's into sports.'

'I don't really know.' She explained Mrs Coppola's ban.

He shook his head and she felt comforted. He said, 'Looking at it from her point of view ... but hard on you, very. The police...?'

'Are chasing after Gus, but I can't believe he did it. Tod won't talk and I'm worried that if this isn't cleared up, or even if it is, he might never get over it. Also, someone sent him a book of stamps the other day, and I'm scared it's a message to Tod. Suppose this man tries again? He's damaged the boy so much already, but suppose ... oh, it's too awful to think about. And yet, I can't help thinking about it. I've got this sense of impending danger. Don't laugh, I really have.'

'I'm not laughing, Mrs Quicke. You're very close to the boy, and you're probably picking up what he's thinking and feeling. You've tried to tell the police what you think?'

'They're not listening. They're fixated about Gus and I'm absolutely sure it's not him. The stamps are the only clue I've got. Armand, who lives next door to me, and the organizer of the stamp fair locally, have given me the names of all the people they can think of in the neighbourhood who collect stamps, and I've been chasing around trying to talk to them. But either I'm not asking the right questions or they're all in the clear.'

'Right. Well, first things first. I'll ask Jojo to look out for Tod. It might help. Jojo's well grown for his age and he's a kindly lad.'

'Thank you.'

'Now let's have a look at this list of yours.'

She handed her notes over with a feeling of relief. This man was actually going to help her. Fantastic.

'Let me see...' He studied her notes for a minute. 'I've only been here two years. I know of these people of course, though not intimately. I take a stand at all the local fairs, though I'm more of a postcard man, myself. I pick them up at jumble sales, car boot sales and the like. It's surprising what price a rare postcard can fetch. Now ... your list seems complete except for...' He scribbled a name down, drew a box around it, and then crossed it out. 'No, he died, didn't he, sometime last autumn?'

He tapped his pencil on the paper, scribbled down another name and crossed that out, too. 'No, you're not looking for a woman. Forget her.'

He tapped with his pencil on the paper, drawing a box round the first name on her list. 'Pearsall. I see him at all the fairs, but...'

'Above suspicion. I visited him. He wasn't at all helpful, either. What about the others?'

He drew a box around another name, and then drew a butterfly next to it. 'Logan.' He looked up at her and smiled.

She smiled back. 'I visited Mrs Logan. He wouldn't have the opportunity to meet Tod, or the time, or the energy. Besides, he's babysitting for his brood on Tuesday nights, which was when Tod was attacked.'

'You're right. It couldn't possibly be him.' He crossed out Logan's name.

'Fenwick.' He drew a box round that name. 'Have you been to see him?'

Ellie laughed, shaking her head. 'I don't think it's him, do you? I visited him yesterday and was shown some of his treasures as a special treat. I got the impression that he's not interested in people, only in stamps.'

'Correct. He's a serious player in the game.' He drew the outline of a stamp around the name of Fenwick, and filled it in with cross-hatching. 'I know him by sight, but I've never been to his house. You're privileged, if you've been invited in. It's a rare bird that gets invited there. He's really at a national level in the stamp world, not like me or Logan. He goes to the national shows, writes learned articles on rare stamps, occasionally reviews the design of new stamps, that sort of thing. Retired, no job.' He flicked away with his pencil, covering the margin with a lattice of lines.

'Surely you don't like him for it?'

'No.' He leaned back in his chair, twirling his pencil in his fingers. 'I agree with you. He's totally single-minded. Tunnel vision. He eats, drinks and sleeps stamps. He was married once I believe, but his wife went off and I can't say I blame her. His whole life revolves around stamps.'

He laughed. 'I remember Logan trying to show him photos of his latest production – why, his youngest must be nearly three months now – Fenwick wasn't interested. Fenwick was quite annoyed with him. But there, we come in all shapes and sizes, don't we? That leaves Cunningham. Have you visited him yet?'

'No, he's the last on my list. What's he like?'

'Colonial stamps. Lives in the past. Retired major type, into Saga holidays. Wife is a watercolourist, not bad. Grown-up children, grandchildren come to stay. Writes letters to the local paper and sometimes even gets them printed in *The Times*. A disciplinarian with a soft centre. I can't see him abusing children, myself. He's a – er – bum-and-tits man.'

'You mean he likes buxom wenches?' Ellie was not at all shocked.

The Reverend Greenway laughed and drew a drum round the retired major's name then crossed it through with a double line.

'Forgive me,' said Ellie, 'but would you recognize a child abuser if you met one? My friend Liz Adams talked to me about them – she's an experienced counsellor – and said they could be all sorts.'

He gazed out of the window. 'I was abused myself as a child. A family friend. I told no one and after going through a bad patch, I decided I wasn't going to let it ruin my life. But when I grew up and was called to the ministry, I read up on the subject. I was afraid I couldn't be objective if I had a parishioner who was a paedophile, you see. I wanted to understand them as best I could without being one. But the subject is so vast ... I can only generalize.

'Yes, I've had contact with one or two in the line of business. One was just a miserable misfit, anxious to please. A tentative groper, you might say, easily discouraged, hooked on the Internet porn sites. The other appeared normal but was abusing the younger members of his extended family, which was fairly horrible. He was into girls. It seems they don't usually mix girls and boys. One or the other. I did come across a man once who was obsessed with young boys. He used to take jobs which brought him into contact with them, professionally. He's still in jail.'

'None of those I've seen fit the bill.'

He concentrated on the point of his pencil. 'Well, there is Armand himself. I know he gave you some names and seems anxious to help, but that might be a cover and he does have access to children.'

'The children are of the wrong age,' said

Ellie. 'I've thought it through, and it's not him. No opportunity, nowhere to abuse the boy in safety and just, well, not the type.'

He wrote Armand's name at the bottom of the sheet. After a moment he put a large tick beside it. And then crossed it out. 'No,' he said. 'I really don't see it, either. And that leaves Pearsall, whom you say can't have done it.'

She looked at the paper. He'd drawn wriggly lines all round Pearsall's name but hadn't crossed it through.

She frowned. It couldn't be him. She said, 'What does he buy?'

'Canadian, very high-powered, which doesn't fit. Again, someone who uses stamps to attract boys' attention would want to buy large packs of stamps, cheap. He doesn't.'

'He could get them on the Internet, couldn't he? Then no one would know. Why do you think it's him? Nobody else does.'

'Who said I thought it was him?'

'Your doodles do. He's the only name that you haven't crossed out.'

He met her eyes squarely. 'I don't know.'

'You don't like him.'

He spread his hands wide. 'I didn't say that.'

'But you don't.' He didn't reply. Well, she hadn't liked him, either, but...

She said, 'Liking or not liking is no grounds for thinking him guilty. He was once in a position where he could have had his pick of children to abuse, but apparently he didn't.

Though I suppose the pupils at the High School might be too old for him, if his tastes run to young boys. And of course his wife was alive till eighteen months ago and he might have started after that. He does live alone and he does have a big detached house, where nobody could hear if anything were to go on. I haven't uncovered any link between him and Tod except stamps, and that's not reason enough to suspect him.'

He looked out of the window. 'Sometimes grief over one's partner's death can drive you in on yourself, make you reserved, sound cold, even.'

'Yes.' That hadn't been her experience but everyone was different.

He pushed the paper towards her. 'What are you going to do?'

'I don't know. We have absolutely no proof. Having a feeling about somebody isn't proof. If I told the police I'd a feeling about Pearsall, they'd laugh themselves silly. I'll try to warn Mrs Coppola. And I'll pray.'

'I will, too, if you like.'

'Thanks. All contributions gratefully received.' She might make a joke of it but she would definitely value his prayers.

He got to his feet. 'Well, I suppose I'd better get to Tesco's ... Can I give you a lift anywhere? When I tell my wife I've spent the morning talking to a five times millionairess...'

'But I'm not,' said Ellie, at last finding the right words. 'Reports of what I am about to receive under my husband's will have been greatly exaggerated. It's getting difficult. People seem to think I can give them anything they ask for, but I can't. I will have a trust fund for charities in due course, but I haven't got that set up yet.'

'Oh, I see,' he said. And he obviously did. He laughed. 'What a shame. There was I going to touch you for some new wiring for our church.'

She liked him enormously. 'Why don't you write in to the trust when it is set up and we'll see if we can manage something towards it?'

Seventeen

The Reverend Greenway drove an ancient estate car with a rattling exhaust. He dropped her off by the police station and she went in to see if they had managed to rescue her silver christening cup and vase. They had. The cup and vase looked slightly tarnished, even insignificant, laid out like that. She signed a statement confirming that they were hers, and was told they'd be returned to her in due course but at the moment they were evidence. There was no news of Gus. She didn't know whether to be glad or sorry about that.

She walked slowly along to Aunt Drusilla's. It hadn't rained for almost twenty-four hours – a minor miracle. The forsythia was brilliant this year. Some crocuses were still around; just. Someone had a bush of witch hazel in full flower – a lovely sight.

Aunt Drusilla's front garden looked as dreary as usual. What would she do with it, if it were up to her? Tear all the laurel out and plant beds of polyanthus, perhaps? Mixed with forget-me-nots?

A mother's-union conference was taking place in the hall. There was Aunt Drusilla enthroned in a big, high-backed chair and there was Rose, darting about with a pad of paper and a pencil. There also was Mrs Dawes, massive in a tartan poncho, and Rose's haughty daughter, Joyce. Surprise, surprise! They were discussing arrangements for the wedding reception.

'Our largest flower arrangement ... here.' Mrs Dawes indicated the foot of the stairs. 'Then you can have the reception line in front of it.'

'I'd prefer it in front of the windows.' Joyce was frowning, discontented as usual.

Rose darted at Ellie and gave her a kiss. 'Isn't this fun?'

Mrs Dawes inclined her head graciously in Ellie's direction and Ellie realized that Mrs Dawes was sending her a signal. Mrs Dawes was going to overlook her friend's recent flightiness and poor judgement because Mrs Dawes had been invited to create flower arrangements in this big house.

'Who's going to pay for such large arrangements?' asked Ellie, knowing how little Rose had to live on.

Mrs Dawes and Joyce both looked at Ellie, clearly thinking that she ought to offer to do so. Ellie smiled blandly back. 'Oh, I remember now. It's the groom's privilege, isn't it?'

'Ellie, my dear,' said Aunt Drusilla, lifting her cheek for a kiss. 'Joyce reminds me so much of your Diana. Shall we go into the sitting room and leave them to it?' She got to her feet with only the slightest of assistance from her stick and led the way to the sitting room.

'The room looks different,' said Ellie.

Aunt Drusilla gestured to two large bowls of flowers, which contrived somehow to lift the heavy magnificence of the room into splendour. A cafetière and all the trimmings for making coffee were on a table nearby. 'That girl Rose was up at the crack of dawn, bringing me a cup of tea. I'd forgotten to ask her to fill up the Teasmade, so it was most welcome.'

'She didn't wake you?'

Aunt Drusilla chuckled. 'No, no. I don't usually sleep after six o'clock. It was delightful. She wanted me to have breakfast in bed but I struck at that. My father always said it was a sign of moral weakness to have breakfast in bed. I never understood his reasoning, but that doesn't matter. Rose is going to do me a power of good. I shall have a little nap after lunch – which she's promised will not be out of the frozen-food cabinet – and then we'll be ready for the electrician at five, and the man to see to the gutters at six.'

Ellie sat down with a thump. 'Electrician? Gutters? You're never going to do something about the state of this place, are you?'

'Yes, dear. Don't you think I should?'

'You are a wicked old woman. You'll wear Rose out and then what will we both do?'

'I'll see she doesn't do too much and she'll see I don't do too much. Thank you, Ellie. Pour yourself out some coffee. It's freshly ground. Rose went to the shops for me first thing this morning, though I understand I can now order on the Internet, which may be more convenient in the long run. Now how are you getting on?'

Ellie had nothing to do but put up her feet and obey...

'Sad for you about little Tod,' said Aunt Drusilla, unerringly putting her finger on the sore spot. 'I hope the lad pulls through.'

'Yes. Aunt Drusilla, I have a meeting with the curate this afternoon about the money they want for rebuilding the church hall. Any advice?'

'Show them Frank's will and leave it at that.'

'I thought I might make it up to a thousand.'

'I don't see why you should but if you do, count me in for another five hundred. I haven't attended church for years and I don't intend to start going now, but I wouldn't mind them putting a plaque up somewhere with Frank's name on it.'

Ellie took the dirty coffee cups out to the kitchen. Mrs Dawes and Joyce had disappeared and Rose was busying herself in the kitchen, preparing lunch. As always, Ellie was depressed by the gloom in the kitchen.

'Rose, are you sure you can put up with this?'

Rose had seen the Promised Land. She led Ellie over to the window overlooking the garden. Ellie saw what she always saw: a large square of grass surrounded by some unremarkable shrubs and a few mature trees.

Rose saw something different. 'Look! Trees! I used to dream about trees when I was up in my little flat. Look how they're all coming into leaf! And there are birds nesting in them! It's the most exciting thing that's ever happened to me.'

'But Rose, this house is...'

Rose returned to peeling potatoes. 'It needs new electrics, new gutters, a couple of new bathrooms and this kitchen refitted. After that Miss Quicke is going to bring in some decorators, but she's going to let me choose all the wallpapers and new carpets for my own rooms. She's been so good about letting Joyce have her wedding reception here.'

'She'll wear you out.'

'I'll see she doesn't. We two old ladies will have little naps when we need them, and she's going to pay me an enormous amount of money, just for the pleasure of being able to live in this lovely big house and look after her. And stuff Madam at the charity shop!'

Stuff Madam, indeed, thought Ellie as she did a little shopping in the Avenue. Paying off old scores was delightful. She considered the windows of the charity shop and made her way in. There was a rail of curtains for sale at the back – perhaps she might find something there to replace her torn ones, just till she could get new ones made.

There were no curtains there in the green that she fancied, though she lingered for a while considering a pleasant oatmeal-coloured fabric that might do. Unfortunately it was neither wide nor long enough.

'Well, look who's here!' demanded Madam. 'What's the millionairess doing, slumming?'

Several shoppers looked round to see who was making the fuss and Ellie steeled herself to face their curiosity. The words slid into her mind and she let them fly out of her mouth.

'Oh, I'm back to being the poor relation again, you know. Everything is to go into a trust. I daresay I shall be looking for a job soon.'

'What?' Madam gobbled in her annoyance. 'But I thought, we heard that...'

'Rumours.' Ellie sighed and shook her head. There was a cream-coloured duvet cover with Disney characters on it, plus pillowcase, which she rather fancied. She pulled it out to check that there were no stains on it. There weren't. It would do nicely for the little bedroom now baby Frank was growing so fast. 'I'll have this, I think. Any reduction for past staff?'

'I – er – no, of course not. You won't be coming back here to work, I can tell you that.'

'Of course not.' Ellie opened her eyes wide. 'I did enjoy working here once in the days when I didn't have to earn money. But that was a long time ago. I've just heard that dear Rose has got herself a nice little job looking after an elderly lady, with board and lodging included. I suppose I must look around for something like that myself.'

Madam went a most unbecoming scarlet. The other staff and the shoppers remained as if frozen, listening hard.

Ellie brushed past Madam with the duvet and paid for it at the till.

Giving Ellie her change, the woman behind the till whispered, 'Is it true, then? Well, best of luck, Ellie. You deserve it.'

'Thank you, dear,' said Ellie, and swanned out of the shop, trying not to giggle. Their faces! It would be all over the parish within an hour. With luck.

At five to three the doorbell rang and there was Timothy with Archie Benjamin.

Timothy said, smiling, 'The architects are out of the office today and couldn't be reached, so I haven't been able to get them to come earlier. They should be here at four as arranged. Hope this doesn't put you out too much.'

Archie showed his glinting gold tooth. 'Hope this won't take long. I promised to take the little woman out this afternoon.'

Ellie smiled, appreciating that they were laying down their battle lines. 'Do come in. I won't offer you tea or coffee because this is just a business meeting, isn't it? I apologize for the noise – the tiler is working in the new conservatory – an extravagance which I really can't afford, but there ... the mortgage company were happy to oblige with a little extra. Won't you be seated?'

Two pairs of eyes opened wide at this reference to the mortgage company. Timothy shot a worried look at Archie, who frowned and looked down at his fingers.

'Now,' said Ellie, taking the initiative. 'Archie, I understand that you had an interesting talk with my husband just before he died. I was there every day with him in hospital and I didn't see you. Perhaps this conversation took place before he went into hospital?'

'Poor fellow. Nasty business. Best leave him alone with his family at the end. We were talking, just in general terms, about his health. As old friends do.'

'Of course. And that's when he said that he was leaving me well provided for...'

'And that he was doing something big for the church.'

'Of course. He'd worked so hard for the church, hadn't he? It was very much on his mind. But he didn't mention an actual figure, did he?'

'Well, yes. Of course he did.' He produced a triumphant smile for her. 'A million pounds.'

'Are you sure?'

'I couldn't be mistaken about that. I was quite taken aback at first. I mean, I had no idea he was such a warm man. He must have been worth, well, three million at least to make such a donation.'

'Can you think which day of the week it was?'

'Probably the Sunday before he went in. I could look it up in last year's diary, but I think I can safely say it was the Sunday before he went into hospital. Over coffee, after church.' Archie fingered the buttons on his waistcoat and looked smug.

Timothy looked bewildered, his head turning from side to side as if he were a spectator at Wimbledon.

'Dear me, what a tangle,' sighed Ellie. 'I really don't know what to think. Frank wasn't the changeable sort, was he? He made up his mind and then he stuck to it. Yet his will doesn't say anything about leaving a million pounds to the church.'

Timothy bit his lip. 'It doesn't?'

Archie smiled fatly at her. 'I know what he promised. I expect this was an old will...'

'He gave the instructions to our solicitor in writing during his last illness, and the will was signed while he was in hospital. He sent me out of the room while the solicitor was in with him and I knew nothing about it until afterwards.'

'But you intend to honour his promise?'

Ellie said, 'There's a clause in his will which gives a donation to the church. Naturally that will be honoured when probate is granted.'

'There you are, then,' said Timothy, being all hearty.

Archie plucked at his lip. 'A million pounds, as he promised?'

'Five hundred. I'm so glad that he remembered the church in his will. It seems only right and proper, don't you think?'

'Only five ... hundred ... pounds?' squeaked Timothy.

'I think I would like to add a little more to that...'

'Yes?' said Archie.

'...making it up to a round thousand. And if you agree to put up some sort of plaque to my husband in the church hall, then Miss Quicke will also add five hundred pounds. That makes fifteen hundred pounds in all.'

Archie went a dull red. 'He promised me...'

'I expect he talked in vague terms about wanting to leave me well provided for and about making a donation to the church, which is exactly what he did.'

'But you inherited...'

'Enough to keep me comfortably but not enough to throw money around. By no stretch of the imagination was I left three million pounds. Do you know, I was so shocked when Timothy told me your plan that I even considered selling this house in order to let you have the money? It would mean I'd have to go to live with relations and find myself a job of some sort, but I did think about it. Then I realized that even if I sold this house – and you do know I only own half of it, don't you? – it wouldn't make up the million pounds you needed.

'Then I thought, but this is not what Frank wanted for me and I realized there must have been some misunderstanding. I rang Gilbert Adams and asked him about it, and he was quite clear that Frank knew what he was doing and that his Last Will and Testament must be observed.'

'But...'

'Now, my solicitor suggests that some of the money I will eventually inherit is put into a trust fund for disbursement to deserving cases. I can't touch that money yet of course but I suggest that when the time comes, Archie applies to the trust for something towards the rebuilding fund; perhaps another couple of hundred pounds? I'm sure they will consider the request for a small donation favourably if I put in a good word for you.'

Archie was staring into a future which looked distinctly unhappy. Ellie felt almost sorry for him.

'I'm afraid you've been misled into thinking I could solve all your financial problems. It's so easy to indulge in wishful thinking, isn't it? You all wanted me to be the goose that laid the golden eggs, but it turns out I'm just the goose.'

Timothy had the grace to try to laugh at this but Archie looked thunderous. He was not going to forgive her for making him look a fool. The story would be all round the parish by nightfall. He might even have to resign as church treasurer.

Ellie didn't want that. He was a good treasurer and that's what the church needed. 'Like Frank, I have the greatest respect for you as treasurer, Archie. I'm sure you'll be able to pluck the necessary funds out of thin air.' No, that was a bit close to the knuckle. 'Of course, you may have to scale down your plans for the rebuild, but I'm told that fundraising unites a church beautifully.'

'The architects,' said Timothy in a hollow voice. 'They must already be on their way.' Poor man, he could see that the failure of this plan would count against him in his plan to be appointed vicar.

Ellie stood up, forcing them to stand as well. 'Why don't you take them across to the old hall and have a site conference?'

Archie fought for words, glaring at Ellie.

She had one last subversive thought and held out her hand to him. 'Friends?'

She guessed he wouldn't take her hand and he didn't. Then she was ashamed of herself. She had provoked him rather.

Timothy, however, was recovering himself better. He held out his hand to shake hers. 'Well, thanks for ... for being so straight with us. We'll see you on Sunday as usual?'

She nodded. By Sunday everyone would know she wasn't going to give the church a million pounds and that she wasn't on the list of the richest women in England. They'd know about the trust fund and they'd know they couldn't expect her personally to underwrite their financial problems. That suited her.

Archie wasn't finished yet. 'You should have told us earlier. What fools we're going to look...!'

'You should have asked. You didn't even check my husband's will. I think I see the architects' car arriving, so I'll leave you to deal with them. Have a nice day.'

* * *

When they'd gone, she sat down and had a good laugh. Which turned into a bit of a weep. But not much of a one. Dear Frank, she thought. If only he were there to see the problems she'd inherited along with his money. Archie was never going to forgive her. No. A pity. But not the end of the world.

She got some tea for the tiler, who had nearly finished, and some for the builders, who had arrived to fix the drainpipes on the outside of the conservatory. They'd already installed a connection to the nearest drain. The sun made the conservatory beautifully warm and she liked the pattern of the floor tiles now they were down. She rather thought she might have to have blinds fitted in the summer. That was all right with her.

She watched Tod cross the Green on his way home from school. Alone as usual. Again, he avoided looking up at her as he turned into the alley. Oh dear. But perhaps that nice Methodist minister would be able to get his son interested in befriending Tod. Dear Lord, please ... And keep him safe. I expect I imagined that there was still danger to Tod. I hope so...

Ellie felt her pain ease a little.

After tea she forced herself to work in the front garden. It was dreadful having to cut down and clear away broken plants, especially shrubs which had been just about to flower. She had to leave most of the larger plants for a man to deal with but she thought some of the bulbs might recover, with luck.

It was getting cold and dark.

There were lights on inside Tod's house. Soon Mrs Coppola would be home from work. Ellie had told the Reverend Greenway that she would try to warn Mrs Coppola, who would no doubt be very rude in return. Ellie gritted her teeth. She must give it a try and then, if anything were to happen to Tod ... No, don't think like that. Nothing's going to happen to him.

Ellie went in, cleaned herself up and told the tiler how much she admired the new tiles and the builder how much good the new drainpipe would do. The drainpipe would take water off the roof of the conservatory and fill a capacious water butt before emptying into the drain. Everyone was being very jolly.

Once the workmen had gone, the house seemed remarkably silent. Waiting for something, almost. She put the radio on. Turned it off again. She might live in a close community but she had no one to talk to.

She felt restless. She rang the police station to see if there were any news of her other stolen valuables. They said they'd contact her if there were any news, but oh yes, they'd caught up with Gus sleeping rough somewhere on the south coast, and were hoping to charge him pretty soon.

Poor Gus, she thought. Poor lost little waif – except that I wish he hadn't seen fit to steal my bits and pieces.

It was all wrong, what the police thought. Now if they'd only followed up her idea about the stamps ... but they didn't believe in it. A bird in the hand, that's what they liked. After all, Mr Pearsall was untouchable, living in his big respectable house in a respectable neighbourhood. There was no proof. Absolutely none.

Then she remembered the smell. When the cleaner had opened the door leading out of the hall, there had been a waft of air which had brought with it a strong, antiseptic smell. Possibly from the room she'd gone into, and possibly from the man himself. Not Dettol. Not Flash or anything like that.

She had it now. It was chlorine.

You didn't use chlorine to wash down a hall floor. You used chlorine to purify water, particularly in swimming baths. So why was there such a strong smell of chlorine in Mr Pearsall's hall?

Tod's swimming trunks and towel stank of chlorine when he came out of the swimming baths. They were missing.

Swimming baths. Tod had gone swimming, had left alone and vanished. Stamps. Tod had loved his collection dearly but had jettisoned it after he'd been abused.

Did Mr Pearsall by some chance go swimming about the time that Tod did?

Had he bribed Tod with stamps before and after the event? No one else fitted the profile. Gus certainly didn't.

Oh, this was pure surmise. How could she

find out if it were true?

She must ask Tod. It was the only way. He might try to pretend he didn't know what she was talking about but now she had guessed enough of the story, perhaps she could get through to him.

She picked up a notebook and pen, but left the lights on because she was only going up the road. Notebook in handbag, sling it across your body. Stupid girl, you should have put your jacket on first. Never mind, jacket can go on top. No need for an umbrella.

As she banged her front door shut, she saw a long silvery car draw away from the front of Tod's house. Another visitor for Mrs Coppola? Or ... hadn't she seen a car like that in Mr Pearsall's drive?

The car was going away from her, but she could have sworn that as it passed under the street light, she saw Tod in the back. She couldn't see the driver because of the head-rest. It wasn't a plainclothes police car. They didn't use that sort of vehicle. Number plate ... no, it was too far away for her to read it.

She paused, undecided. The lights were still on in Tod's house. She went down the path and rang the doorbell. He would come to the door and laugh at her fears, invite her to come and see him play a complicated game on his new computer. Or slam the door shut in her face because his mother had forbidden him to see Ellie.

No reply. The door was slightly open, so she went in.

The lights were on everywhere. The television was on. A bottle of Coca-Cola was sitting on the floor, half drunk. A biscuit half eaten. There was no one at home.

Eighteen

Hungry boys don't leave biscuits half eaten. Perhaps he was in the loo?

Ellie went upstairs, calling for Tod. The rooms were all empty. *Marie Celeste*, she thought.

She knew – she thought she knew – where he'd been taken. If it was him in the car. It might not have been. He might just have popped out to a friend's house.

She rang the police station. Nobody she knew was on duty. She could tell by the weary tones of the desk sergeant that he was fed up with her ringing him. She said she thought the boy Tod had been enticed away by a man in a silver car, no she didn't know the make or the number, but she thought he might have been taken to a house by the park, near the tube. It was owned by a Mr Pearsall, she had the number of the house somewhere but not on her.

He took down the details and said they'd get someone on to it but they had a major incident on their hands at the moment, so...

Do it yourself, she thought. She scribbled a note for Mrs Coppola, who probably wouldn't get it till far too late, and ran out of the house. Then ran back in and called a minicab. Only, now it was the rush hour and they hadn't got a cab for fifteen minutes. She would get there quicker running ... well, walking a bit and then running a bit ... got a stitch. Stop and breathe deeply.

On again. Oh, Tod...!

It was quite dark now. Overcast, too. It was going to rain again, probably. Lord, help me and Tod in our hour of trouble. Please, Lord, don't let him be hurt again, let me be in time, though Lord alone knows what I can do when I get there, but maybe something...

She reached the house at a stumbling run and leaned on the gatepost to catch her breath. There were lights on inside the hall and on the first-floor landing, but nowhere else. She leaned on the doorbell.

The silvery-grey car stood outside, ticking itself gently into silence as the metal contracted. She memorized the licence number, not that she had any means of giving it to the police, but it seemed a sensible thing to do.

She leaned on the doorbell again. Still no sound from within. Was this all some hideous mistake? Perhaps it hadn't been Tod in the car at all and it was just a coincidence that Mr Pearsall happened to have a car which looked the same as the one which had passed down her road and stopped outside Tod's house at the time that Tod disappeared.

No, it wasn't a mistake.

She looked around desperately for someone, anyone, a passer-by, a man parking his car, to tell them, warn them, ask them to ring the police again.

The door opened, slowly. But it opened wide.

'Yes?' The man in grey, cold and cautious. Alone. No Tod. The hall tiles sparkled behind him in the light of a chandelier above his head. A large oak table in the centre of the hall held library books, gloves and a man's cap. She sniffed the air, and again caught a whiff of chlorine, much fainter now, but still recognizable.

'I'm so sorry to trouble you but I was supposed to collect Tod from his mother's house tonight and give him supper, but I must have missed him.'

Ellie stepped into the hall, smiling brightly. 'I saw your car drive off with him and thought, Oh dear, his mother will be cross, so I came to collect him, take him off your hands.'

A poor excuse, but perhaps it might work.

He shut the door behind her, with care. All his movements were slow and deliberate. The house was eerily quiet around them.

She said, 'If you've still got his swimming things, I can take those as well. His mother's going spare, missing them.'

His voice and eyes were dull. 'Whatever makes you think I've got them?'

'I smelled the chlorine in here the other day. Do you go to the baths often?'

'I go when I feel like it. Sometimes I help coach the boys. Occasionally I give them a lift home. They're so scatterbrained, that lot. I'm always finding a bundle of swimming things in my car. A boy called Tod, you say? I don't think I know him. I have my nephew here with me this evening. My sister's boy. I expect it was him you saw with me tonight.'

'Have I made a terrible mistake?' She smiled brightly. 'I could have sworn that I saw Tod in your car and he wasn't at home, you see.'

'Yes, you were mistaken. So...' He moved to open the front door again, holding her by the elbow to show her out.

She yelled, 'Tod!' with all her strength. It seemed to take him by surprise, for he fell back. They both listened. Was that an echo? Someone banging on a door?

Their eyes met. Both knew that the other knew. The grey man shut the door and locked it. 'I can see I shall have to show you my little secret. Come.'

The grey man pulled Ellie across the hall to a door and opened it. It was a small cloakroom, with no outside window. The smell of chlorine grew stronger. He switched on the light from the hall and a fan started up. There were a number of pegs holding men's outdoor clothes, but in the far corner were some bulging plastic bags.

'Is this one Tod's?' he asked, throwing one of these bags at her. 'Or perhaps this one? Or this?'

She blinked. She opened the first bag and found a boy's swimming trunks inside, wrapped in a red towel. Not Tod's. The second bag contained Tod's swimming trunks and blue towel, marked with his name.

'These boys are so careless,' he said, in the same even tone. 'They leave all sorts of little mementoes behind. I have quite a collection of them. Locks of hair, sometimes. Tod has quite spoilt his good looks, hasn't he? I was quite shocked when I saw him again this evening. He was such a good-looking boy when I first spotted him. Polite, too. Sometimes they aren't at all polite to their elders and I have to teach them manners. He was a delight to teach, I must say.'

'What have you done with him?'

'Why, nothing that he didn't want to do, I assure you. Did you think I was a pervert?' He laughed, a dry sound.

Ellie wondered if she were dreaming. The man was so quiet, so orderly, so gentlemanly. Had she made a terrible mistake?

'Come, I'll show you.' He switched off the light and led the way across the hall and up the stairs. Like the staircase at Aunt Drusilla's, the treads were wide and gently curved. It was a pleasure to climb them, if you weren't worrying about what would happen when you reached the top. Now she could hear someone thumping up above.

Mr Pearsall didn't pause at the first-floor landing but switched on some more lights and turned right ... and up a second flight. This time the stairs were steeper and not so gentle. The banging got louder and now Tod could be heard shouting.

On the second floor Mr Pearsall turned right again, went down a short corridor and continued up a third flight of stairs. This flight was steep and uncarpeted. The servants' stairs.

At the top the grey man took out his bunch of keys and unlocked a stout wooden door.

The room had once been a nursery, perhaps. The windows were blacked out. A rocking horse stood in one corner. From the ceiling hung various straps and chains. In one corner was a bed and in another a camera on a tripod and lighting equipment.

Tod was crouched in a corner, using a small chair to beat on the wall. 'Let me out!'

'It's all right now, Tod,' said Ellie, not moving from the doorway in case she got locked in as well. 'Come over here. We're leaving.'

'No, no.' The grey man shook his head. 'You've got this all wrong. Tod came here willingly, didn't you, Tod? You got into my car of your own accord and you came up here with me on your own two feet. Didn't you?'

Tod had been crying. He stood up now, letting go of the chair. 'You promised me...'

'Silly boy. I promised to let him have some pretty pictures, didn't I? And that's exactly what he will have to take home with him, to remind him of me.'

'And the negatives?' said Tod. 'You promised me...'

'Dear boy, if only it were as simple as that.

But you've destroyed your pretty looks, haven't you? You're not much use to me now, unless...'

'No, don't make me!'

Ellie was getting frightened. 'What is it you want him to do? Pose naked for you?'

The man and the boy looked at her with a strange pity and she realized that the games Mr Pearsall played were outside her knowledge. She said, 'I don't think I want to know.'

'My dear lady, you have earned the right to know. I insist you know. Tod here—'

'No!' cried Tod and made a rush for the door. Mr Pearsall caught him by the wrist and deftly turned him round, holding the boy's hand up behind his back.

'Now, now. Don't let's be in a rush. I think this dear lady has earned the right to see what's on my computer, don't you?'

Tod went limp. Mr Pearsall thrust Tod down the stairs, turning off the light behind him. Ellie followed. Down and down. They came to the ground floor and turned into a room at the back of the house. Ellie could hear the trains running along the tube line close by, but the windows were covered with drawn blinds.

The room was a luxurious study, equipped with all the latest computer technology.

'Go on,' said Mr Pearsall, pushing Tod on to a chair in front of a computer. 'Switch on. You know how.'

Tod gave Ellie a miserable look and did as he was told. Mr Pearsall stood behind Tod and waited. He was smiling. 'Go on, Tod. Don't be shy.'

'No,' said Tod, sounding far older than his years. 'I did it before because you made me and I didn't know what I was going to see. Now I do know, and I won't do it any more. You can't make me.'

'Can't I?' Softly.

'Not with Mrs Quicke here, you can't.'

'She's not going to talk about it, is she? She knows that if she talks everything will come out and those pretty pictures of you will be circulating the globe, being looked at by hundreds and hundreds of people, all knowing who you are...'

'Stop it!' cried Tod. With all his strength he tugged the computer off the desk and threw it on to the floor, taking printer and keyboard with it.

'You...!'

Ellie pushed the chair at the grey man, shouting, 'Run for it, Tod!'

Tod scrambled out of the room and ran across the floor. She stood in front of the grey man, keeping between him and the door. She could hear Tod's footsteps on the tiles. Mr Pearsall picked himself up and flicked dust off his jacket.

He made no move towards her but said apologetically, 'He won't be going anywhere. The front door's locked and so is the back. All the windows have locks on them. I'm very security conscious. He'll come back to me, you'll see.'

'That won't do you any good, now he's broken your computer.'

He waved his hand at some filing cabinets. 'Computers can be replaced or mended. The pictures are all on disc, or hidden safely away upstairs.'

Tod shouted from the hall, 'I can't get out! What do we do now?'

'We leave,' said Ellie, trying not to panic. The grey man's calm assurance was frightening.

'Of course. Did you think I'd try to keep you here against your will?'

'With the pictures. And the negatives.'

'Don't you want to see them first?'

Tod's voice came from the hall. 'Don't trust him, Mrs Quicke. He talks and talks and he makes you think it's all right to do what he wants, but it isn't!'

Ellie tried to think quickly. You're absolutely right, Tod. But once we're out of here, with whatever prints and negatives we can get hold of, then it's straight to the police for us...

'Prints and negatives, please,' she said.

'Of course. But first some pictures of you, don't you think? For insurance that you won't be going straight to the police.'

'You're mad,' said Ellie. 'I wouldn't pose for you for all the tea in China.'

'That's what they all say at first, but a few minutes thought will show you that you have no option.'

Ellie bit her lip. If I were the swooning type, now would be a good time. But I'm not. She looked at her watch.

'Any minute now...' she said.

'Police?' For the first time he showed signs of uneasiness. He fiddled with his tie.

'I left a note for the boy's mother as well.'

'She's usually back very late, sometimes not till he's gone to bed. I always pick them from single-parent families. They're only too happy to be fussed over by their precious Daddy.'

'And of course there was the bond of the stamps this time.'

'I buy them in bulk on the Internet for my niece who runs a stamp club at the school. Sometimes I go along to the baths when she takes her class there. It's best to see them in swimming trunks before you decide whether it's worth your while to groom them for play.'

'The police told me they had a major incident to deal with first, but would be along after that.'

He took two steps to the door, bit his lip and turned on her so quickly that she hadn't time to escape.

She screamed, 'Run, Tod. Hide!'

She heard Tod scream in response and his footsteps pounding up the stairs.

The grey man slapped her, first one side and then the other. 'I wouldn't normally hit a woman, but you have provoked me beyond endurance.'

His attitude was that of a dispassionate adult chastising a naughty child. He thrust her out into the hall and across it into the cloakroom. As he closed the door he said,

'Forgive me, but I have to leave you in the dark while I find the boy and get one or two things together.'

She tried to rush him, but he pushed her back with ease. He was a lot stronger than he looked.

'Sorry about this,' he said. 'You've forced my hand, and left me no option but to burn the evidence. Not just the pictures, of course. You and the boy as well. You needn't worry about me. I'll take my stamps along when I leave – best exchange currency there is. You really ought to have listened to me, but there...'

He sighed and shut the door. She was totally in the dark. She lunged for the door and beat upon it. She found the doorknob and turned it. There was a keyhole just below the doorknob. But no key in this side of the door. And no light switch. That was in the hall.

She felt around for the lavatory seat, dropped it and sat down. He was bluffing, of course. He'd let her out in a minute. Or Tod would release her.

She felt her way to the door again and yelled, 'Tod!' Then she thought, I oughtn't to have done that. She'd told him to hide, and he must know that if he replied, the man would be able to locate him.

The police would come. Or Mrs Coppola.

There was a scraping sound and the door opened, light flooding in. The man thrust Tod into her arms. 'The stupid boy tried to hide under my bed.'

He shut the door on them again.

Darkness. She could feel Tod was crying in her arms. 'There, there,' she said.

'He was too strong for me!'

'For me, too.'

She passed him a tissue from her jacket pocket. His sobs subsided. 'How are we going to get out? He's got the big hall table wedged under the door handle.'

'Let's see if we can shift it together.' They tried. And again. And again.

'It's no good,' said Tod.

'Someone will come.'

'Of course they will.'

Nobody came.

They sat on the floor eventually, Ellie with her arm around Tod. It was very dark and rather on the warm side. She remembered that the light switched on the fan and without the fan, there was no ventilation.

Time passed. She thought, how do we conserve the air that's in here? By expending as little energy as we can?

Tod whispered, 'This is all my fault. He was at the swimming gala. He was with my form teacher. She called him uncle. He gave some of us a lift home. Ms Thomas told him I collected stamps and he said he'd got some swops I could have, so when he turned up at an ordinary swimming lesson, I thought it was all right to get a lift home with him. He did give me some stamps. Good ones. He showed me his computer and let me play games on it. He asked me about my dad and said he'd like to have been my father and perhaps he could be a pretend father for me. He said not to tell anyone, that it was our little secret.

'He said he sometimes helped coach swimmers, and if I was there he'd give me a lift back. He was good to me at first. We had some fine times. He let me see his stamp collection and I helped him with it, a bit. Then he said would I like my photo taken as a surprise for Mum, and I said yes, of course. But he wasn't best pleased with the pictures he took and he said he wanted me to pose as a faun, against a painted background. He said I looked just like a faun in a book he had. I had to take off most of my clothes but of course he'd seen me at the swimming baths, so it wasn't very different, was it? I wasn't sure about it at first but he made it seem like I'd be rude to refuse when he'd been so kind to me. So I did, though it was dead embarrassing.

'After that, I didn't see him for a while and I sort of forgot about it. But then he turned up again one day and said I ought to see the pictures as they were amazing, and he could give me a copy that evening. I hadn't got anything much else to do and you were out, so I went with him.'

He was silent for a while. She stroked his head.

'There was another man there this time. They wanted me to pose with him but somehow I didn't want to. I'd grown up a bit since that first time, I suppose. But there were two of them and I couldn't help it. They made me take off my clothes and the other man did nasty things and I screamed and tried to get away so they said I was a naughty boy and if I wouldn't let them do what they wanted, I'd be punished. So they tied me up by the wrists and then...'

His whole body convulsed, remembering.

'Yes,' she said. 'Did it hurt a lot?'

'Yes and no. It was weird. The other man kept saying that no matter what I said, I was enjoying it.' He shuddered again. 'Mr Pearsall didn't do anything to me himself. He just sat there, filming it. Ugh!'

'Shush, shush.'

'When they'd finished, they let me get dressed again and said I could see myself on the Internet the next day. They were laughing. They had a drink together. Mr Pearsall said he was going out somewhere that night, but he'd drop me off at the church. He said he'd see me again. He said that no matter how much I'd pretended I didn't like, it, I really did. That I'd be back for more soon.

'I wanted to die. I got to the bottom of your garden but there weren't any lights on in the house and I could see you were out. There was no one at home, either. Mum had said she was going to be out late. The shed was nice and quiet. I got in, but then I thought people could easily find me there, so I opened the window, put the padlock back on the door, crawled through the window ... and then I slipped and hurt my head as I was getting in. I thought then that I'd be able to die. I pulled the rug round me and got under the table and tugged the pots back in after me. Midge came and sat on me and purred. I don't remember anything after that.'

She rocked him in her arms. What misery!

Eventually they heard the front door bang shut. And smelled smoke. The man had done exactly what he'd said he would do. He had fired the house and left them inside.

Someone must come soon.

Smoke seeped under the door.

She'd always been afraid of fire. She got the boy to help her, and in the dark they felt around on the hooks to find something, anything, to prevent the smoke suffocating them. They took the towels out of the plastic bags and stuffed these under the door. The sides of the door fitted pretty well. Not so much smoke came in now. Would it be better to die of suffocation than to burn alive?

Ellie tried the door again, and again. The house was empty, except for Tod and herself. The door was a heavy, panelled, solid affair. Immovable.

They were shut into that small room with no means of escape. There was no window, and the fire was gaining ground around them.

Hysteria threatened.

Calm down!

How long since that fiend in human form

had shut them in? How long would it take for the fire to reach her ... or the smoke to suffocate her ... and Tod?

Breathing wasn't getting any easier...

Then she remembered it. She shucked off her jacket. In her haste she'd put it on over the handbag which she'd slung across herself before she left home. Fumbling around in it in the dark, she told herself to keep calm. Trembling fingers wouldn't help.

'What is it?' Tod asked.

'Looking for something.'

She picked up and identified item after item by feel. Small change purse. Wallet. Notebook. Make-up bag. Indigestion tablets. Diary. Pen. Cheque book.

She laid them down on the floor beside her.

It was a deep bag. She'd never liked very deep bags. Things got lost at the bottom. She tried not to cough. It distracted her. Her eyes were streaming.

Diana's mobile phone. The phone Gus had stolen and left behind in his bedroom. She'd meant to mention it to Diana or hand it in to the police, but had forgotten all about it.

She'd always said she couldn't work one of these things to save her life, but in this instance, she thought she could probably manage it ... if the battery weren't quite dead...

'Tod, do you know how to work a mobile phone?'

'Give it here.' She found his hand and

pressed the phone into it. He turned it round and pressed a button which lit up a tiny screen. Now there was enough light to locate the ranks of buttons. He said, 'Nine, nine, nine? Right?'

'Fire service *and* police, don't you think?'

Ellie was holding a party to celebrate the completion of her new conservatory. She had bought some pleasantly rustic chairs and matching table to furnish the place. On the right-hand wall, a pottery lion's head trickled water out of its mouth and down into a deep cistern in which seven goldfish swam around a miniature water lily. On either side of the French windows, large teak containers held a lemon and an orange tree and from deep troughs overlooking the garden, sprang climbing geraniums, stephanotis and jasmine.

It had all cost a hideous amount of money but Ellie was – if a little guiltily – enjoying it enormously.

The French windows from the sitting room had been thrown open, and Tod was helping to pass round plates from the buffet of sandwiches and canapés which Ellie had bought from Waitrose. Ellie picked up Midge, who had been about to jump on to the table to investigate the sandwiches and pushed him out into the garden, locking the cat flap after him.

Inside the sitting room, the Reverend Gilbert Adams was in charge of the drinks table, talking to Bill, Ellie's solicitor. They were getting heated about a white wine Bill had been advised to buy. Liz Adams was asking Tod about the extra cricket practice he was putting in nowadays, courtesy of his new friend Jojo. Tod had had a decent haircut, and looked thinner in the face.

Mrs Dawes poked at the labels on the plants. In a minute she would tell Ellie that she'd chosen the wrong variety or that she, Mrs Dawes, could have got them cheaper somewhere. Armand was checking out the water feature. He and Kate wanted a conservatory something like Ellie's though they intended it not for plants, but for use as an outdoor dining room. He seemed to like the water feature, however, so perhaps something like it would be incorporated into his plans.

Aunt Drusilla said she thought the plants were a little overdone but dear Rose, sitting beside her, thought they were just lovely.

Diana was there; from the look on her face, you'd have thought her drink was battery acid. Stewart was joggling little Frank who was almost asleep in his pushchair, the dear little boy. Diana looked as if she'd rather be elsewhere.

Kate put her arm round Ellie. 'You're looking much better, dear. I was worried about you.'

'I'm fine. Have some more of these smoked-salmon titbits. Such an extravagance but we have a lot to celebrate, haven't we?'

Ellie was particularly thankful that Tod was beginning to pull out of his depression. Liz had arranged a couple of sessions for him with a local therapist, but Ellie was privately convinced that his burgeoning friendship with Jojo would do as much if not more than therapy to complete his recovery. Or get him through it as well as possible. Ellie didn't think you could ever really forget it, or get over it. But you could deal with it. Not let it ruin your future.

Roy got his glass refilled and started talking to Armand about the benefits of joining the golf club. As if Armand would be interested. But Armand was on his best behaviour today and probably wouldn't say anything untoward. She hoped.

Ellie picked up a tiny sausage roll and popped it in her mouth. She had a moment's sadness thinking of poor Gus, once more on the difficult cycle between drink and theft. She'd refused to prosecute him for the things he'd stolen from her, even though the police had not been able to recover her jewel box or the lapis lazuli necklace. She'd put it down to experience, and drawn a line beneath it.

At least the registration number of the car which she'd given the police had led to Mr Pearsall's arrest at the airport, and the fire had failed to destroy more than the kitchen and bedroom above it, so that his secret files were still intact and would be used against him at his trial.

'A toast!' cried Gilbert, from behind the drinks table. 'Or rather two toasts. One to our hostess with the mostest ... of course. And the other to the man the Bishop is about to appoint to my old church here. A good man. I know him of old.'

'Not Timothy, we assume?' said Rose.

'Certainly not. But I expect Timothy'll get another move up the ladder when he's seen the new man safely in. So here's to Ellie, and to the future!'

'To Ellie. To her shining future!'

'Thank you all,' said Ellie, blushing. 'Now I've got a toast to propose myself. As you know, there's been a lot of rumours going around about the money I inherited from my dear husband. Taking advice from all and sundry...'

'We're all very sundry here,' said Roy, who was on his third glass of wine.

'Don't be silly, Roy,' said Aunt Drusilla, who had barely touched her first.

'...and aiming to get the people who'd like to help me spend it off my back, Bill has proposed and I have agreed that most of the money goes into a trust fund. Kate here will see that the money is invested wisely and check the feasibility of the applications made to the trust. Gilbert will advise on all moral issues...'

She smiled and raised her glass to Gilbert who had whole heartedly commended her decision about the church hall.

'...and then there's me.'

Gilbert crammed a sandwich into his mouth and said, 'Kate's the head, and Ellie's the heart, so what am I?'

'The stomach, dear,' said his devoted wife Liz.

'Great idea,' said Roy, though he looked disappointed. He would have liked to be a trustee, too. As would Diana. Stewart smiled and lifted his glass to Ellie, but Diana put her glass down and turned away. In a minute she would make an excuse to leave.

Tod pulled at Ellie's arm. 'Midge wants to come in.'

'He can't, dear. Not with all this food around. He'll have to wait.'

'Three cheers for Ellie!' Roy raised his glass, and everyone else responded.

Tod screamed, 'Look at Midge!'

Foiled from entering through the cat flap, Midge had retreated some way down the garden, turned round and was galloping towards the door at speed. With a bound, he reached the door handle and pulled it down under his weight. Momentum carried him into the conservatory. He dropped off the handle, leaving the door open, and made a beeline for the buffet.

'Oh, Midge,' said Ellie. 'Whatever am I going to do with you?'